Rex Lovell.

He was standing with his back to her, but Jennifer didn't need to see his face to know it was him. No matter how handsome, his face had never been his most memorable feature, she thought, as her gaze slid down his broad shoulders. Not by a long shot.

Rex had been born to wear jeans. Lean hips, long legs muscular enough to challenge wash-softened seams, and his way of planting his booted feet and cocking his hip gave the world the impression he didn't give a damn what it thought of him.

Blindfolded, she would have known his voice. No one else in her whole life had ever made her feel so caressed—or so invaded—with words alone.

Rex Lovell was definitely one of a kind.

The wrong kind.

Dear Reader,

Welcome to Silhouette **Special Edition** . . . welcome to romance. Each month Silhouette **Special Edition** publishes six novels with you in mind—stories of love and life, tales that you can identify with—as well as dream about.

And this December brings six wonderful tales of love! Sherryl Woods's warm, tender series, VOWS, concludes with Brandon Halloran's romance—*Cherish*. Brandon finally meets up again with his first love, beautiful Elizabeth Forsythe. Yes, Virginia, as long as there is life and love, dreams *do* come true!

Heralding in the Christmas spirit this month is *It Must Have Been the Mistletoe* by Nikki Benjamin. This winsome, poignant story will bring a tear to your eye and a smile to your lips!

Rounding out this month of holiday cheer are books from other favorite writers: Trisha Alexander, Ruth Wind, Patricia Coughlin and Mona van Wieren.

I hope that you enjoy this book and all the stories to come. Happy holidays from all of us at Silhouette Books!

Sincerely,

Tara Gavin
Senior Editor
Silhouette Books

P.S.—We've got an extra special surprise next month to start off the New Year right. I'll give you a hint—it begins with a wonderful book by Ginna Gray called *Building Dreams!*

PATRICIA COUGHLIN

GYPSY SUMMER

Silhouette®

SPECIAL EDITION®

Published by Silhouette Books New York

America's Publisher of Contemporary Romance

To three special writers and special friends,
Dee Holmes, Kristine Rolofson and Rebecca Sinclair

SILHOUETTE BOOKS
300 East 42nd St., New York, N.Y. 10017

GYPSY SUMMER

ISBN: 0-373-09786-7

First Silhouette Books printing December 1992

All the characters in this book have no existence outside the
imagination of the author and have no relation whatsoever to
anyone bearing the same name or names. They are not even
distantly inspired by any individual known or unknown to the
author, and all incidents are pure invention.

®: Trademark used under license and registered in the United
States Patent and Trademark Office and in other countries.

Printed in the U.S.A.

Books by Patricia Coughlin

Silhouette Special Edition

Shady Lady #438
The Bargain #485
Some Like It Hot #523
The Spirit Is Willing #602
Her Brother's Keeper #726
Gypsy Summer #786

Silhouette Books

Silhouette Summer Sizzlers 1990
"Easy Come..."

Love Child

PATRICIA COUGHLIN

is also known to romance fans as Liz Grady and lives in Rhode Island with her husband and two sons. A former schoolteacher, she says she started writing after her second son was born to fill her hours at home. Having always read romances, she decided to try penning her own. Though she was duly astounded by the difficulty of her new hobby, her hard work paid off, and she accomplished the rare feat of having her very first manuscript published. For now, writing has replaced quilting, embroidery and other pastimes, and with more than a dozen published novels under her belt, the author hopes to be happily writing romances for a long time to come.

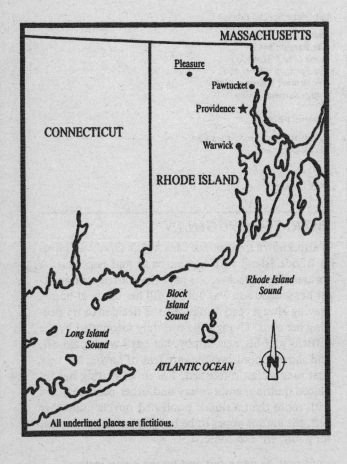

MASSACHUSETTS

CONNECTICUT

Pleasure

Pawtucket

Providence ★

Warwick

RHODE ISLAND

Rhode Island
Sound

Block
Island
Sound

Long Island
Sound

ATLANTIC OCEAN

N

All underlined places are fictitious.

Chapter One

" Are we there yet?"

Jennifer McVeigh clenched the steering wheel of the rented Thunderbird and counted to ten, which coincidentally was the number of times she had answered that same question during the thirty-minute drive from the airport to Pleasure. The town, not the mood.

As it had the previous nine times, the question came from four-year-old Ryan, the younger of her two sons. He and his brother, Jeff, just turned six, were seated in back, their sandy hair tousled, their blue eyes discouragingly bright.

"Haven't you two ever heard of jet lag?" Jennifer grumbled.

"What does that mean?" asked Jeff, as solemn as ever.

"It means that after that long flight from California you should both be worn out and taking a nap instead of antsy enough to keep asking if we're there yet."

She caught the emphatic shake of Ryan's head in the rearview mirror.

"No. No nap. Naps are for babies," he insisted.

This, Jennifer noted affectionately, from a child whose soft, plump cheek was creased from resting against the well-worn security blanket he had clutched throughout the entire trip. Jeff was already too conscious of other's opinions to carry his "softie" so openly. Only he and Jennifer knew about the strip of faded satin blanket binding tucked deep inside the pocket of his shorts.

"So are we there yet?" Ryan asked again.

Jennifer sighed. "Almost. Ten more minutes and we'll be there, and the surprise I told you about is coming up even sooner than that . . . on the right."

"Is this my right?" asked Ryan, slipping from his seat belt and leaning forward to dangle his left hand in front of her.

Jennifer swatted it aside so she could see the road ahead. "No. That's your left. You write with your right, remember?"

"But I can write with this one, too."

She removed Ryan's other hand from her line of vision. "That's nice, sweetie."

"She means write right, you dork," Jeff chimed in. Now they were both out of their seat belts, and, after a long day confined to one cramped space after another, they were none too eager to return to them. Inside Jennifer, responsibility warred with fatigue.

"You can only write right with your right hand," Jeff continued with the pompous authority only a six-year-old addressing his kid brother can muster. "Right, Mom?"

Boy, she hated this part of being a mother. "Not exactly, some people write best with their left hand."

"Like me," proclaimed Ryan proudly, if incorrectly.

"Yeah," Jeff agreed, "dorks like you."

"And like you," Ryan shot back. "Like you, like you, like you."

"Enough," Jennifer ordered, whizzing past a sign that read Pleasure—5 Miles. Alleluia! "I want both of you to sit back, zip your lips and buckle up."

"Aw, Mom...."

"My belt hurts my stomach and—"

"Pronto. Or else," she added because they expected it.

Ryan's eyes gleamed. "Or else what?"

Usually she managed to fulfill her role in the game by coming up with something suitably outrageous and comical, but she was feeling the strain of the day-long journey from California to Rhode Island even if they weren't. "Or else I'll tie knots in the line on the fishing poles Uncle Greg promised you."

"You wouldn't."

"Try me, partner."

They stared at her in shocked silence. Fishing, something which they had never done and considered extremely exciting, was number one on the list of reasons for moving back to her hometown. At least for Ryan. Jeff's cautious enthusiasm had dimmed considerably when he learned the fishing would be done from his uncle's boat rather than the safe, solid shores of the lake that gave the small town its name.

Jeff wasn't particularly fond of new experiences. Actually he avoided them with a mulelike determination, surprising in someone so young. Nice when the new experience involved a book of matches or crossing a busy street unsupervised; not so good when it incited a battle on the first day of kindergarten and many days thereafter.

In September, Jeff would start the first grade. She hoped. A sympathetic kindergarten teacher had helped all of them survive last year, but she had warned Jennifer that things would be different in first grade. Jeff's underlying problem, according to the Los Angeles child psychologist she had resorted to consulting, was a basic lack of security. Jennifer knew he was insecure, and she knew why. What she didn't know, then or now, was how to overcome it, only that she had to do everything in her power to try. Even if that meant coming home.

The fishing line threat worked, more or less. Jennifer opted to ignore the way Ryan was sticking his tongue out sideways in an attempt to provoke his brother. Two years of preschool had sharpened his combative instincts and Ryan was as impulsive and daring as Jeff was timid and thoughtful. Maybe, she thought, that was because he didn't have Jeff's unfortunate firsthand knowledge of how arbitrarily and irreversibly disaster can strike.

Jennifer prayed the truce would hold at least until they could get out of the car and stretch their legs. If she had her way, she would stop at the market in town, then head straight for the lake house where she could fix a quick dinner and tuck the boys into bed early, leaving the welcome-home visits until tomorrow. Unfortunately, here in Pleasure, she seldom got her own way. The McVeigh clan would heed her wishes, she was sure, but her own parents were another story. Jim and Victoria Cahill were convinced they knew what was best not only for Jennifer, but for their grandchildren and just about everyone else in the western hemisphere, as well.

Following the familiar curves in the country road, she tried to shake off the irritating memory of their recent phone conversation and her mother's determination to ready the house for their arrival and pick them up at the airport. There was, she insisted, no need for Jennifer to rent a car, no need for her to walk into an empty house and

start making beds and definitely no need to be so contrary
and stubborn about every little thing.

But there was a need, and Jennifer just hoped her
mother had understood and accepted it when she told her
that she preferred to handle things herself. She needed to.
Just as she needed to face that empty house alone this first
time, to prove to her parents—and maybe herself—that she
could do it, that she was capable and in control, that she
was all grown-up. The small bungalow by the lake had
been a wedding present from her parents, a none-too-
subtle incentive for Jack and her to visit often, and they
had. For Jennifer, the house held many happy memories
of their brief time together.

A cascade of bright yellow on her left caught her attention and drew a smile. The last time she was here was two
and a half years ago. It had been winter and the forsythia
bushes that grew wild along the roadside had been nothing but bare black branches. Not that she would have noticed if roses had been blooming through the snow on the
steps of the town hall. She had come then to bring Jack
home for the last time, a widow at twenty-seven.

Although she and Jack had built a life for themselves in
California, it had seemed right that he should be buried
here in the small town where both their families had lived
for generations, where he and Jennifer had grown up and
gone to school together and fallen in love. Now Jennifer
was doubly glad she had made that decision. She was
bringing their sons back here to make a fresh start, with the
desperate hope that being surrounded by a large extended
family in a small, safe town where nothing seemed to
change but the seasons, would compensate a little bit for
the loss of their father.

On her last trip home, she had stayed with her parents
and she had permitted them to run the show, numbly al-

lowing herself to be led through the funeral services and the endless details and decisions. Then she had shocked everyone by leaving the morning after the funeral.

"But you'll be all alone. What will you do? How will you live?" her mother had demanded over and over again as she and her father reluctantly drove Jennifer and the boys to the airport.

"I'll manage," Jennifer had insisted. She hadn't said more because truthfully she'd had no idea what she was going to do. She only knew that if she succumbed to her own fear and to their pleas for her to do the sensible thing and move home, she would lose herself forever, and maybe her sons, as well.

"If you stay, it will be just like old times," her mother had promised in a desperate last-minute appeal by the boarding gate.

Jennifer had simply smiled and clasped Jeff's hand more tightly, Ryan snuggled safely in her arms. That was exactly what she was afraid of.

It was not that she was one of those people who combs through their childhood memories looking for reasons to be neurotic. She'd had a very happy, pampered childhood. The only child of a successful attorney and his blue-blooded wife, she was blessed with everything she wanted, or at least with everything her mother thought she ought to have.

"Jennifer, dear, wouldn't you rather have the pale pink dress that matches the new ribbons I bought you?" she would ask when Jennifer had her eye on the red striped one hanging next to it.

"Jennifer, wouldn't you rather take ballet lessons like all the other girls, instead of bouncing around on a silly trampoline? Just the thought of all that jumping makes me dizzy."

And in the end Jennifer came around to seeing that of course her mother was right. She was by nature easygoing and eager to please; her mother was overconfident and overbearing, although always in her own subtle, nice-as-pie way. It had never been much of a battle. Not until she moved two thousand miles away and took a deep breath did it even occur to Jennifer that for years she had been smothered. Separation was like stepping from the shadows into the sunshine.

On her own, married to a man who was as much friend as lover, she blossomed. It was liberating to discover that she preferred bright colors to pastels, Mexican food to pot roast, and wearing her pale blond hair long and straight instead of in the face-framing curls she'd always been told were so becoming. Her own unique style exploded from within and she bravely held her ground during their trips home and her parents' visits to the West Coast, enduring her mother's disapproval of most of what she said, wore and ate, with a smile and the knowledge that it would soon be over.

Then, in an instant, Jack's death had turned her world upside down and shaken loose everything in it. As heartsick and confused as she had been in the weeks after, Jennifer had understood that if she moved home, it would never be over.

But that was then, she assured herself firmly. Things were different now. She was different. Older, for one thing. Thirty just sounded more serious and impressive than twenty-seven. And she'd been a mother nearly three years longer—a single mother at that. She'd encountered all the minor mishaps and emergencies that went with the territory, and handled them in her own way. And she'd found a career she loved and that paid the bills very nicely. Actually she'd stumbled into it by accident, but it was a career just the same. And luckily it was work she could do here as well as in California.

Yes, all things considered, she was ready to return on her own terms. Now if she could just convince the chorus line of butterflies in her stomach of that, she'd be doing just fine.

Spotting what she'd been watching for up ahead, Jennifer gratefully pushed aside thoughts of the past and the future, and slowed down.

"All right, you guys, take a look at this."

The boys let loose with the expected giggles and shouts.

"What is it? What is it?" demanded Ryan.

"It's a mailbox."

"Mailboxes are blue," Jeff pointed out. "And big."

"It's not that kind of mailbox," she explained, laughing and coming to a full stop. "This is a box where the mailman puts the mail when he delivers it."

"How come he doesn't put it through the hole in the door?"

"Because this is the country. In the city he puts it through the slot in the door because the houses are close together. But out here, where they're all spread out, he rides by and puts each family's mail into a box like this one. Well, not exactly like this one. This one is special, that's why I wanted you to see it."

She shifted into Park so they could get a good look at it. Everyone stopped to look at the LeBlancs' mailbox. The family expected it.

The box was a homemade contraption at least three feet wide with an assortment of levers and gears and plywood figures that whirled into action whenever the wind blew or the door was opened. Rose LeBlanc decorated the box according to the season, which explained the presence of Uncle Sam and the abundance of red, white and blue bunting and spinning pinwheels. The Fourth of July was only five weeks away.

"Is that the president?" Ryan asked in a rare tone of awe.

"No, honey, that's Uncle Sam."

"You never said we had an Uncle Sam, too."

Jennifer smiled. For weeks they had been struggling to memorize the names of everyone in their father's large family. "He's not really an uncle. He's a symbol of the United States." Please don't let him ask what a symbol is, she thought wearily.

"Mom?"

"Yes, Ryan?"

"Can we get out and touch him?"

Jennifer groaned inwardly. "Wouldn't you rather hear what a symbol is?"

"No. I want to touch him. Can we, huh? Can we?"

"I don't want to touch him," Jeff said immediately.

"Chicken," cried Ryan, following with a loud, annoyingly accurate clucking sound. He got a lot of practice.

"I am not a chicken." Jeff's eyes were a dark, fierce blue. "I just don't want to touch some dumb old mailbox. That doesn't make me a chicken. Does it, Mom?"

"Of course not," she responded as instantly and firmly as she always did in this all-too-familiar exchange. Her denial didn't matter. With each passing day, each new small crisis, all of them believed it less. Impatiently she shifted into Drive and pulled away in a storm of flying gravel.

"Hey," wailed Ryan, "I thought we were getting out."

"Well, you thought wrong." Jennifer felt a quick stab of guilt. She shouldn't take her frustration out on Ryan because she was so worried over Jeff. "We can't get out to take a closer look today, because we have so much to do.

But I know the lady who lives in that house and someday we'll stop by and I'll ask her to show you how it works.''

Ryan looked only partially placated. Jeff appeared apprehensive about returning, although Jennifer suspected that beneath the layers of caution and mistrust he was every bit as eager to explore the fascinating mailbox as his brother was. Her heart ached for him.

A half mile down the road they finally reached the sign reading Welcome to Pleasure, Rhode Island—Population 836.

Make that 839, Jennifer amended silently, with the same mixed feelings and second thoughts that had plagued her since she'd decided to make this move. Then the road twisted sharply to the left and delivered her to the edge of the town itself, really no more than a widening in Route 44, a four-block stretch of the usual small-town assortment of stores and offices. Ordinary and extraordinary at once.

It was a scene worthy of Normal Rockwell's brush. A slice of Americana. Home. A lump formed suddenly in Jennifer's throat. She couldn't have felt more at home if a banner had been spread across the road to welcome her, and in that instant she knew without a doubt that she was doing the right thing.

She drove slowly, savoring the sights and the recollections they inspired. The white church steeple silhouetted against the late-afternoon sky, the striped pole in front of the barber shop, the sturdy iron swings in the park. At least half a dozen flags danced in the breeze, and red geraniums spilled from wooden planters on every street corner. Each image represented a piece of her past—and Jack's, thought Jennifer. Now it would all be part of their sons' childhoods, as well. And just in time. Life here was orderly and dependable, exactly what they needed right now.

Parking in front of Hindley's Market, where you could find everything from lamp oil to herbal tea, she gave each boy a quarter and left them in the entry, happily playing Ninja Warrior. There was something wonderful about a town that was modern enough to have video games and old-fashioned enough that you could take your eyes off your kids for a few minutes without worrying about them.

After greeting and catching up with Mary Hindley, who had run the store for as long as Jennifer could remember, she hurriedly filled a hand basket with bread, milk, peanut butter and a few of life's other essentials. The basket was overflowing by the time she finally headed back toward the check-out counter, and she was suddenly brought up short by yet another piece of her past. Only instead of sweet nostalgia, this one brought Jennifer an instantaneous feeling of cotton-mouthed, heart-thumping panic.

Chapter Two

Rex Lovell.

He was standing at the counter with his back to her, but Jennifer didn't need to see his face to know who it was. His face, she thought as her gaze slid down from his broad shoulders to his muscular torso, was not Rex's most memorable feature. Her mouth puckered appreciatively. Not by a long shot. Rex had been born to wear jeans. Lean hips, long legs just muscular enough to challenge the wash-softened seams, and a way of planting his booted feet and cocking his hip that gave the world the impression he didn't give a damn what it thought of him. The world was right.

Whatever Rex was saying to Mary was lost on Jennifer, but not the pitch of his voice or the unhurried cadence of his words. Blindfolded, she would have known that voice. No one else in her whole life had ever made her feel so caressed, or invaded, with words alone. Rex Lovell was one of a kind.

The wrong kind, according to most citizens of Pleasure. Rex had been Jack's cousin, the black sheep of the respectable McVeigh family. Funny, she seldom thought of Rex as a McVeigh. Probably because the other label applied to him was so strong it had always overridden whatever else he might be. *Gypsy*.

Half Gypsy really. His father had belonged to a band of Gypsies that had passed through Pleasure late one summer to help with the apple harvest. The way Jennifer heard it from her mother, Henry Lovell stayed around long enough to charm Laura McVeigh into falling in love with him and get her pregnant. There was a hurried wedding, but true to what just about everyone in town predicted, it didn't last.

Jennifer could still see her mother's smug expression as she asked, "What else could you expect? The man was a Gypsy for heaven's sake."

Victoria Cahill always managed to imbue the word *gypsy* with all sorts of mysterious evil, but somehow Jennifer could never quite see it that way. To her, *gypsy* meant only one thing—Rex, a rebellious, romantic figure with his long dark hair, gold earring and red bandanna defiantly setting him apart from everyone else in the small, conservative town.

As small as it was, Pleasure had social classes so rigidly defined they might as well be different worlds, and for most of Jennifer's life, Rex existed on the fringes of her world. He was the sort of disreputable, vaguely dangerous character she was always being warned to stay away from. Jack had understood that, perhaps better than she did.

Although he and his cousin were close, sharing a passion for cars of every shape and size, he never suggested double-dating with Rex and one of the older—twenty-two-

or twenty-three-year-old—girls he seemed to prefer to anyone at school. No one, not even Jack, had ever suspected how, during that last summer before college, the boundaries between Jennifer's world and Rex's had briefly given way.

Standing behind Rex now, the memory of those days brought Jennifer the same rush of heat and regret as always. She anxiously shifted her grip on the basket. There was no way she could avoid speaking to him, but she would at least like to do it with a modicum of dignity and reserve, rather than with her cheeks flaming.

Pulling herself from her own thoughts, she heard Mary snap, "There's no need to be rude."

"I'm sorry," Rex replied, his soft tone laced with amusement. "I wasn't trying to be rude, only helpful. Would you rather see for yourself? Pat me down, maybe."

Puzzled, Jennifer looked on as he lifted his hands away from his sides and stood in front of the counter expectantly.

When Mary simply glared in response, his head tipped to the side. "No? All right, how about this?" He quickly turned his jean pockets inside out, holding loose change, a few folded bills and a pocket knife in his outstretched palm. "See? It's like I said. I'm an innocent man."

Mary folded her arms tightly across her chest. "I never said a word otherwise, Rex Lovell."

"But you were thinking it," he countered as he tucked his pockets back in. "Admit it, Mrs. Hindley. You were thinking maybe I'd gotten light-fingered around the licorice back there, or that maybe I'd stuck a shoehorn in my pocket or a couple of penlight batteries."

"As if you could know what I was thinking," said Mary, her round face sporting an uneasy frown.

"Of course I know," Rex said. "Gypsies can read minds as easily as palms. Remember that, Mrs. Hindley."

Leaving the older woman flushed and angry, he picked the pack of Marlboro cigarettes from the counter and turned to leave, stopping short at the sight of Jennifer.

"Hello, Rex."

"Jenny," he said, his deep voice soft. He had the most extraordinary golden brown eyes she'd ever seen, and they lit briefly at the sight of her before once more becoming as hard and unreadable as brass. He tilted his head as he glanced down at her from a seven-inch height advantage, the edges of his lips curved in a smile that did little to put her at ease. He said nothing.

"So," said Jennifer, nervously twisting the handle of the basket, "it sure is a surprise to see you here."

He nodded. "That seems to be the general consensus in town. And not a very pleasant surprise at that."

In spite of the fact that she wasn't sure she was pleased to see him herself, Jennifer felt a polite urge to say so. Just as she opened her mouth however, Mary cleared her throat, reminding both of them of her presence, and reminding Jennifer that whatever she said, especially to Rex Lovell of all people, would be repeated and dissected and embellished everywhere from Betty's Beauty Nest to the filling station. Jennifer had come here to simplify her life, she reminded herself, and she wouldn't do that by waving a red flag her first day back.

"I have to go," she said abruptly. With an apologetic gesture in the general direction of the door, she added, "My sons..."

"Right," said Rex, his eyes narrowing almost imperceptibly. "I understand. See ya."

He stepped closer, and Jennifer involuntarily shrank backward, then felt very foolish when he flashed her a sardonic look and took great pains to maneuver through the narrow space without touching her. God, she was an idiot.

Glumly she placed her groceries on the counter to be totaled and bagged, all the while enduring Mary's soliloquy about how bad pennies always turn up where they're least wanted. She left the store feeling rotten over the brush-off she'd given Rex.

"Let's go," she called to the boys.

"But I'm still playing," Jeff protested.

"You're still playing with that same quarter?" she asked, knowing their skill level defied such a possibility.

"We got another quarter," Ryan informed her. "From the man."

"What man?" she demanded with a frantic glance around. "You took money from a man you don't know?"

"We didn't take it from him," Jeff explained. "He just put it in for us and said 'Have fun.'"

"And he winked, too," added Ryan.

"What did this man look like?" she asked, her panic easing slightly. Even before Jeff began describing Rex, she knew it had to be him.

Why did he have to go and be nice to her kids and make her feel even more guilty? Because she deserved it, she acknowledged, waiting until Jeff lost his third and final warrior and then hustling the boys out to the car.

No matter who was looking on, she should have had the decency to treat Rex like what he was, an old...she searched for the appropriate word, finally settling on the safe, cowardly, *friend.* She should have told him that it was nice to see him again. She should have asked what he'd been up to in the past twelve years and what he was doing in town. She should have introduced him to the boys.

Right, she told herself, slamming the car door harder than necessary. Then the town's most notorious "bad boy" could welcome them to town before their grandparents had a chance to. That would sure get things off to a fine start.

How was it, she wondered, that something as trivial as a chance meeting could become so complicated and emotionally charged? The answer was obvious. Because this was Pleasure, of course. Resolutely pointing the car in the direction of the lake, she muttered to herself, "Welcome home."

Just outside of town, the road forked. To the left lay the country club and the elegant brick Colonial where she'd been raised. Jennifer turned right, toward Pleasure Lake, following the tree-shaded road that ran past the town beach and twisted into the low hills overlooking it. The houses were more modest here, and separated by stretches of undisturbed woods rather than manicured lawns.

Her own house, a small A-frame with a loft she'd promised to convert into the bedroom of the boys' dreams, was located in the hills, a safe distance from the lake itself. The closest water to the house was the brook that trickled through the ravine between her property and the next.

Jennifer frowned, suddenly recalling that the Lovell house sat on the property adjacent to hers. Unlike the newer houses that had cropped up around it, the Lovell house was a large two-story Dutch Colonial. Laura Lovell had lived there alone after Rex left town at eighteen, a huge chip on his shoulder, and it had remained empty since her death several years ago. Had Rex decided to move home, too? she wondered.

Impossible. There was nothing for him here, and besides, his return would be big news in Pleasure and her mother definitely would have mentioned it—unless of course, she didn't know yet. Rex himself had described his return as a surprise. As if she didn't have enough to think about with Jeff and her folks and getting settled in a new house, now she had to worry about Rex Lovell living practically on her doorstep and all that went with it.

And all that went with it. And what exactly was that? Guilt, she thought immediately. Guilt and secrets and mistakes. Plenty of mistakes, all of them her own. Now that she thought about it, maybe it was a good thing Rex was around after all. Maybe she would finally have an opportunity to clear the air between them by apologizing to him for the way she'd treated him, not only today, but twelve years ago.

"All right, troops," she said, turning into the long narrow drive that led to the house. "Close your eyes and give me a drum roll."

A knot formed deep in her stomach as the peak of the roof came into view, but for the boys' sake she was determined to hide her feelings. How many times had she pulled up here? Parked in this very spot? Of course always before, Jack had been the one behind the wheel and she had most likely been dozing after the long trip. "Wake up, sleepyhead," he would say. "We're here." And then they would jump out and start unloading the car laden with Jack's camera equipment, Jack's water skis, Jack's... Jennifer swallowed hard.

"All right, enough drum roll." The racket behind her ceased. "And now, the moment you've all been waiting for... we're here."

"Surprise!"

The front door of the house swung open and, too late, Jennifer noticed the fender of her father's Lincoln Town

Car protruding from its hiding place around back and—dead giveaway—the balloons tied to the lamppost.

"Surprise," her mother shouted again. Her father stood beside her, grinning sheepishly.

"Grandma! Grandpa!" shouted the kids as they spilled from the back seat.

Jennifer followed more slowly, observing her parents and her children knotted in a huge bear hug on the front steps. All right, it was sweet, it was thoughtful, and it was precisely what she had warned them she did not want. So, did being grown-up mean she should remind them of that and ruin the moment for everyone?

Smiling around gritted teeth, she stepped forward to join the hug.

"Hello, Dad," she said, reaching him first.

"Hello, sweetheart."

"Oh, Jennifer," her mother said, her arms outstretched, "you look wonderful. Shaggy, but wonderful." She brushed Jennifer's hair back from her forehead and raised it off her shoulder on one side. "I'll bet Clairise could give you a marvelous perm."

"I don't want a marvelous perm," Jennifer replied, her smile suddenly feeling like a lead weight. "I don't want a perm at all."

"Of course," her mother said brightly. "Straight is nice, too. And just look at my little men, how big they've grown. What on earth has your mother been feeding you?"

"Pa-ghettios," Ryan shouted. "I love pa-ghettios."

His grandmother's brow wrinkled. "Pa-ghettios? Oh—you mean, SpaghettiOs," she said as if that were something that came from a sewer instead of a can. "Oh, well, I suppose you can't work and do everything else, too."

Everything else meaning being a good mother, Jennifer translated silently.

"Shall we go in?" Jennifer said before there was bloodshed.

"Of course." Stepping aside to let her go first, her mother said, "Now don't be angry, Jennifer. I just made a few, teensy-weensy preparations for your arrival. This place was so stuffy from being closed up that I was afraid your allergies would act up and—"

"I don't have allergies, Mom, and I fully expected the place to be stuffy. I would have thrown open a few windows."

"Well, your father and I did that for you."

"Thank you, but you really shouldn't have."

"It was no trouble," she said, purposely misunderstanding. "And there are a few things in the fridge to get you started—milk, a casserole and there's even a welcome-home cake. Homemade," she added, tossing a secret little smile toward Ryan, who was exploring the cabinet beneath the sink.

Jennifer glanced around for Jeff, but didn't see him, and it suddenly occurred to her that she was inside. She'd been so preoccupied with her own anger that stepping across that threshold hadn't been as traumatic as she'd feared.

She looked on in amusement as her mother tried to persuade Ryan that he didn't really want to wash the floor with furniture polish. *You've met your match, this time, Mom,* she thought, before taking mercy on her.

"Ryan, cease and desist."

"I want to wash the floor."

"And I want the Hope Diamond," she said, removing the can of polish from his hands. "Them's the breaks, kid."

"I want to go fishing," he said immediately.

"Not today."

"Tomorrow?"

"We'll see. Why don't you go outside and see what Grandpa and Jeff are doing?"

"Okay."

As he bounded out the back door and across the deck, her mother came to stand beside her and together they watched him through the kitchen window.

"I hope he doesn't go near that brook," her mother said.

"Why? Has it gotten deeper than two inches while I was away?"

"Water doesn't have to be deep to be dangerous. He could slip and hit his head on a rock or get lost or—"

"I'm sorry," Jennifer broke in. "You're right. I'll warn both the boys to be careful. I'm just a little tired and cranky. It's been a long day."

"Of course, darling, what can I do for you?"

"Nothing really. I just want to get the boys settled and hit the sack myself."

"Which is precisely why your father and I are not staying."

She picked up her purse from the table, a sleek designer bag the exact same shade of caramel as her slacks and sweater. She was the same height as Jennifer, five-six, and at fifty-five, still as slim. With the same pale blond hair, deep blue eyes and fine bone structure, they were as alike physically as they were different in most other ways.

Slipping the purse strap over her shoulder, she touched Jennifer's cheek lightly. "I hope you're not upset that we stopped by. I just had to be the first to see my little guys."

"That reminds me," Jennifer said, shooting a glance toward the thick barrier of cedar trees off to her right. The

Lovell house was hidden beyond. "Did you know that Rex Lovell was in town?"

"I heard only this morning. Can you imagine? After all this time. I don't mind telling you I wish he wasn't going to be staying right next door to you and the boys."

"So he is living there," Jennifer remarked thoughtfully.

"Just temporarily. He's supposedly here to fix the place up to sell it. And about time. Of course you can hardly expect a boy who doesn't even see fit to come home for his mother's funeral to be conscientious about anything else."

"Rex is hardly a boy any longer."

Her mother arched a meticulously shaped brow. "You've seen him?"

"Just for a minute, at Hindley's."

"How did he look? Claire Renault says his hair is still too long and he was still dressed in the same ratty-looking dungarees."

"I thought he looked wonderful," Jennifer snapped. "Of course he didn't have a Polo shirt stretched across a potbelly, which, judging from Dick Renault, is what Claire looks for in a man."

"Actually Dick has lost some weight. He went on that same liquid diet that Oprah went on. I hear it wreaks havoc with your system, if you know what I mean. At any rate," she said, pulling a compact from her purse and absently powdering her nose, "at least this means you won't be living next to a vacant property. Maybe a nice family will buy it, with children for the boys to play with."

"Mmm, that would be wonderful," murmured Jennifer, her thoughts on the house's current resident rather than whoever might live there in the future.

"In the meantime," her mother continued, "if he bothers you in any way, call your father. Better yet, call the police. Carl Haggard will know how to handle that Lovell character.''

Jennifer turned from the window. ''What do you mean . . . *bothers me?*''

''You know, bothers you or the children.''

''Mom, this isn't some stranger we're talking about. I know Rex. He was Jack's cousin and—''

''A fact the McVeighs would doubtless rather forget.''

''That's cruel. He hasn't done anything but return home, to a house he owns, and already the rumor mill is grinding at full speed.''

''Well, there's certainly plenty to grind,'' her mother said in the maddeningly serene tone she always used to counter criticism. ''Everyone knows the man has done nothing of consequence with his life. Laura Lovell herself told me he linked up with his father after he left town and simply roamed around the country doing Lord knows what. He's simply unsavory.''

''Because he'd rather travel than punch a time clock?''

''It's not just that. It's why he prefers it. For heaven's sake, Jennifer, have you forgotten the man's background? He's a Gypsy. And if you ask me, blood tells.''

''Well, as a matter of fact I didn't ask—''

''What's a Gypsy?''

Jennifer stopped short and turned to find Jeff standing in the open archway between the kitchen and living room. ''Jeff. I thought you were outside with Grandpa.''

He shook his head. He looked tired and pale. ''I was in here. Looking around. What's a Gypsy?''

Jennifer made the mistake of giving her reply some thought, providing her mother with an opening.

''Gypsies are very strange people,'' her mother said, moving closer to Jeff.

''Mom, don't tell him that,'' said Jennifer quietly.

"It's the truth. They don't live in houses or have jobs like normal people," she went on.

Jeff frowned, and Jennifer saw his hand slide into his shorts pocket in search of the ever-present blanket binding. "What do they do?"

"Nothing very good," said his grandmother. "They travel from place to place, causing trouble mostly. They work at this and that when they need money, and when they don't have any money they just take what they want."

"That's stealing," Jeff pronounced solemnly.

Jennifer made an exasperated sound. "It's also ridi—"

"When I was young," continued her mother, "we were taught to stay away from Gypsies because they steal little children."

Jennifer whirled around to glare at her. "Mom!"

"I don't want any Gypsies to steal me," Jeff cried, on the verge of tears. "I don't. I hate it here, Mommy. I want to go home where there aren't any Gypsies. I hate it here." Throwing his small arms around Jennifer's legs, he gave in to a flood of tears.

She smoothed his head, banking down on her own anger in order to comfort him. "No one is going to steal anyone. Grandma was just joking with you. Right, Grandma?" She shot her mother a look.

"Of course. Why, Grandpa won't let any old Gypsy steal our—"

Jennifer cut in impatiently. "There are no such things as Gypsies who go around stealing children. Of course you always have to be careful like Mommy taught you and not talk to strangers, just like back in California."

"I hate it here."

She stroked his silky hair. "Jeff, sweetie, we just got here."

"I don't care. I hate it here. I hate it because there are big trees and Gypsies and...and because my Daddy's not here. He's not," he said, lifting his head to stare up at her, his blue eyes filled with a searing pain. Everything inside Jennifer twisted in agony. "I know he's not, because I looked. I looked everywhere, Mommy."

Chapter Three

Afterward, Jennifer decided she shouldn't have been so utterly stunned to hear that somehow, some way, Jeff had come to Pleasure hoping to find his father here waiting for them.

"Ignore him," her mother had whispered to Jennifer on her way out. "He'll forget all about it in a day or two."

Jennifer wasn't so sure. The psychologist had explained to her that until around age eight, children process information through what is referred to as "magical thinking," with themselves as the cause of everything that happens in the universe. *If I didn't wet the bed, Mommy and Daddy wouldn't be getting a divorce. I'm adopted because I cried too much when I was a baby.* Or, in Jeff's case, *If I'm brave and move to this scary new place, Daddy will be waiting when I get there.* Too bad life wasn't as magical as a child's dreams.

She had done her best to make both boys understand that Jack's death was real and permanent. Perhaps it was easier on Ryan because he'd been younger when it happened and couldn't really recall his father being part of his life. Jeff remembered all too well. And although he had accepted the tragedy stoically, time and again, in dozens of small ways, Jennifer was reminded that what he knew in his head and what he believed with his heart were two different things.

Maybe this time she was even to blame for his heart-wrenching misconception. In her eagerness to give him and Ryan some sense of connection and roots, she had emphasized to them that Pleasure was the place where their Daddy had grown up, where he'd learned to fish and fly a kite and play ball—all the things she dreamed of for them. Maybe she had gone too far.

It was just so damn hard to know the right things to do and say... and to not say. She understood that Jeff was troubled and that many of his fears and doubts were related to his father's death. And why wouldn't they be? she thought miserably, considering the circumstances.

Jack had been a television reporter for a network affiliate in Los Angeles, with a bright future ahead of him. Not content to merely parrot the news, he was always chasing the toughest stories, always the first on the scene of breaking news, always pressing the boundaries. That's what got him killed. At least that's what the police told her afterward, as they tried to piece things together and figure out what he was doing inside the police barrier.

He'd been covering a standoff outside a gun shop, where two escaped convicts armed with assault rifles and explosives were holding several hostages. No one was quite sure how much explosive until they made good on their threat to detonate it, killing everyone inside, as well as two

members of the SWAT team—and Jack. The teenage baby-
sitter who was minding the boys that afternoon was busy
talking on the telephone at the time and had no idea that
in the next room, three-and-a-half-year-old Jeff was sitting in front of the television mesmerized, watching as a
fiery red-and-black monster filled the screen and made his
father disappear forever.

Jennifer shivered violently and wrapped both hands
around her mug to warm them. She'd forgotten how chilly
June nights could be in New England. And mornings, she
reminded herself with a yawn. It was 2:00 a.m. and she was
sitting on the deck, exhausted and unable to sleep. The
surrounding woods were black and full of night sounds.

After she'd finally soothed Jeff and convinced her parents that she could handle the situation better alone, she,
Jeff and Ryan had settled down to a dinner of peanut butter and jelly sandwiches and potato chips. Next to hot
dogs, it was the boys' favorite meal, and still the mood was
not the happy one she'd envisioned on the first night in
their new home.

When it was time for bed, Ryan conked out as soon as
his head hit the pillow, but Jeff suddenly decided there
were monsters under his bed, just waiting for her to tiptoe
away to pounce. He refused to sleep in the loft and after
nearly an hour of useless cajoling, Jennifer gave in and did
what she'd sworn she absolutely was not going to do again,
allowed Jeff to sleep in her bed. He'd finally drifted off,
but now she was too frazzled to sleep.

After tossing and turning and worrying about how she
was going to accomplish all she had to do tomorrow if she
didn't get some rest, she'd finally gotten up and made a
cup of instant cocoa using hot tap water. It was that or
nothing since the stove refused to turn on. Along with

everything else she would have to remember to call and arrange to have a repairman check it out.

She eventually went back to bed and crawled out the next morning with only about two hours' sleep...and looking it.

"What are you doing?" Ryan asked, watching her from the doorway as she muttered and patted the skin beneath her eyes.

"Trying to make the wrinkles go away," she replied. "Got any ideas?"

"Yeah. Try this." He puffed both cheeks up with air.

Jennifer copied him, then nodded at her reflection. "Not bad. Thanks, pal. What do you want for breakfast?"

"I don't want breakfast. I want to fish."

"So what else is new?"

"New York," said Jeff, coming out of her bedroom. "New Jersey."

"Morning, sleepyhead," she said, tousling his hair on her way to the kitchen. "What would you like for breakfast?"

"New Zealand," he continued.

"Enough. Give a kid a globe and he turns into a comedian... someone who tells jokes," she explained before Ryan could ask. "All right, for breakfast we have..." She swung open the cupboard door. "Captain Crunch and... Captain Crunch. That sure simplifies matters."

Blurry-eyed, she aimed the cereal in the general direction of their bowls and added milk.

"I want to watch 'Ninja Turtles' while I eat, okay Mom?"

She nodded, and Ryan scampered across the room to turn on the television. Silently Jeff lifted his bowl and turned his back to the screen—something he always did when a television was on in the same room he was in. Jennifer sighed and headed for the shower.

It took most of the morning to run through her long list of errands and necessary chores. She drove into town to register the boys for day camp and swimming lessons. The camp, sponsored by a local church, ran from eight to noon and they could start Monday. A blessing, since Monday was also the day the moving van was supposed to arrive with their things and the day she was hoping to get back to work.

After a quick lunch in town they went to visit the McVeighs.

Jennifer had wondered what it would be like to be there without Jack, but his parents' joy at seeing their grandsons again was so overwhelming, it was impossible to feel anything but happy. Annie McVeigh was a round, cheerful woman who loved to garden and loved being surrounded by her family. The boys melted into her welcoming hug as if they'd seen her only yesterday. After being examined and exclaimed over, and devouring the cookies and lemonade she offered, they ran off to play on the elaborate wooden swing set Burt McVeigh had built, and was continually expanding, for their legion of grandchildren.

"That one," Annie said to Jennifer as she watched Ryan swinging on the overhead rings, "has a lot of his daddy in him."

"You got that right," Jennifer agreed, smiling.

"And Jeff," she said with a soft sigh. "Jeff needs time, that's all."

Jennifer glanced at her. She hadn't attempted to explain about Jeff and her concerns about him to anyone back home. Well, she had confided in her mother once, but just as she had last night, her mother had insisted that Jeff was fine, that all children went through stages. And so, Jennifer—knowing that this was no normal stage and knowing that her mother couldn't accept that—couldn't accept that there could be anything wrong with her family that she couldn't simply will to right itself—had shut up about it. Now it seemed that after only a few minutes' observation, Annie had picked up on the emotional distress her mother refused to see.

"It's been hard for Jeff," Jennifer told her quietly. "It still is." She briefly revealed some of Jeff's fears and how she hoped moving home would help ease them.

Annie nodded. "You did the right thing, Jennifer. Both those boys need men in their lives, and heaven knows they have enough McVeigh uncles and cousins to handle that. And as for Jeff, well, it's never bad to feel things as deeply as he feels them. Time . . . that's what he needs. You mark my words."

Before the afternoon was over, Annie and Burt had made plans to take the boys fishing and to have them and several of their young cousins sleep over some weekend soon, maybe even outside in the tent if it would be warm enough. Jennifer saw Jeff's eyes cloud, but at least he didn't reject the camp-out proposal outright and she left there feeling more hopeful than she had since she arrived in town.

At home, she unloaded groceries from the car and put them away while Jeff and Ryan went to explore the section of the brook within sight of the house.

"Be careful," she warned, "and stay together . . . and keep your sneakers dry. I'll just finish putting this stuff away and I'll start dinner. How do hot dogs sound?"

They shouted their approval as they disappeared over the grassy bank that sloped gently down to the brook.

Jennifer relished the relative quiet, with their distant laughter and shouts a reassuring drone in the background. It was as perfect as a moment stacking canned goods could be, until Jeff's frightened scream ripped the late-afternoon peace.

Jennifer froze, and then lunged for the back door, racing across the deck and meeting the boys just as they crested the hill.

"What is it?" she gasped, falling to her knees and grasping Jeff by the shoulders. "Did you hurt yourself?"

"N-no." He shook his head frantically, his eyes wide with real fear. "I saw a bear. Down there." He pointed behind him.

"A bear?" She heaved a relieved sigh. "Honey, there aren't any bears around here."

"There are so. I saw one. I did. Ryan saw it, too."

She turned to Ryan. "Did you see a bear, too, Ry?"

He nodded. "A big black one. Right over there."

It was remotely possible, she supposed. Once, years ago, there had been a moose hanging around these parts. She debated calling the police, then decided she first ought to be sure what she was talking about.

"Show me where you saw this bear," she instructed, taking them firmly by the hands.

Ryan tugged her forward while Jeff hung back.

"No," he said. "I don't want to go back down there."

"Jeff, I'll be right beside you. I just want to know exactly where you saw the bear so I can tell the police where to look for him. Okay?"

Frowning, his small body stiff, he reluctantly edged forward. Jennifer's own heart was pounding and she glanced from side to side cautiously, as if expecting something to spring from behind a tree any second.

"There," Ryan shouted suddenly. "He's right there."

Jeff's grip on her hand tightened. "Mommy, Mommy..."

"Holy..." She stopped dead in her tracks and instinctively yanked the boys behind her, much to Ryan's annoyance. For an instant she actually thought it was a bear, or at least a bear cub. Then the animal turned and faced them directly, revealing what was clearly a canine snout. "It's just a dog," she breathed.

A closer look cut her relief short. It was in fact a very big dog, and headed their way. With its gaze locked on the three of them, it lumbered across the brook and onto the bank only a few yards away, still coming at them.

Torn between the desire to bolt and the knowledge that running was the worst thing she could do, Jennifer held the boys' hands tightly and had begun to slowly back her way up the bank when a short, clear whistle sounded from the other side of the brook.

"Bear. Come."

Two crisp words and immediately the huge dog wheeled around and loped back across the brook, coming to a stop beside the man waiting there. Across the same distance, Jennifer's gaze locked with Rex Lovell's. He patted the big dog's head without looking down, and Jennifer thought he murmured something low and soothing to the animal.

For a moment, she lost all awareness of the boys still clinging fearfully to her and the gentle rushing sound of the water moving over earth and rocks and the warmth of the late-afternoon sun overhead. It was as if she'd stepped into a memory... a soundless, timeless world of pure feeling.

Ever since their encounter in the market, the knowledge that Rex was nearby had hovered at the edges of her thoughts. Guilt, she told herself over and over. That's what kept him on her mind. She would see him again and apologize, and that would be that.

Now she was seeing him again, and as soon as the tightness in her chest permitted her to speak, she would deliver the apology she had rehearsed. But that definitely would not be that. Standing a dozen yards away, doing nothing more intimate than watching her, Rex was making her feel exactly the way he'd made her feel at eighteen—excited, and a little afraid and as if she were in way over her head, with absolutely no idea how to save herself.

He started toward them just as Ryan squirmed free of her hold. Sensing there was no real danger, she let him go and waited anxiously as Rex crossed the brook with two steps, the dog close at the heels of the heavy tan work boots Rex wore with the usual snug jeans and faded chambray shirt.

He was darkly handsome, his features strong and sharply etched, a lucky blend of his varied heritage. His brows were black and, she recalled, often more expressive than the hooded eyes beneath them. His mouth was wide and distracting, his square jaw covered with at least a day's black stubble. As he drew closer, she began to smile, then noted that his own expression was grim. She let her smile slip from her face.

"I'm sorry if you were frightened," he said, joining them. His pale eyes held hers. "Of the dog, I mean."

"The kids thought he was a bear," explained Jennifer.

Rex didn't laugh at their mistake. His expression stubbornly solemn, he nodded at Jeff who was peeking from behind Jennifer "That's understandable. I thought the same thing the first time I saw him. That's why I named him Bear."

"Can I pet him?" asked Ryan, the usual eagerness in his tone.

"Sure. Sit, Bear." The dog quickly sat and looked toward his master for approval. He had a red bandanna knotted around his neck. "Good boy," Rex murmured. "Now, paw."

He raised one huge black paw.

Ryan's eyes grew wide. "He knows what you say."

"Most of the time. He wants to shake hands with you."

Ryan stepped forward and curled his hand around the dog's paw as best he could.

"This is Bear," Rex told him, rubbing the dog's head. "Bear, meet..."

His pause prodded Jennifer to remember her manners. "I'm sorry. Rex, I'm sure you've already guessed, but these are my sons. This is Ryan," she said, placing her hand briefly on his shoulder, "and this is Jeff. Boys, this is Mr. Lovell."

He bent down slightly to offer his hand to one boy at a time. "Hello, Ryan...Jeff."

"H'lo," replied Ryan. "You're the mister who gave us the extra quarter."

At last Rex smiled, almost in spite of himself, it seemed to Jennifer. "That's right. Did you win your game?"

"Nope," Ryan replied, then immediately turned his attention to Bear, who returned the favor by licking his face.

"Jeff, say hello to Mr. Lovell," Jennifer prompted.

His expression stormy, he repeated, "Hello, Mr. Lovell."

"If it's okay with your mom, you can call me Rex." He lifted his gaze to meet Jennifer's. "They look like Jack."

Before he said it, his chest lifted with a deep breath that reminded her that Rex had been Jack's friend as well as a distant cousin. She smiled faintly. "Yes, they do. I'm not always sure if the resemblance is a blessing or a curse."

He nodded, seeming to understand. "How are you, Jenny?" he asked with a quiet urgency that told her it wasn't a cliché or superficial request.

How could she answer in kind with her heart pounding and her kids underfoot and her thoughts atangle of all the things they'd said to each other in the past and all the things she wanted to say to him now?

"I'm okay," she said finally, deciding there was enough of the truth in that to suffice. "Most of the time I'm okay."

And the rest of the time? Thankfully he didn't give voice to the question that burned in his eyes.

Jennifer cleared her throat and pulled her clammy hand loose from Jeff's. "I want to thank you for the note you sent after... that is, when Jack died. You'll never know how much it meant to me."

"I wanted to come here... to see you, but..." He hesitated, running his hand through the dark hair Claire Renault thought shaggy. Claire Renault was an idiot. "But I didn't."

"I understand. I probably wouldn't have remembered anyway. I was sort of numb at the time, and there were so many people around. I got your note later, when all the fuss was over and I was beginning to realize what it really means to be alone and wondering how on earth I was going to make it through the next twenty-four hours." She managed a small smile. " 'Keep kicking or you'll sink....' That was exactly what I needed to hear."

Keep kicking or you'll sink. That's how he had ended the condolence note he'd written her. It was also what he used to say to her twelve years ago, during the long, hot summer afternoons when they met secretly at an isolated part of the lake and when he'd taught her to overcome a paralyzing fear of the water. And of him.

It was those times Jennifer recalled now as they stood staring into each other's eyes, the memory of the words intertwined with the memory of all those private swimming lessons...his hands supporting her body beneath the water, the sleek, rough feeling of his legs when they accidentally, inevitably, became tangled with hers, the heat of his breath on her face when he murmured words of encouragement and when he...

Jennifer straightened suddenly and just as abruptly Rex seemed to surface from private thoughts of his own. He turned away from her to look toward the brook where Ryan was trying to get Bear to drink from his cupped hand.

"Yeah, well," he said, "it's good advice, I suppose."

"It worked for me," Jennifer replied as lightly as she could manage. "Up to that point, I'd been just drifting along, going through the paces, but I decided then and there to start kicking again. Of course at first it was more of a stumble, but..." she threw her hands in the air "—at least I haven't gone under."

Rex smiled. "I guess that's what counts." He slid his fingertips into the snug front pockets of his jeans and rocked back on his heels. "So, are you back for good or just for the summer?"

"For good. There's family here and..." Cautiously she glanced down at the top of Jeff's head. "I just decided it was best for all of us. How about you? I hear you came back to get your mother's house ready to sell."

"That's right. This seemed as good a time as any to get rid of it."

"Are you taking a vacation from work?"

His smile was cold. "Don't you really mean to ask if I have a job to take a vacation from?"

"No," she denied, flushing.

"Funny. That's what most folks around here wonder."

"Aren't you being a little defensive?"

"You get that way when you're used to defending yourself."

"Well, you certainly don't have to defend yourself from me."

He gazed at her with silent skepticism.

"I only asked to be friendly," she insisted, "and to catch up on lost time."

"Uh-huh. You were real friendly to me the other day."

Her face grew hotter. "Look, I'm sorry about that. I just— There's no excuse for the way I acted, and I'm sorry."

Rex shrugged. "I'm sorry I called you on it. You don't owe me anything."

Don't I? thought Jennifer. At the very least she owed him an explanation and another apology, but this probably wasn't the best time or the place to go into all that.

"Anyway," he offered, "I wouldn't say I'm taking a vacation so much as I'm squeezing this in around work. I run a small business in upstate Massachusetts and I expect to be back and forth a lot."

"Sounds like—"

"Are you a Gypsy?" Jeff demanded suddenly.

Rex stiffened.

Jennifer glared at her son. "Jeff! Rex, I'm sorry. He doesn't..."

He shook his head to silence her. Bending his knees, he hunkered down so he was level with Jeff. "As a matter of fact, I am," he told him. "Half Gypsy anyway. The other half of me is Scotch and Irish, just like your daddy. Just like you."

That news only seemed to add to Jeff's dismay. He thrust his chin forward belligerently, and at the same time he clutched Jennifer's sleeve with his fingers. "I don't want you to steal me. Or my brother, either."

Rex shot Jennifer a narrow-eyed look.

She squirmed nervously. "My mother..."

His lips twisted, and he muttered something under his breath. "What makes you think I might steal you or your brother?" he asked Jeff, his tone interested, nothing more.

"Because that's what Gypsies do," Jeff retorted.

"I see. You know a lot of Gypsies, do you, Jeff?"

Jeff shook his head.

"I get it. You know only a few who steal children?"

Again Jeff shook his head, his feet shifting uncomfortably. "But my grandma said that's what Gypsies do."

Rex nodded. "I'll tell you something, Jeff, I'll bet your grandma doesn't know too many Gypsies, either. But I do, and you know something? I don't know even one who's ever stolen a child."

"But she said they did."

"I'm sure she did. I'm sure she thought she was telling you the truth, too, just like you thought you were telling your mom the truth when you said you saw a bear down here a while ago. Right?"

"I thought it was a bear."

"I know you did, Jeff. But thinking something doesn't always make it so. And sometimes all it takes to figure that out is a closer look."

His expression softening as he pondered that, Jeff's hold on Jennifer loosened marginally. She smiled gratefully at Rex as he straightened.

"Thanks, I tried telling him the same thing, but I don't think it got through to him half as well. You're pretty good with kids."

Almost before the words were out, it occurred to her to wonder why that might be. Was he married? A father?

Living with someone? His dismissive shrug revealed nothing in that direction.

"I figure kids aren't much different from grown-ups. If you stick with the truth you can't go wrong."

Was there a pointedness to that remark, and to the way his gaze rested on her expectantly? she mused.

It was a relief when Ryan wandered over at that moment to announce that he was starving. "And so is Bear," he added. "Can he come to our house and eat with us? Bear likes hot dogs, too."

Jennifer's mouth quirked. "He told you that, did he?"

"Uh-huh," Ryan insisted, nodding vigorously. "He does like hot dogs, doesn't he?" he asked Rex.

"If it doesn't climb out of his dish, Bear likes it," Rex replied dryly.

So he wasn't going to let her off the hook with this dinner invitation, and she could hardly invite Bear to join them without including his master. Her heart picking up momentum at the thought of having Rex in the small confines of her kitchen, she tossed her hair back over her shoulder and looked at him.

"Well, we're only having hot dogs, but if..."

The sound of tires spinning on the gravel drive above drew all their attention in that direction as her father's car pulled into view and parked.

"Grandma. Grandpa," the boys called as they bolted to greet them.

Damn, thought Jennifer, feeling every nerve in her body tighten. Now what was she going to do? Rescind the invitation she'd already half extended? Or traipse up the hill with Rex in tow and shout, "Guess who's coming to dinner?" Right, and end up with dinner table tension you'd need a machete to hack through. Not to mention the possibility of another embarrassing scene with Jeff. She was going to have to have a serious talk with that kid.

After struggling briefly to come up with a tactful excuse to offer Rex, she turned back and discovered she needn't have bothered. He was already gone, back on his own side of the brook with Bear at his side, two dark, menacing forms moving through the foliage and the shadows.

Chapter Four

*S*teal children?

Rex had to hand it to Jennifer's old lady. He'd been fielding accusations and slurs all his life, but it was the first time he'd ever had to deal with that one head-on.

He crossed the back porch in two strides, slamming the screen door so hard, the bottom hinge snapped. He swore violently. Just what he needed—one more thing to be repaired, cleaned or painted before he could put a For Sale sign in front of this place. Sometimes, when he counted the broken blisters on his hands or when the fumes from the paint thinner got to him, he wondered why the hell he was bothering in the first place. The easiest thing in the world would be to hire a Realtor to sell the house as is, a handyman's special.

More like a handyman's nightmare, he thought, staring at the ancient Formica backsplash, which was curling loose behind the sink. Grabbing hold of it, he ripped it off the wall with one powerful yank, something he hadn't planned to do for a few weeks yet, when he'd progressed as far as the kitchen. Impulsive actions. Jennifer always did have that effect on him.

He flung the Formica aside and swatted at a fly that had come in through one of the many torn window screens. As for why he didn't just get whatever price he could for the dump and bid "good riddance" to Pleasure once and for all, the answer was painfully obvious. He never made things easy on himself.

With that, he thought of Jennifer again, and the look that had come to her face when her parents showed up and caught her with him, and he swore again. He hadn't needed to read her mind to know what she'd been thinking, and so he had walked away and spared them both the embarrassment of her having to tell him to get lost for the second time in as many days.

Before her folks had arrived though, she had looked at him in a very different way. He'd recognized the look no matter how much she'd tried to hide it behind a friendly smile. He'd had women look at him that way before. Hell, he'd had Jennifer Cahill—correction, Jennifer *McVeigh*—look at him that way before. He knew it meant that somewhere deep inside she was having the same primordial reaction to him that he was having to her.

And he knew that when push came to shove, it didn't amount to a pile of crap. The biggest favor he could do himself was to wipe from his mind the fact that she was living next door, close enough that he could almost smell her, that teasing scent that always made him think of lemons and sunshine.

Sunshine. He gave a harsh laugh. Corny as it was, that was what always came to mind whenever he weakened and allowed himself to remember Jennifer. Maybe it was be-

cause so much of their time together had been spent outside, beneath the kind of hot summer sun that makes
everything heat up and slow down. Maybe it was simply
because of her smile and the way it had the power to break
through everything else in his life the way the sun can break
through the clouds after a sudden storm.

Some women had great eyes or cheekbones or mouths.
Jennifer had all those, too, but she also had great teeth—
perfectly straight, white, *expensive*-looking teeth. But
then, he reminded himself, everything about Jennifer was
expensive. Too expensive. Snap out of it, Lovell, he
thought as he kicked aside the piece of Formica. Just this
once make things easy on yourself.

To distract himself he went out to the back porch where
a dozen cans of Ivory Bisque paint were lined up. When he
was finished here, every wall in the house would be clean
and Spackled and painted the same shade of Ivory Bisque.
An eight-room clean slate waiting for someone to make a
fresh start, all traces of his life here either painted over or
thrown away. Just the way he wanted it.

The house hadn't always been like this. It had origi-
nally been his mother's family home, and when he was a
kid she'd worked hard to keep it up. Why give the town
something else to talk about? she used to say. But then he'd
gone away and she'd grown older, and of course, having
the house remain vacant for so long hadn't helped any. As
always, the thought of his mother living here alone brought
Rex mixed feelings. If he'd stayed, he could have fixed the
roof and the ripped screens for her, but he could never
have been a different kind of son, the kind of son she'd
deserved. His only regret was that maybe she had never
understood that. Never understood that he'd left and
stayed away as much for her sake as his own.

Prying the lid off the can he'd been using earlier, he stirred the paint gently with a wooden stick. His mother had loved this place, and the best he could do for her now was fix it up in a way that would have pleased the proud woman she was. No one who walked through here ever had to know how she'd burnt the counter beside the stove with a hot frying pan, or how she'd gotten by with only two of the four burners working, or how the carpet treads on the stairs had been worn right through to the jute backing. Why give them something else to talk about?

He carried the paint upstairs to one of the four large bedrooms. He'd started in the back corner of the house, planning to work his way downstairs and right out the back door to freedom. He painted methodically, his motion with the roller even and controlled, his thoughts chaotic. He'd covered one wall and half of another when he felt a familiar brooding presence behind him. Still holding the roller, he stopped and turned.

"What are you looking at?" he demanded. Perhaps a little too belligerently, judging from the response he got.

"Don't," snapped Rex. "Don't give me that look. You're the reason I got dragged over there in the first place, scaring the kids like that."

Bear whimpered. Smiling, Rex bent to rub his head. "I know you didn't mean it, boy. You and I, we have that sort of effect on folks. We just can't help it, can we?"

The dog sat up a little straighter, his expression eager.

"Forget it," Rex told him. "If I let you out now you'll be right back over there looking for those kids." He nodded at the thumping of the dog's tail. "I know that little guy is fun. Yeah, I know I'm not. I've got a lot on my mind. Go take a nap, why don't you? Later I'll take you for a walk . . . on this side of the brook."

Bear left in a huff and Rex continued painting. Not until the setting sun shadowed the room did he finally think about eating. He covered the paint and dropped the roller into a bucket to soak and went downstairs just in time to see Bear coming through the broken back door.

The big dog froze and hung his head when Rex demanded to know where he'd been. Rex was the only one Bear ever cowered before, and Rex knew that even then it was out of remorse and not fear. It still wasn't a sight he relished.

"Forget it," he said now. "It's not your fault I'm so hotheaded, I broke the door."

The dog perked up and immediately retrieved something Rex hadn't seen him drop. He trotted to Rex's side as fast as a dog his age and with his arthritic hips and other health problems could trot.

"What's this? A souvenir from someone's clothesline?" Rex shook his head as he crouched down and gently pried the scrap of cloth from between the massive teeth.

"You're gonna be real popular with the neighbors, I can see that already." He fingered the cloth. It was a strip about eighteen inches long, faded blue, silky and frayed at the edges. It reminded him of something. He rubbed it back and forth between his fingertips, remembering the feel of something very similar tucked up around his chin on cold nights.

"A piece of some old blanket," he said to Bear. "Where'd you find this?" He frowned. "That's what I figured."

Lifting it to his nose, he sniffed and the clean scent of it filled his head in a way that would have warned off a smarter man. He eyed the dog. "So what do you think?"

The heavy tail beat against the floor.

Rex stood and shoved the scrap into his jeans pocket. "Yeah, me, too."

Jennifer's first thought when she heard the knock on the back door was that her parents had once again ignored her wishes and returned with a pizza or a bucket of chicken. Then it occurred to her that they wouldn't have knocked.

Her second thought, after glimpsing Rex through the window, was the wish that she had taken time to change out of the wrinkled khaki shorts and red T-shirt she'd been wearing all day. Both times Rex had seen her she'd been rumpled. Not that it made a difference, she told herself, finger-combing her long hair even as she pulled open the door.

"Hi," he said, his gaze drifting down her bare legs briefly before he brought it back to meet hers with a sudden frown.

Was there something wrong with her legs? wondered Jennifer, resisting the urge to check and see. Maybe she had something repulsive stuck to her sandal.

"Hi," she replied.

"Look," he said, "this might seem pretty silly, but Bear brought home something that I thought might belong to one of your boys... the little one most likely."

"Ryan?"

He nodded. "Yeah. I thought I ought to check it out, just in case." He stared at her.

"What is it?" Jennifer asked.

He slid his fingers into his jeans pocket and pulled out the remnant of Jeff's precious baby blanket.

"Ohmigosh, that's Jeff's softie," she exclaimed.

"Jeff's?"

Jennifer nodded. "It's a scrap of his favorite baby blanket. Ryan is still comfortable toting around the whole blanket, but Jeff feels big boys don't do that. At the same time, he's not quite ready to let it go completely, and under the circumstances I haven't wanted to force the issue.''

''The circumstances?''

''You know,'' she said, shrugging. ''Jack's death and all.''

''Oh, sure. I can understand that.''

''So we came up with the idea of cutting off a piece of the binding—sort of a portable version. It must have fallen out of his pocket when he was down by the brook.''

''I'm glad Bear picked it up,'' he said, handing it to her.

''You're glad? Bedtime is tough enough around here without losing the little bit of comfort Jeff seems to draw from this.''

''What kid ever wants to go to bed? Especially in a new place where there's so much to do and explore.''

''If only that were Jeff's...'' She halted, shaking off her wistful tone. ''Anyway, thanks a lot for bothering to return it. I owe you one.''

His golden eyes glinted. ''In that case, got any hot dogs left over?''

''All of them actually. The stove's not working and I was so busy running around all day that I forgot to call to have it checked out. And since my microwave is on a moving van somewhere between here and L.A., cooking is out of the question until the van arrives next week.''

''So you haven't had dinner, either?''

''Let's just say we're existing on Captain Crunch and peanut butter,'' she replied as the boys appeared behind her. While Jeff lingered at her side, Ryan immediately went to hug Bear, who seemed just as overjoyed to see him.

''Easy, honey, don't squash him,'' she admonished.

"Not much chance of that," remarked Rex. "Bear's pretty sturdy."

"Still, I always worry when they're around strange dogs...that is, dogs they don't know."

"Is that why Jeff is so afraid of dogs?" he asked, something in his direct stare at odds with his mild tone.

"Not at all. Jeff is simply more cautious than his brother. That doesn't strike me as such a bad thing, especially when we're talking about a pretty big, pretty fierce-looking animal."

"Appearances can be deceiving," Rex said softly.

Their gazes remained locked.

"I know that."

"Do you?"

Jennifer shivered.

"You're cold," Rex observed.

"No," she denied, then could have kicked herself when his lips lifted at the corners, silently suggesting other reasons she might shiver in his presence.

"Anyway," he said, "I didn't come here to stand around talking about Bear."

Jennifer's eyes widened in alarm. She wished she'd thought to ask him not to mention to Jeff that he knew about the blanket. The poor kid worried enough as it was. To her relief, Rex caught her look and with a barely perceptible nod, conveyed that he understood.

"What I really came for," he said, "was to see if I might borrow a few hot dogs to roast. Maybe you'd even like to join me?"

"You mean at your place?" asked Jennifer.

"No," he said quickly. "Not there. I thought I might make a camp fire. Anybody interested?"

"Me," shouted Ryan. "And Bear, too."

"Okay, there's two volunteers. Jenny?" he inquired.

No one called her Jenny. No one but Rex ever had, and the memories evoked by the name washed over her disturbingly.

"Sure," she said. "I haven't had a hot dog cooked over a camp fire in years."

Rex crouched down. "How about you, Jeff? Want to try cooking your own hot dog?"

"I don't know."

"Ever had a hot dog cooked on a stick over a fire?"

Jeff shook his head.

"They're the best. And if you don't like it, you can always feed it to Bear. What do you say?"

Jeff darted a glance at Jennifer.

"It'll be fun, sweetie."

"Okay," he said quietly. "I'll try."

"Good," said Rex. "We can start by gathering the wood for the fire."

Jeff, appearing startled to learn he was expected to take an extended role in this new venture, kept glancing in Jennifer's direction as soon as they went outside. But Rex continued talking in the same calm, unhurried tone, explaining that they had to find dry wood a certain size and pile it just so in the spot he pronounced perfect after leading them around the yard, eliminating one potential site as too bumpy, another as too damp.

It was, Jennifer observed, a crash course in fire building, complete with all the safety warnings she herself would have delivered, but given in a practical, understated way. She was assigned to keep watch over the fire as they hunted for long narrow sticks suitable for spearing the hot dogs and holding them over the flames. Jeff's face erupted in a smile when he was the first to find one Rex considered worth whittling to a point, using the fascinating pocket knife he carried with him.

Men's stuff, she thought, watching Jeff hover at Rex's elbow as he skillfully wielded the knife. The sort of stuff they had been missing out on. And the main reason she had brought them here. The only catch was that in her wildest dreams she hadn't imagined that the man to supply the missing ingredient would be Rex Lovell.

The hot dogs were an overwhelming success, with Bear eagerly gobbling up all the mistakes and leftovers. The dog claimed the choice spot between the kids, and Jennifer watched with happy amazement as Jeff progressed from cautious pats to the relatively safe terrain of Bear's hefty sides, to actually letting the dog eat from the palm of his hand.

"It tickles," Jeff said to Jennifer, his tone sturdy, his eyes bright with excitement and wonder in a way that was all too rare.

Afterward, Rex taught them how to bank down the fire and smother the embers with sand.

"Does Bear have to go home now?" Ryan asked.

"I'm afraid so. It's past his bedtime—and yours, too, I'll bet."

"I don't want to go to bed."

"Me, either," said Jeff, his small face tensing.

"Well, I'm sure your mother does. She's had a long day trying to keep up with a couple of hotshots like you."

She was tired. Still, it disturbed Jennifer that she couldn't decide which she dreaded most, Rex's leaving or another game of musical beds with Jeff. On his small face she saw his pride at being called a hotshot vie with anxiety. Anxiety won.

"C'mon, Bear," said Rex, getting to his feet. "We better get out of here and let these guys get some sleep."

Ryan reluctantly gave the dog a final hug.

Jeff hung back. "I'm not going to bed," he blurted. "I hate that bed. There are monsters up there."

"Monsters?" squeaked Ryan.

This is what Jennifer had feared would happen, the spread of monster fever. "Ryan, there are no such things as monsters."

"There are so monsters," insisted Jeff. "Just like there are Gypsies. They're under my bed."

"You've got Gypsies under your bed?" Rex asked him with feigned surprise.

Jeff giggled in spite of himself. "No. Monsters. There are monsters up there."

"I see. You've seen these monsters, have you, Jeff?"

He shook his head. "Not exactly."

"Heard them?"

"Sometimes."

"What do they sound like?"

"I don't know. Things."

"Loud things?"

"I don't know. Whooshing things mostly, I guess."

"Sort of like the noise the wind makes at night?"

"Right, like that."

"You don't suppose maybe what you hear is the wind?"

He shook his head frantically. "It's monsters. I know it is."

Rex pondered that. "Then if you're absolutely sure it's monsters making the noise," he said finally, as matter-of-factly as if Jeff had announced that his bike had a flat that needed fixing, "there's only one thing to do."

Jennifer stood by, a little skeptical about where he was going with this.

"I know," said Jeff. "Sleep in Mommy's bed."

"I see. There are no monsters in Mommy's bed?" he asked, directing the question to Jennifer.

"Not at the moment," she shot back.

"That's good news." He turned to Jeff. "But sleeping with your mom isn't the solution I had in mind. I thought you might want to take care of this problem all by yourself."

Jeff looked doubtful. "How?"

"Do you have any monster repellent on hand?" he asked.

Jeff looked to Jennifer for a response.

She shook her head. "I'm afraid not."

She smothered a laugh as Rex rubbed his jaw thoughtfully.

"Me, either," he said. "I guess we'll have to whip up a batch."

"You know how to make monster repellent?" Jeff asked, clearly in awe. Ryan just gazed at him. Jennifer was certain Ryan didn't even know what *repellent* was, but if it interested a man who owned a great dog like Bear, it interested him, too.

It took the next twenty minutes to produce the substance Rex assured Jeff would ward off any and all monsters that might be in the area. Jennifer, a tentative accomplice, was sent to find a spray bottle while the men, armed with flashlights, went in search of the secret ingredient, leaves and green berries from an elderberry bush. Under Rex's direction, Jeff and Ryan enthusiastically crushed and stirred and added water.

"Yuk," said Ryan when he held aloft the finished product, a watery, brownish green potion with bits of leaves and berries floating on top.

Jeff scrunched up his face. "It looks gross. And it smells funny."

"Do you expect monsters to run from something that smells pretty?" Rex asked. "Quit belly-aching. Nobody's asking you to drink it. We're just going to spray it around your room.''

"Great," muttered Jennifer, trailing along as they headed for the loft. "Who needs air freshener?"

The boys took turns spraying beneath their beds, in the closet, the windowsills and every other conceivable nook or cranny where a clever monster might hide. Finally Rex commandeered the bottle and placed it on the nightstand between the boys' beds.

"For an emergency," he said. "But I can tell you right now there won't be one. This place is one hundred percent monsterproof."

"That means there aren't any?" inquired Ryan.

Rex grinned at him. "That's what it means, pal."

"It also means it's time to hit the sack," added Jennifer, turning down their covers. Ryan hopped onto his bed and she held her breath, filled with relief and amazement when Jeff followed suit.

She tucked them in and delivered good-night kisses as fast as she could, not wanting to do or say anything that might break the magic spell. As far as she was concerned, that's exactly what it was—magic, and Rex was the man responsible.

She paused halfway down the stairs, fully expecting Jeff to call her back. The silence was almost a physical relief.

"Monster repellent," she whispered with a shake of her head. "I don't believe it."

Rex shrugged.

"But what if he—"

"Shh."

He pressed his finger to Jennifer's lips to stop her, and the light contact pulled at her in a strange way, a warning that she hadn't outgrown all the weakness of her youth. Rex cocked his head to urge her downstairs.

"I'm sorry," he said when they reached the kitchen. "What were you going to say?"

"I forget," she was forced to admit. His gaze touched her lips briefly, as if to speculate about the reason for her sudden memory lapse.

"Anyway, thanks for coming up with that monster repellent idea. I don't think I could have taken another night like last night."

"Does he usually sleep in your bed?"

"No," she replied edgily. "He did for a little while after Jack died and then again last night. This monster bit is something new. I tried telling him there are no such things."

Amusement lit his eyes. "No such things as monsters lurking in the night? Waiting to pounce on the innocent and unsuspecting. Are you sure about that, Jenny?"

"Yes. I just hope that spraying for them doesn't backfire by convincing him I was lying and they really do exist."

Rex shrugged. "From what I saw, denying their existence wasn't getting you anywhere. Sometimes showing someone how to deal with a potential problem is all it takes to make the problem go away."

"How come you know so much about kids?"

"I don't know all that much."

"Don't be so modest. Do you have kids of your own?"

His earlier amusement vanished in a harsh laugh, and Jennifer found herself biting her lip in anticipation of an answer she didn't want to hear.

"Do I really strike you as a family man?" he asked, his tone dry.

"I don't know. But you sure are good with kids."

"Other peoples'. I'm not the marrying kind, Jenny. I never was."

"People change."

"Not that much. *Jal a drom*," he said softly, the unfamiliar words sounding like music.

"'*Jal a drom*,'" she echoed. "What's that?"

"It's our expression for the Rom way of life. Rom means Gypsy," he explained. "It roughly translates to *travel the road*, but it's much more than that. It sums up all the joy and freedom that goes along with that life."

"*Jal a drom*. I like it."

"Me, too," he said bluntly.

"That potion, is that a *Rom* tradition, too?"

"More or less. Elderberries are what my Rom grandmother used to treat babies with colic. It was the closest remedy I could think of for this situation."

Jennifer laughed. "I don't care if it was used to cure hoof-and-mouth disease. It worked."

They stared at each other through an awkward silence.

"So," they both said at once, then both shrugged, and followed the lone word with more silence.

"Would you like a cup of coffee or something?" she asked finally. He hesitated, and for a second she was afraid he was going to say no, was afraid he was going to leave and was afraid of how that was going to make her feel.

"Coffee sounds good," he said.

Jennifer filled the drip-pot with water. "Decaf?"

"It doesn't matter. If I can't sleep, I'll work and be finished that much sooner."

"How's it going?"

"I just started really. But I'm in no hurry. If it takes the rest of the summer I won't mind."

Me, either, thought Jennifer as she counted scoops of coffee. She heard Rex moving around the kitchen, stopping occasionally.

"Didn't you say something about a moving van full of stuff coming next week?" he asked.

"That's right."

"Where are you going to put it?"

Jennifer laughed. "Well, it's not actually a vanful. I sold a lot of the things I had in California and others went with the house. I just shipped things that were really special either to me or the kids. I plan to get rid of some of this stuff to make room, change the look a little.... I've sort of outgrown these gingham curtains and duck prints." She swung a critical gaze around the open area of the kitchen, dining and living rooms. "I think that when everything is finished coming and going I'll still have one or two empty places to fill."

"Do you know what you're going to do with the stuff you're getting rid of?"

"I haven't really thought about it. Why?"

"I've been getting rid of a lot of stuff myself since I got here, and I know a place that will take whatever you've got. If you like I'll take care of it for you."

From out of nowhere, more of her mother's past comments about Gypsies came at her. *Schemers, that's all they are. Always looking for a handout.* She slammed the mugs onto the counter, hard enough to raise his eyebrows.

"Fine," she said. "I'll let you know when I'm ready."

They carried their coffee outside to the deck and sat side by side on the steps leading to the yard. Bear dozed nearby. For a while they sat without talking. Dozens of questions ran through Jennifer's head. There was so much she wanted to know about him and about how and where he'd spent the past twelve years, but she was afraid of asking the wrong thing and putting him on the defensive once again. Finally he broke the silence.

"Do you have plans for the summer?" he asked.

"Well, starting Monday, when the kids begin camp, I plan to get back to work. I have a big deadline coming up in the fall."

"You work?"

Even in the dark she could see the glint of surprise in his eyes.

"You sound shocked. Oh, I get it. You expected me to spend the summer lying by the pool at the club, sipping frozen daiquiris. Jumping to conclusions, wouldn't you say?"

"I suppose I deserved that."

"You bet you did."

"Sorry. Tell me about this deadline you have. What do you do?"

"It's sort of hard to explain."

He stretched his long legs out along the steps. "I'm in no hurry. Are you?"

Jennifer shook her head. "No. No hurry at all."

"Good. So," he prompted. "The deadline."

"Right. That's for a book I'm working on."

"You're a writer?"

"Not exactly," she acknowledged, thinking of all the editorial and technical assistance that would be involved in getting this book to the stands. "The books are just something that happened."

"Books?" He sounded both impressed and amused.

"This is my second. It all started a few months after Jack died, when I realized I had to do something to supplement the life insurance he left. With no experience and two kids, my options were not exactly wide open."

"Did you consider moving home then?"

"Every day," she said wryly. "That was my greatest motivation for finding a job. You know my parents."

Rex laughed softly.

"Anyway, I began looking around, and the jobs I was qualified for, I didn't want. The ones I wanted, I either wasn't qualified for or they didn't pay enough to even cover day-care expenses. Finally I got desperate enough to sit and make a list of all my marketable skills—short list," she added, "and I knew I was in trouble. You may be surprised to learn that there's not a big demand out there for people who can embroider Peter Rabbit on overall bibs."

"Might be a better world if there were," commented Rex.

"Be that as it may, around the time I decided I was unemployable, Jeff's birthday came rolling around. Things were tight, which meant I couldn't afford to hire a pony or a Teenage Mutant Ninja Turtle to entertain at his party. So I came up with the idea of a dinosaur bash."

"I'll bite."

"I used some gray sheets to turn the dining room into a cave and I baked dinosaur-egg cupcakes and served prehistoric cherry punch. The day of the party I helped each guest make a dinosaur costume out of an old T-shirt and some cut-up sponges. We called them…are you ready for this? Spongeasaurus."

He laughed. "Spongeasaurus, huh? How did it go over?"

"A major hit," she told him. "With the kids *and* their moms. One, a real lady exec type, even offered to pay me to plan and arrange her son's party a few weeks later. She didn't have to hit me over the head with the possibilities the idea presented and so Parties To Go was born."

"Let me get this straight. You plan kid's birthday parties? That's it?"

"Well, I've expanded a bit since then, but basically, that's it. It may not be Nobel Prize material, but believe me, it is a marketable skill. And, thanks to my mother, one I come by naturally."

She briefly explained how children's parties had evolved into organizing larger, adult gatherings and finally into the lucrative world of business entertaining.

"Where does the book fit in?" he asked when she finished describing a few of her more outrageous ventures.

"I have my friend Molly to thank for that. She lived next door to me in L.A. and she introduced me to her sister who was visiting from back East and just happened to be an editor with a major New York publisher. She took a look at the photo album of past parties I showed to prospective clients and thought it had book potential. It came out last year, entitled *Throwing a Kid's Birthday Party Without Going Broke or Crazy.*"

"And now you're writing the sequel."

"Close. I'm working on a book of wedding ideas."

"*Getting Married Without Going Broke or Crazy?*" he joked.

"I'm not sure that's possible, but at least readers might pick up a few hints."

"No kidding, Jenny, I think it's terrific that you could turn things around that way. It looks like I worried for nothing."

"Did you? Worry about me, I mean?"

He looked away from her into the darkness. "I guess it's fair to say I thought about you from time to time."

"What did you think about me?"

He faced her. "I don't remember. Right now I'm thinking that it's getting late. I ought—"

"No fair," she said, surprising both of them by placing her hand on his arm as he started to stand. He froze, his muscles so tense, they felt like granite beneath her fingers. "You know all about me now, not to mention being privy

to my kids' innermost fears, and I still don't know anything about what you've been doing the past twelve years.''

"Nothing nearly as impressive as you've done, believe
me.''

"I'm sure that's not true. You said you owned your own
business.''

He gave a short laugh. "That was an exaggeration. It's
more like me and a couple of assistants and a dozen or so
free-lancers spread across the country who I call on when
I need them. I'm a pyrotechnician,'' he said, watching for
her reaction.

Her forehead wrinkled. "A pyro... Fire?''

"That's right. Fitting, huh?''

"Rex, I...''

"Although in this case it's not really fire that's involved, but fireworks.''

"That's where I've heard that word before. A pyrotechnician is someone who puts on firework displays,
right?''

He nodded. "You got it.''

"That's fascinating. How did you get into it?''

"Sort of the way you got into the book business,'' he
said wryly. Briefly he told her about the years since he left
town, satisfying a lot of her earlier curiosity in the process. He had hooked up with his father and the band of
friends and relatives he traveled with and had at last indulged a long-standing desire to learn more about the
people and culture that had caused him to be branded an
outcast all his life.

At the time his father and the others were working with
Leo Olivetti, a man who arranged firework displays
throughout the country. Rex joined on and took to the
craft naturally, staying with Leo even when his father and
the others eventually moved on in search of greener pas-

tures. Neither of Leo's sons was interested in the business, and when it came time to retire, Leo went with Rex to the bank and worked out arrangements for him to buy the Olivetti Fireworks Company.

"It's not much," he concluded, "just a few old storage barns in upstate Mass., far enough out in the country so that no one would be hurt if anything goes wrong."

"Do things go wrong?" she asked. "It sounds dangerous."

He shrugged. "Life's dangerous. You just have to know what you're doing."

"But I would think that this would be your busiest time of year. How can you afford to take time off now? Or is that why you're in town? To handle the Fourth of July fireworks?"

"Hardly," he said, his short laugh bitter. "Not that I wasn't jerk enough to bid on the job. It seems the town council has a long memory. They turned me down flat, even though I intentionally lowballed the bid."

"I guess you really wanted the job. It's understandable, this being your hometown and all, and—"

"I didn't give a damn about the job," he broke in harshly. "Or this town. I just wanted to see for myself how small-minded people here could be. And I did."

Jennifer took a deep breath. "Rex, I'm so sorry. I—"

"Stop," he ordered, the word sounding clear in the darkness. "Don't you ever pity me. The fact is I've got more work for the Fourth than I can handle . . . jobs as far away as Denver and Fort Meyers, Florida. I've been crisscrossing the country for months, romancing town councils, putting in bids and signing contracts."

"Sounds like you have to do a lot of traveling."

He glanced sideways at her. "That must be why I'm so good at it. It's in the genes. Anyway, I can't be at all the jobs at once, so I design and organize the materials, ship it to the site and use free-lancers whom I trust on the other end to handle the actual display. That way I'm here to control all the details in case there is a glitch somewhere...and to answer your question, that's why I can afford to take some time off right now to work on the house.''

"But don't you ever get the urge to be there and do the job yourself? To see it and hear the noise and smell the gunpowder?''

"Yeah, I get the urge sometimes, and when I do, I take off and handle a job myself. That just isn't possible right now," he added tersely. He glanced at Bear and as if they shared some sort of mental telepathy, the dog lifted his head, his eyes like fire in the darkness.

"Look, I really ought to shove off so you can get some sleep, too," he said to Jennifer.

She glanced up at the loft window. "Thanks to you, it looks like I will get a good night's sleep. I don't know how to thank you.''

"Don't you?" he countered.

Jennifer hadn't realized how close they were sitting, until he turned and she felt his breath on her face.

"I guess I could offer you another hot dog," she said in a wooden attempt at humor.

"I don't want a hot dog," he said.

What do you want? The question pulsed inside her. She couldn't ask. Wouldn't ask. She didn't want to know.

It didn't matter.

"I want what I've always wanted," he said without having to be asked, and without warning he leaned toward her in the darkness. She felt his hand slide under her hair, cupping the back of her neck, heat and hunger in his touch. "I want you, Jenny."

Chapter Five

Rex moved in on her slowly, letting an eternity tick away before his mouth touched hers. Jennifer knew she should protest, tell him no, push him away. But she didn't do any of that. Instead she made the same mistake she had made twelve years ago. She closed her eyes—so that just in case there was any smugness in his she wouldn't have to confront it until later—and she let him kiss her.

His mouth was as warm and as soft as she remembered, but nowhere as patient. On that long-ago night he had taken his time, kissing her until she felt feverish, as if the exploration of her lips and tongue were fascinating enough to satisfy him for hours. Tonight his kisses were demanding from the start, the movement of his hands on her shoulders and back urgent, as if he'd been awaiting precisely this moment to break a twelve-year celibacy. Of course Jennifer was worldly enough to know that was not even close to the truth.

For one thing, he was far too practiced at this. It seemed to her he always had been, although as an eighteen-year-old virgin she hadn't been in much of a position to judge. Having been with only her husband in the years since, she didn't have all that much more experience to draw on now, but there was no mistaking the fact that Rex was graceful and adept in a way she wasn't, with the act of bringing as much of his body as possible into intimate contact with hers.

His tongue thrust against hers with a rhythm that made her weak, and made her remember. Her awakened senses recalled things her mind didn't: the scrape of his whiskered jaw, the silky texture of his hair, even the surprising soap-and-water smell of him. Memory mingled with new sensation, creating a mood of unreality that permitted her to cross boundaries she never would have if she'd been thinking straight.

Her body recalled the tactile sensation of the warm leather upholstery in his old Buick against her bare skin, and the excruciating thrill of having him unsnap her jeans and slowly lower the zipper. She remembered how her stomach muscles had clenched and quivered in response to the contact with the back of his fingers. She was quivering the same way now, even though all their clothes were on and properly buttoned and zippered.

With her eyes still squeezed shut, she sensed Rex moving, swinging his leg across hers, and then he was pressing her down until her back was flat against the wood decking, and he was flat against her, bracing his weight on his hands as his kisses turned teasing. He nuzzled her nose and eyelids and the spot in her throat where her pulse fluttered. His lips were soft against her skin, and the front of his jeans was very, very hard as he slowly rocked his hips against hers.

Desire beyond her control spread through her, overriding caution and reason. She didn't want to control it; she didn't want to stop the sweet melting inside and send him away and be alone. Again. It had been so long since she'd been touched and held. To ask her to stop now would be like asking a man lost in the desert to please step over a cool stream and keep on trudging.

Jennifer was tired of trudging up the series of hills her life had become. For just a little while longer she wanted to drift on the pleasure created by Rex's callused fingertips as they slowly found their way beneath the neckline of her T-shirt.

His touch made her senses sizzle, and she unwittingly arched against him in longing. Rex groaned and pushed his hand deeper inside her shirt, his fingertips skirting the crest of her breast. With excitement coursing through her in more powerful waves, Jennifer clung to his shoulders, eagerly returning his kisses and sliding her tongue along his jaw, tasting the hot salt of his damp skin and then suddenly the cold metallic tang of the small gold hoop that pierced his ear.

She froze, the past and present colliding violently as she recalled exactly whose hard, big body had her pinned to the deck.

My God, how could she have forgotten herself this way? She was no longer a misguided teenager, secretly infatuated with the town's most notorious bad boy. She was an adult, a woman with responsibilities...two of which were sleeping in the room directly above them. What if Jeff had woken and glanced outside? What would he think?

What would anyone think who saw her rolling around on the deck with a man she hadn't seen in years? A man who'd been wrong for her back then and was even more wrong for her now? She'd returned to Pleasure to provide a secure, stable life for her sons, not to get involved with a man who had no real ties here...or anywhere for that matter, and who'd made it clear he liked it that way. A man who had a track record of taking off without warning. A wanderer. A Gypsy.

"Stop," she said, although at that moment he was doing nothing more than holding himself in absolutely still suspension above her, obviously watching and waiting to see what had caused her to freeze up on him.

"Why?" Lingering passion was evident in his raspy voice, and in the thundering heartbeat he was still close enough for Jennifer to feel. "Why, Jenny?" he asked again, not quite as gently.

"I came to my senses, that's all."

He laughed unpleasantly. "Oh, really? I guess I ought to be grateful that this time you came to your senses before we got our pants off."

"That's crude," she snapped, shoving at him.

"But true."

With one fluid motion Rex rolled to his feet, leaving Jennifer scrambling to do likewise.

"I suppose we should talk about that," she said awkwardly.

His expression blanked. "What?"

"For pity's sake, Rex...*that. This.* What happened twelve years ago."

He rested his hip against the deck post. "What happened?"

"We made love," she snapped. "Remember?"

"Nope."

"Fine, play games if you like. It won't change the fact that that's what happened." Hurt and bewildered, she started to move past him toward the back door. Rex grabbed her arm.

"Not by a long shot, honey. *Making love* requires two people who are involved heart and soul. There was only one person's heart involved that night in my car. We screwed, lady."

Fresh pain ripped through Jennifer, making her thankful it was too dark for him to see her face clearly. "All right, call it what you like. The fact remains that there's obviously still something between us, some...spark...."

"That's one name for it, I suppose." He tapped out a cigarette from the pack in his shirt pocket and lit it. For a minute Jennifer watched the smoke curl above his head, hoping he might be gentleman enough to take the lead from here. Of course he didn't.

"Anyway," she said, when the silence grew too uncomfortable for her to bear, "I just thought that it might clear the air once and for all if we talk about that night...and about what happened afterward. Rex, I—"

"Let me get this straight," he said, cutting her off. "You want to talk about how you let me screw you and then you returned the favor by letting me take the rap for a fire I couldn't possibly have set because we were together at the time it happened?"

"But you didn't take the rap for it," she protested. "In the end they found out it wasn't you."

"No thanks to you."

"Rex, you don't know how awful I felt and—"

"Is that or isn't it what you wanted to talk about?"

"I wanted to—"

"Is it?"

"Yes."

"Then, no thanks. I had my fill of all that the first time around."

"Rex, wait," she said, this time grabbing his arm as he started to go, with Bear instantly lumbering to his side.

"I've waited twelve years to apologize to you for the way I acted back then, for being such a coward."

He swung around, and the narrow beam of light from the kitchen caught his face, illuminating the fierce expression in his eyes and the tight, hard line of his jaw.

"I don't want an apology," he told her. "I've already made it as plain as I know how to what I do want from you. I haven't changed much. I'm still the guy who wants what he can't have, who can't keep his hands to himself, who your folks warned you to stay away from. If you're interested in giving me what I want—*again*—fine. If not, stay here on your own side of the brook and I'll stay away. Cross it and I'll figure you're fair game."

Idiot. The word thundered inside Rex's head as he plunged through the dark woods between their two houses, heedless of the branches that slapped against his face and arms. A couple of hours in Jenny's presence and he felt like a dumb kid again, wanting and reaching out to take and being reminded all over again that they weren't even in the same league. And running away afterward.

Jenny was not the woman for him. Never had been, never would be. And deep down she knew it as well as he did, even if that very tempting body of hers sometimes forgot and matched him craving for craving. The fact that their hormones were so in sync, resulting in a wild attraction beyond any definition of lust he knew, only added to the sad irony of the whole thing. Hormones aside, Jenny was born to be with a very different sort of man, a man like Jack had been. It wasn't only a cruel fate, but a sadistic one that had first taken Jack from her and then conspired to have the two of them land back in town at the same time.

Rex was suddenly filled with the urge to keep running, to toss his few belongings into the back of his pickup truck and take off. Just like the last time. By now he'd reached his back steps however, and Bear's labored panting reminded him why that was out of the question. Squatting down, he stroked the dog's sides, feeling how they heaved after even such brief exertion. No, no matter how much he wanted to get away, he wasn't going to condemn Bear to spending this summer cooped up in an apartment and a small fenced-in backyard.

"You like it here even if I don't, don't you, pal?"

Bear nuzzled his hand and lay down.

He would stay all right, but he would also keep his distance from Jenny in the future...even if he couldn't get her off his mind, even if he continued to wake up dreaming about her and seeing her image on every damn white wall he painted. He could handle it. After all, it was only for the summer. Maybe not even that long. And he owed Bear that much.

Besides, Jenny had been warned. Stay away. He'd said it and he'd meant it. In his mind the brook became as solid and unbreachable a boundary as the Berlin Wall had once been. As long as Jenny stayed on her own side, she would be safe. They both would be.

Swell, thought Jennifer more than once during the long night. Jeff was back in his own bed, and now she was tossing and turning for a different reason. And the worst part of it was that she wasn't sure precisely what that reason was. Was she angry with Rex for taking the liberties he had? Or with herself for permitting them even briefly? Or was her slow burn really due to the fact that they had been short-circuited at all?

There was no denying the heavy, restless feeling down low in her body. It had been stroked to life by the pressure of Rex's arousal, and it didn't seem likely to subside anytime soon.

She'd been a widow for nearly three long years. Between the kids and her work, she'd managed to sandwich in a scattering of dates, but none of them had ever led to anything more intimate than a good-night kiss at the door. She was no stranger to unfulfilled longings. This wasn't the first night she'd lain awake imagining a man's face hovering above hers in the shadows of her bedroom, the musky smell of his lovemaking, the feel of his hands gliding over her thighs and between them. It was, however, the first time the face and hands she imagined belonged to a man other than her husband. And it scared the hell out of her.

Rex was dangerous. Oh, not in the way her mother claimed. But dangerous for Jennifer. Or maybe it was imply that she was a danger to herself when he was around. She couldn't explain it any more now than she could twelve years ago. She only knew that Rex unleashed a part of herself she didn't know very well. And she didn't think this was the right time in her life—or Rex the right man for that matter—to go exploring it. There was, she decided sometime before finally sinking into an exhausted, frustrated sleep, only one thing to be done. She had to avoid Rex Lovell at all costs....

That turned out to be easier than Jenny anticipated. Surprisingly, annoyingly easy. Almost, she thought with totally irrational disappointment that grew stronger as the days went by, as if Rex was also going out of his way to avoid her.

On Monday the kids began camp as scheduled and the movers arrived with her things, totally decimating her plan to get back to work on the book. Spatial visualization wasn't her strong suit and, as predicted by Rex, the small house was soon overcrowded with duplicate furniture and all the other things that it had seemed absolutely essential to hang on to just a couple of days ago.

Jennifer spent the next two days in a room-by-room, search-and-discard mission. Some items were dispatched with secret glee—like the magazine rack-floor lamp that had been a wedding present from her Aunt Mildred—and others, like the kids' baby clothes and high chair, she put aside with teary-eyed resolve. The house was just too small to accommodate an abundance of sentimental value.

Everything that was on its way out was piled temporarily in the living room. How temporarily was the question.

"Wonderful," her mother said when she stopped by and saw the nearly ceiling-high assortment. "You need to make a clean sweep of things. Let's deep-six these curtains while we're at it, shall we?"

Her enthusiasm hit a nerve. Jennifer glanced at the flowered drapes she had been about to strip from the windows earlier when something made her say, "I happen to like those curtains."

"Oh, Jennifer, honey, they're so...busy."

"I also happen to like busy. *I'm* busy. In fact I'm behind schedule," she said almost rudely.

"I guess that means you don't want to come shopping with me?"

"No thanks."

"We could look at curtains."

"No. Thanks."

"Oh, all right. Although what good is it having my daughter home at last when I never get to spend any time with her?"

"I just have a lot to do right now, settling in, catching up on my work. But we'll go shopping, Mom, I promise."

"When?"

"Soon."

"I guess that will have to do. In the meantime, can I help with anything? Maybe I could call the Salvation Army for you and have them pick up all this stuff and get it out of your way."

"No," replied Jennifer. "I... I've already made arrangements to get rid of it."

Very vague arrangements, she thought after her mother had left. But since Rex had offered to handle it for her and she had agreed, it didn't seem right to go making alternate plans without checking with him first. And since he didn't have a telephone and she couldn't set foot on his side of the brook without sending inappropriate signals, she wasn't sure exactly how she was going to accomplish that.

Maybe she ought to pin a note to Bear's bandanna. Obviously the big mutt didn't share his master's qualms about hanging around there. He came around mornings, looking for the boys and moping off when he didn't find them. Afternoons, when they were home from camp, they were as inseparable as peanut butter and jelly.

"They'll get ticks from that animal, you wait and see," her mother had warned when the kids jubilantly introduced her to their beloved new friend.

Jennifer shrugged off the remark, but she did make a point of checking them at bathtime each night. So far, she hadn't seen any ticks, but even if she did, she figured it was worth the trouble to see Jeff romping so carelessly through the woods, with Bear alternately being pressed into service as a dragon, a circus lion or Wonder Dog. The dog dozed on the deck while the boys ate dinner, eagerly gobbling up the scraps they sneaked him afterward. At dusk, a familiar sharp whistle would pierce the air from somewhere deep on the other side of the brook and Bear would reluctantly trot off toward home.

Jennifer made it a point to be outside when the whistle sounded, but try as she did, she never caught a glimpse of the man it belonged to. Of course, the only reason she even tried was because she was sick and tired of whacking her shins and hipbones on the furniture crowded into the living room. She refused to think about why she didn't just do as her mother continually suggested and have it hauled away by someone else. She would give it until Monday morning, she decided late in the week, and if she didn't run into Rex by then, the Salvation Army would win by default.

On Sunday she took the boys to church in the morning and then to the McVeighs for a family dinner, which included the whole clan. Afterward, Jack's brother Greg offered to take them, along with a few McVeigh cousins, fishing on his boat. Ryan was so ecstatic that Jennifer warned Greg to tie him to the rail, but it was the blend of wistfulness and anxiety on Jeff's face that worried her most. All her instincts warned her to go along, but she allowed the others to persuade her to stay behind.

"You deserve a few hours off duty," her sister-in-law Jeanne insisted.

"And there will be plenty of men there to keep an eye on them," Annie added.

Jennifer had to agree that was true. Still she felt torn watching them drive away, and when a silent, red-eyed Jeff was returned home not even a half hour later, she kicked herself for not following her own instincts and being there when he needed her.

He refused to talk about what had happened, and truthfully Jennifer hardly needed to hear his uncle's explanation to piece it together. Jeff had simply balked at the last minute and refused to set foot on the boat with the others.

"I hate fish," was all he said, then or when they returned home later and Ryan babbled nonstop about the rods and reels, the funny-looking lures and the tiny bathroom in the bottom of the boat. "Fishing is for dorks," Jeff told him.

But later, when the two boys were alone on the deck, Jennifer heard him asking Ryan if it was true he got to turn the wheel and steer the boat.

"Yup," Ryan replied proudly. "Twice. I got my turn and yours."

Even through the window screen, Jennifer could see Jeff's bottom lip tremble, and she had to bite her own.

She wished old Bear was there to cheer him up. He hadn't been around since yesterday morning and the kids seemed to miss him as much as if he'd been gone for months. Jennifer assumed Rex was off taking care of his business and the dog was with him. He'd said he would be back and forth between Pleasure and his business in Massachusetts. She had to hand it to him, the man told it like it was.

The late-afternoon heat lingered, and to distract Jeff from what she was certain were mixed feelings of regret and anger over the botched fishing trip, she suggested they pack sandwiches for supper and have a picnic on the beach. Too emotionally weary to make small talk with anyone who happened to be at the town beach, Jenny headed instead for a small private inlet where the beach was sandy and the water sloped gently. It was a perfect place to learn to swim. She ought to know since it was where she had learned. Where Rex had taught her. It was also closer to home than the public beach, she rationalized, telling herself that the fact that it held powerful memories had nothing to do with her deciding to go there.

She parked the new Volvo wagon, which had replaced the rented Thunderbird, at the edge of the road, and they carefully made their way along the path to the shore. The leafy branches overhead formed a shadowy tunnel. As she stepped back into the sunlight, Jennifer blinked to refocus, and suddenly there he was, emerging from the water right in front of her, tall and lean, the body that haunted her dreams covered only by a pair of black cotton shorts.

Was she dreaming now? she wondered with a sudden clutch of panic for her own sanity. She might have thought so, might have believed she had been thinking about Rex so often, wondering if and when she might see him again, that she had somehow conjured him up out of memory and air and water. Except that the body before her was not the body of her memories.

Though strong even back then, the muscles of his arms and shoulders had lacked the sharply sculptured definition they had now. His chest was also broader now, and more muscular, and covered with a wider wedge of black hair. He froze when he saw Jennifer, as if he, too, were struggling to bring the past and present into alignment in his head.

Managing a smile and a wave, Jennifer moved closer. "How's the water?" she called out.

The question reverberated in her head, opening old doors. It was the same question he'd asked her that first afternoon.

She had come here alone that day. A childhood scare at the club pool had left her with a fear of the water, a fear her mother encouraged. When she learned that swimming was a required part of freshman gym class, she made up her mind to conquer her fear in her own way ahead of time. Rex was alone, too, left behind at day's end by the town work crew that thought that forcing the Gypsy to walk home was a great joke.

He had come from the direction of the road, coming up behind so quietly he scared her. But then to be fair, she would have been scared even if he'd approached with a brass band. She knew who he was.

How's the water?

Deep.

Yeah? It looks to me like it's barely up to your waist.

Well, that's deep when you can't swim.

How easily she had admitted that to him, something she never admitted to anyone, preferring to say that she just didn't like getting wet. And how easily things had progressed from there, like something rolling downhill.

"It's deep," Rex said now, and watched closely for her reaction to his reply.

Jennifer quickly looked away, peering farther along the shore to where Ryan and Jeff were trying to teach Bear to jump over the stick they took turns holding.

She laughed out loud. "Boy, are they glad to see him."

"Looks like the feeling is mutual."

She sensed Rex leaving the water and approaching. She didn't turn, not quite certain what her reaction to all that wet, brown skin might be.

"They're great kids, Jenny," he said.

She knew it wasn't just a glib compliment, because of his tone and because this was Rex, who as far as she knew never indulged in the sort of lip service that held polite society together.

"Thank you," she said. "I think so, too."

"Jeff's sleeping okay?"

"Fine."

"No more monster sightings?"

"No, we spray nightly. They've already had to whip up another batch of repellent."

"Yeah, I helped them find the elderberries for it."

"You helped them?" she asked, turning at last, quickly lifting her gaze from his chest to his face. "When?"

He shrugged. "Couple of days ago, I guess. When they showed up with the bone you sent over for Bear."

"Bone?"

"You didn't send over a T-bone steak bone?"

"No. The kids must have rescued it from the trash."

"Then you didn't know they were coming?"

"Of course not." He eyes flashed. "You don't think I sent my kids over there with some stupid bone and . . . of all the . . ."

"Calm down. I didn't think anything. They showed up with the bone and I thought it was a nice thing to do. They asked about the berries and I showed them where to find them. End of story."

"I wonder why they didn't say anything to me about going to see you?" Jennifer mused aloud.

"Maybe they sensed you wouldn't be pleased."

"Why would they think that?"

"Maybe," he said dryly, "your mother's been talking to them again."

"She wouldn't—" Jennifer stopped abruptly. "I'll have a talk with them myself."

The mention of her mother reminded her of the mess in her living room.

"Actually, I'm glad I ran into you," she told him.

"Are you really?"

"Yes," she continued before he drew any wrong conclusions. "You mentioned something about helping me get rid of my extra furniture and stuff?"

He nodded, not showing any disappointment if he felt it.

"Are you still interested? I should warn you that there's more than I thought there would be. I sort of overestimated the size of the house."

"No problem. If I have to I'll make two trips. When do you want me to pick it up?"

"As soon as possible. I think the pile is growing all on its own."

Rex frowned. "I'll need a day or so to make arrangements. How about Tuesday morning, unless you hear from me beforehand?"

"Tuesday's great."

"All right, then."

Silence settled between them. They didn't have much in common to make small talk about, and what they did have in common was off-limits.

"So," she said finally, inanely, "it sure is a hot night."

"Why don't you jump in and cool off?"

"I might."

"Swim much these days?"

She shook her head. "No. I'm usually too busy for things like that."

"Maybe you ought to make time for things like that," he countered with a smoothness that made her wonder what he included in "things like that." Swimming stirred such evocative memories of the two of them that just discussing it with him made her fidget uneasily.

He frowned suddenly. "Do the kids swim?"

"A little."

"A little? Hell, Jenny, you of all people ought..."

"I know, I know. They've taken lessons at the Y, but they only made it to Polliwog status."

He didn't look amused. "I could teach them, if you want."

What she wanted, Jennifer knew suddenly, was to say Yes, teach my kids to swim, hang around our house the way your dog does, light camp fires and scare away monsters and help me fill up the holes in our lives.

But the years of single motherhood had taught her to put what she ought to do ahead of what she wanted to do, and so with a polite smile, she said, "Thanks, but I plan to teach them myself this summer. Sort of a mother-son bonding thing."

"Suit yourself. Just make sure they can hold their own in the water before they wander down here on their own someday."

"Look, I don't need lessons from you in parenting."

"No?" he countered. "What do you need lessons in, Jenny?"

"Nothing. I learned everything you had to teach a long time ago. Now if you'll excuse me, I'm going swimming."

The second she said it, she regretted it. To swim, she really ought to take off her sundress, and that meant pulling it off over her head right in front of him, exposing more than she cared to in the sleek hot pink bathing suit that wasn't quite as sleek as it had been ten pounds ago. She couldn't help it. She was a nervous eater, and the past few months of planning to move back home had provided inspiration for an Oreo cookies banquet.

Still, now that she'd said it, she had no choice but to take the plunge. Quickly yanking the pale blue cotton dress over her head, she dropped it on top of her beach bag and towels and walked, as nonchalantly as it was possible to walk while trying to remember to hold your chin up, stomach in and shoulders back, to the water. At least her thighs were reasonably firm, thanks to her exercise bike. And she'd retained enough California glow to escape the ghostly white look of most New Englanders in early summer.

Not that Rex had that look. His skin was bronze year-round, thought Jennifer, and without warning found herself wondering how much lighter, if at all, the skin beneath his swimsuit was. Given their past, it might have been the sort of information she was privy to, but it wasn't. Their relationship, if you could call it that, had had strange, jagged boundaries.

They had spent all their time right here, isolated and alone, except of course for that last night when he'd driven her home from a party after Jack had had too much to drink. At their early meetings they had talked only about the rudiments of staying afloat. Later, they'd talked for hours, about all sorts of things, some of them things she'd never discussed with anyone else. She'd had the feeling it was the same for him. And yet there were huge parts of their lives they never spoke of, such as her relationship with Jack and Rex's less-than-sterling reputation. And how he felt about it. So, while in some ways she knew him intimately, in other ways she didn't know him at all.

She walked until the water was about waist-deep and then she slid under, letting it close over her shoulders like a fresh, cool sheet on a warm night. Turning, she faced the shore so she could keep an eye on the kids and Rex, monitoring the beach through oversize black sunglasses.

After a while, Bear and the kids made their way back to where Rex sat on top of his discarded jeans and T-shirt. They sprawled in a small cluster, the setting sun glinting off his dark hair and the silky, gold-tinged heads of her sons. The sound of their laughter skimmed over the water's surface to her. What was Rex saying to make them giggle that way? Especially Jeff, who seldom laughed with such abandon.

Whatever the cause, the sound was pleasing to Jennifer, so pleasing she stayed in the water even after her skin had grown cool, kicking to stay warm and drawing some strange sort of comfort she couldn't explain from having them all nearby. Ryan was now busily digging a hole—hoping to reach China, Jennifer knew without having to ask. Bear looked on, his head propped on one paw. Jeff and Rex sat talking, looking comfortable and easy with each other, the way she'd hoped Jeff would be with his uncles.

Rex finally left when the kids decided to join her in the water, and it wasn't until much later, when she was tucking them into bed for the night, that she received any inkling of what Jeff and he had talked about earlier.

"Mom," Jeff said, "how come everything I love has to die?"

"Jeff, honey what kind of question is that?"

His little face darkened. "A bad one?"

"No, of course it's not bad," she said quickly, sitting beside him on the bed and stroking his hair back from his forehead. Already, worry lines had left their faint mark on the smooth skin there, she noted sadly. "I just wondered what made you ask me that tonight?"

"Because of Bear," he replied. "Bear is gonna die, you know. Rex said so."

So it was Rex now, she noted, knowing that Jeff was too well mannered to have started using an adult's first name without permission.

"That's Mr. Lovell."

"But he said—"

"I don't care what he said. I say you call adults by their full name, got it?"

"All right."

"What did Mr. Lovell tell you about Bear?"

"That he's real old and real sick and that that's a bad comba...comba...."

"Combination."

"Right. And that's how come he brought him here to the country, so he could have room to run, like you wanted Ry and me to have room, and fresh air and stuff. On account of he's going to die."

"Honey, everyone has to die sometime."

"But Bear is gonna die *soon,* Mom. Maybe even tonight. Re—Mr. Lovell said so. Maybe we'll just wake up tomorrow and he won't come around. And then we'll always look for him, but he won't be able to come around again even if he wants to because he'll be dead. Isn't that how it works?"

"Well, yes. I believe that once you die, you have to leave this world and go to a different one, a better one."

"Like where Daddy went. Do you think Daddy wants to come and see us?"

Jennifer forced her eyes to stay open until the burning in them peaked and subsided. If she closed them, she just knew they would flood. "Honey, I *know* your daddy wishes he could be here with us."

"Maybe if he wishes hard enough—if we all wish hard—it will happen."

"No, Jeff, people don't come back like that."

His blue eyes shimmered and overflowed, giant tears rolling silently down his soft cheeks. "Or dogs, either?"

She shook her head. "Or dogs, either, sweetie."

"But I don't want him to die."

"I know you don't, Jeff. Try not to think about it anymore tonight. No one knows for sure when anyone else is going to die. Who knows? Maybe Bear will outlive us all."

"Yeah, maybe," Jeff said, but so hollowly that Jennifer had the sudden feeling that he was the adult humoring her. She glanced back at him as she closed the door, noting that he had the same bewildered, forlorn look he'd had after Jack died, and that she had the same bewildered, forlorn feeling of ineptitude.

This was all Rex's fault, she thought suddenly. Is this what he was telling Jeff on the beach? Where did he get off putting thoughts like this in a little kid's head? Especially when she'd hinted to him how badly Jeff had reacted to Jack's death. So what if Bear was old and sick? Couldn't Rex have just let Jeff enjoy in peace whatever time they did have together?

Yes, he could have, and the fact that he didn't made her furious. She paced around the house, glaring at the pile of furniture in the living room as if it, too, was Rex's doing. She half expected Jeff to call her back to his room, too upset to sleep, but when she tiptoed up later to check on him, both he and Ryan were sleeping soundly.

Back downstairs she went to the refrigerator for a soda, changed her mind, then pulled the door open again. Coke can in hand, she stood gazing through the kitchen window to the glow she knew came from the porch light on the Lovell house.

Damn him and his warnings, she thought. Stay on your own side of the brook and I'll stay away, he'd said. Well, she had stayed on her side. He was the one who'd overstepped his bounds and, she decided, slamming the soda can onto the counter as she headed for the back door, she'd be damned if she'd wait until the next time they accidentally bumped into each other to tell him so.

Running, it took only a minute to cover the distance between their houses. Jennifer glanced over her shoulder as she hurried up his back porch steps, reassured that she could see her kitchen light from here and no doubt would hear if either of the boys called. Not that she planned to be here long. She would say what she had to say and get back.

The bell was broken and her knock on the door brought no response, so she tried pounding. Rex's truck was in the drive and a light was on inside, but the tightly closed blinds on the windows prevented her from seeing more. Next, she tried calling his name, but when her voice didn't even elicit a bark or an excited whimper from Bear, she resigned herself to the fact that they weren't home and turned to go.

The pair of dark shadows waiting at the foot of the steps took her by surprise.

"Hello, Jenny," said Rex. "What are you doing here?"

Chapter Six

"You mean, how dare I cross the boundary you set?" Jennifer countered, mockery overlaying the anger in her tone.

"No. I mean what do you want here?"

"Not what you think."

He smiled at that. "Too bad. In that case maybe we should go back to my original question. What are you doing here?"

"I want to talk to you."

"Fine." He climbed the steps and moved past her to open the door to the kitchen. "Come on in."

"I'd prefer to talk out here."

"I wouldn't."

He entered the house, leaving Jennifer alone on the porch to do as she pleased. With an anxious glance back toward her house, she followed in time to see Rex swing open the refrigerator door. This was the first time she had ever been in his house, and in the seconds it took him to fish a beer from the refrigerator, she'd seen all there was to see in the kitchen. Faded, peeling wallpaper, stained porcelain sink, linoleum flooring worn black in the traffic areas.

It saddened Jennifer, not because of its run-down condition, but because of the complete absence of any personal touches. When Rex had said he'd gotten rid of a lot of stuff, he hadn't been kidding. There wasn't so much as a curtain or an old calendar remaining to reflect the taste of those who had lived here. If this had ever been a home, it wasn't any longer.

"Want one?" Rex asked, holding the beer can aloft.

Jennifer shook her head. "No, this isn't a social call. And I've left the kids alone, so I have to hurry."

"I guess you must want to talk to me pretty bad."

"It's important, yes."

He popped the lid on the can and lit a cigarette before lowering himself into a chair at the kitchen table and using his foot to push another toward her.

"So talk."

Ignoring the chair, she asked, "Did you tell Jeff that Bear is going to die?"

He eyed her levelly. "Yes."

"Why?" she demanded, the utter coolness of his response fanning her anger.

"Because he is."

"We're all going to die, for pity's sake. That doesn't mean we have to go around talking and brooding about it...especially not when we're only six years old and we're having a hard enough time dealing with the whole idea of death as it is and—"

"And just why is that?"

The question stopped Jennifer short. She frowned at him, confused. "Why is what?"

"Why is Jeff having such a rough time dealing with—how did you put it—'the whole idea of death'?"

"My God, are you really that insensitive?"

He stiffened, but his hard golden-brown eyes didn't flicker. "Evidently so. Enlighten me."

"Because his father is dead," she snapped. "I'd thought I'd made it clear without going into details, but you want details, I'll give them to you." Gripping the back of a chair for support, she said, "Jeff saw his father die. He was watching TV when it happened and he saw it...the explosion, the fire, all of it. Now how do you feel?"

"About the same as I felt a minute ago. I already knew all that."

"You knew..."

He nodded. "Jeff told me. He told me his daddy was there and then he wasn't, and he told me that he hasn't watched television since."

"I think he's afraid to," she said softly.

"Actually it's because he's promised himself he won't watch until his daddy comes back."

Jennifer stiffened. "Comes back? No. Jeff knows that isn't going to happen."

"Does he?" Rex asked, stubbing his cigarette out in a jar lid he was using as an ashtray.

"Of course," she replied defensively. "I've told him so myself, over and over."

"But does he know it? Does he know it in his gut?"

Without wanting to, Jennifer recalled the day they arrived here and the crushing disappointment on Jeff's face when he told her how he'd looked everywhere for Jack. She covered her mouth with her hands, feeling something inside give way. Her fingers muffled her words as she said, "No, deep down I'm not sure he really does."

Rex stood and touched her shoulders lightly. "Come on, Jenny, why don't you sit?"

"I can't. The kids..."

"Would you feel better if we went outside where you can hear them? I know you can hear, because I hear you, especially at night, laughing and talking, reading to them sometimes."

For a second, her mind filled with a picture of him sitting on his porch, listening to them, and then she nodded and let him lead her outside. Sweeping newspapers and painting rags off an old glider, he made room for her to sit, then claimed the top step for himself, bracing his back against the porch railing.

Jennifer was stunned by his revelations. Getting Jeff to talk about Jack to her or the child psychologist had been a frustrating, mostly futile, task. Dr. Reynolds always insisted that he would open up when he was ready to, and now it appeared as though he had. But why to Rex Lovell, of all people?

"What else has he told you?" she asked Rex.

"Not a whole lot. It's not like we had an hour-long heart-to-heart or anything. Mostly he slips me bits and pieces. I just happen to be pretty good at putting pieces together."

"What other pieces?"

"He's confused about where exactly Jack is."

"I told him that God—"

"I don't mean in an ecclesiastical sense. I mean where exactly. You see, Jeff knows something happened that day he was watching TV and he knows it has to do with his daddy not coming home anymore. But then you all flew here for the funeral, and I have a hunch Jeff thought Jack

would be here, waiting. Then you went back to L.A. and
so he thought, no, he must still be back there. Now here
you are back in the place where he knows his daddy belongs, and still no Jack,. Underneath all that quiet, he's a
pretty mixed-up little kid, Jenny."

"Oh, God," she said, leaning forward and pressing her
fingertips to her temples where a dull pounding had begun. "Jack is buried here, of course. I've told Jeff that.
I've explained everything to him. At least, I thought I had.
Sometimes..." She shook her head, feeling tears of frustration stinging the backs of her eyelids. "Sometimes I just
don't know what else to say to him."

"Look, I know you said you've talked to experts about
this, and I'm sure no expert about kids, but how did Jeff
take Jack's death at the time?"

"He seemed to accept it. He was sad... quiet... maybe
too quiet."

"How was he at the funeral?"

"He didn't go."

"Yeah, that's what I figured." Even in the shadows
Jennifer could see the look of disgust that shaped his hard
features.

"My folks thought it was best for him to stay with a sitter, that it might upset him, even though it had to be a
closed casket because..." She faltered, shuddering. "And
I... truthfully, I was so out of it at the time that I pretty
much went along with whatever they said. Maybe I was
wrong."

"Nobody could blame you for being out of it," he said.
"But, yeah, I think it was wrong for Jeff. Have you at least
taken him to the grave?"

"No. I thought maybe this summer..."

"Do it," he said. "Let him bring flowers, or baseball
cards—whatever he wants. At least that way there'll be

something concrete to focus on, something real that he can fix in his mind, a place where he knows Daddy is now. Not some ghostly mumble-jumble the kid can't get a handle on.''

"I never thought of it that way," admitted Jennifer thoughtfully. "So...simply. Dr. Reynolds thought his problems had to do with underlying insecurities...."

Rex snorted. "That's all fine and good, Jenny. A kid ought to feel secure, like he belongs somewhere. But I think Jeff needs more right now. He needs help understanding exactly what's happened to him. He needs it laid out in black and white, no sugar coating, no pulled punches."

"But Dr. Reynolds was always adamant about not dwelling on it, about looking toward the future, moving beyond grief."

"Maybe I'm wrong, but it seems to me you need to tie up the past before you can think about the future."

Their eyes met and held and for just a second it seemed they might be talking about something beyond Jeff's problems. Jennifer drew a deep breath, but the portentous instant passed, Rex forced it to pass.

"And maybe I was wrong to tell Jeff about Bear the way I did," he continued. "I only did it because I didn't think he needed to be sucker-punched the same way twice. Bear's sick, real sick, and the fact is I'm only here now because the vet said this will be his last summer and I didn't want him to spend it cooped up in my apartment or in a fenced-in yard not much bigger than a sandbox."

"You mean fixing up this place is just an excuse?"

He shrugged. "It had to be done sooner or later. But truthfully, if not for Bear, I'd have gladly put off dealing with it for another five years."

"I'm glad you didn't," Jennifer told him. "And I'm glad now that you told Jeff about Bear, if only because it led to us having this talk. I think you might be right about a lot of things."

He shrugged. "Sometimes an outsider can see things a little clearer."

"I don't think Jeff told you things he's never told anyone else because he considers you an outsider."

"Yeah, well, I talked to him a little about Jack and me, you know, about some of the things we used to do together. Maybe he figured I was safe."

Safe. Jennifer turned the word over in her mind, thinking it was the very last one she would have used in relation to Rex.

"I figured that by telling him about Bear," he went on, "he'd be prepared for the worst when it happens. That way, maybe he'll see death more as something natural, part of life, not something that sneaks up on you and makes the people we love disappear without warning."

Jennifer reached down and stroked Bear's head. "You're sure the vet's right about him?"

"Yeah," Rex replied. "I'm sure."

His voice was octaves lower than Jeff's but in it she heard the same tremor of raw emotion she'd heard in her son's a while ago. It hit her suddenly what losing Bear would mean to Rex. The bond between them was obvious, and when you came right down to it, what other emotional bond did Rex have in his life?

He loved the dog very much, enough to rearrange his life to see to it that Bear's last weeks were happy ones. Enough, Jennifer thought, that even talking about it must bring him pain, and yet he'd done exactly that in order to spare Jeff pain in the future. She felt a rush of gratitude as strong as the anger she'd felt earlier.

"I wish…" she began, then faltered. "I wish that if this has to be his last summer, it could go on forever."

Rex smiled at her. "Yeah, I know what you mean. At least it's turned out even better than I hoped, thanks to the kids. He really loves them."

"It's been good for them, too. Now I really ought to go," she said, getting to her feet. "I never leave them alone like this."

"It's just next door."

"And across the brook," she added, reaching the top of the steps just as he stood so that they both halted, startled and uneasy to be suddenly standing so close.

"Right…the brook. Look, Jenny, about the other night…"

"Yes?"

"I… Forget it. Come on, I'll walk you home."

I'll walk you home. There was something so innocent about the sound of that. And yet there was nothing innocent about her feelings as she preceded him down the stairs and fell into step beside him. Her heart was racing, and a jolt of electrical awareness shot through her each time their shoulders brushed on the narrow path.

At the brook he took her hand as she picked her way across a trio of flat slippery stones, and he didn't release it until they had climbed the short hill to her back door. Of course that might have been simply because they *were* climbing a brush-covered hillside in the dark, but it also could have been because he wanted to hold her hand for a while longer and it was that second possibility that made Jennifer feel tingly and a little breathless as she turned to say good-night.

With him standing on the ground and her on the deck step, the height difference between them was negated, putting them face-to-face in a way that suggested new possibilities. For a second they stood staring into each other's eyes, breathing those possibilities in the intimate warmth of each other's breath. Then Rex took a step backward and Jennifer quickly moved to the deck proper, distance and safety reestablished.

"See you Tuesday," he said.

"Tuesday?"

"The furniture," he reminded her. "I made arrangements to take it on Tuesday like I told you."

"Sure, of course. See you Tuesday."

Tuesday. Jennifer went inside, feeling Monday looming ahead like a tedious, twenty-four-hour obstacle to be gotten over. Why was that? she wondered, ignoring the telltale snicker within. Maybe it was simply because she'd be glad to have her living room back again. Right, said the snickering voice as she confronted her flushed reflection in the bathroom mirror. Get real.

Before she went to bed, she climbed the stairs to check the loft. Ryan was burrowed into a sea of stuffed animals and Jeff was lying on his back, arms flung wide, looking utterly at peace with the world.

If only he could be that way when he was awake, she thought wistfully, then straightened from kissing his cheek and gazed down at him with renewed determination. He was going to be, damn it. She was going to see to it. She was going to start by taking the boys to visit Jack's grave. Maybe Rex was right about this and maybe he wasn't, but since listening to the experts and her mother's advice hadn't solved the problem, his way was certainly worth a try.

On Tuesday, Jennifer had just hauled herself out of bed, made the coffee and jumped into the shower when she heard the doorbell.

"Mommy," called Ryan from the loft. "There's somebody..."

"I know, I know," she called back, jabbing wet arms into the sleeves of a white terry-cloth robe. She glanced at the clock on her way past. Who came knocking on someone's door at five minutes of seven in the morning? Her mother? It better not be. She couldn't afford any delays this morning. She had just enough time to get herself and the kids ready and get them to camp by eight. Surely Rex wouldn't...

It was her last frantic thought before she yanked the door open and found him waiting on her doorstep. He would.

He was wearing blue jeans and a short-sleeve white polo shirt and one look explained to Jennifer why the man never dressed up. Why bother? When it came to plain masculine appeal, it just didn't get any better than this.

"Hi," he said, removing his sunglasses and slipping the end of one earpiece between smiling lips. Without the dark glasses, it was easy to see how his gaze was drawn to the top of her head. "Cute," he said.

Jennifer quickly yanked off the pink ruffled shower cap she'd forgotten she was wearing, and then plucked out the assortment of hair clips and pins she'd used to secure her long hair under the cap, shoving them into her robe pocket.

"I was taking a shower," she explained, as if he might have mistakenly thought she'd donned the cap so they could shoot the cover photo for her book.

His smile broadened, causing the grooves that bracketed his mouth to deepen attractively. "Am I too early?"

"Well, to be honest, when you said Tuesday morning, I hadn't realized you meant sunup."

"The sun's been up for hours.... And so have I." He sniffed the air. "Is that fresh coffee I smell?"

"Mmm-hmm."

"Great."

"Come on in, why don't you?" she invited dryly as he stepped past her into the kitchen.

"You go on ahead and finish your shower. I'll wait on myself."

"How gracious of you." She shut the door with a resigned sigh. "The boys are still in bed...that is, they were in bed," she amended as they came hurrying down from the loft.

"Rex...I mean Mr. Lovell's here," shouted Jeff.

Ryan grinned sleepily and looked around the kitchen. "Where's Bear?"

"Mr. Lovell left him in the truck," replied Rex, deadpan. "He was afraid Mrs. McVeigh wouldn't want him shedding all over her house."

The boys giggled, aware that some sort of teasing was going on, even if they didn't fully comprehend it. Jennifer met his gaze over their heads.

"They have to have manners," she said.

"Yes, ma'am. I won't argue with that. And on the subject of manners," he added as she turned to go, "here I am helping myself to coffee without thinking of you."

"It's not quite ready yet," she pointed out.

"No problem. If you like, I can bring you up a cup when it is ready." His eyes glittered at her across the kitchen.

"No, I wouldn't like," she retorted.

But the fact is that in spite of her resolutions and her own common sense, she did like it when Rex flirted with her or in some other way acknowledged that there was something different in the air whenever they were together. She liked it too much.

She cut her shower short, threw on a pair of clean jeans and an expensive embroidered T-shirt she'd bought for a going-away party thrown by their California neighbors. It was a shirt she ordinarily would not have worn to load old furniture onto a truck. In the bathroom she applied blush, mascara, lip gloss and after-bath splash, and then sauntered toward the kitchen as if she always looked so pulled together when she drove the kids to camp.

"All right, guys," she called out as she approached, "what's it going to be for breakfast?"

"French toast," the boys replied in unison.

"In your dreams. We've got ten minutes and counting."

Then she noticed that they weren't requesting French toast—they were already eating it. Rex stood at the stove, a plaid dish towel slung over one shoulder, eating out of the frying pan.

"Oops, my manners," he said when their gazes met. The boys laughed in the background. "At least I remembered to save you some." He nodded at a plate on the counter where three perfectly browned slices were arranged.

"You cook?" she asked.

"I live alone," he reminded her. "If you want to eat something besides fast food and canned beans, you learn to cook."

"I'm impressed. This looks great," she told him as she carried her plate to the table and sat down. Rex put the pan in the sink and ran water in it, then poured coffee for both of them and joined her.

"I'm saving the rest of mine for Bear," announced Ryan.

"Dogs don't eat French toast," Jennifer said without thinking.

"Bear does," the other three at the table informed her at once.

She rolled her eyes. "Fine. Save it for him."

Ryan grinned. "You're a good mommy. And pretty."

"Yeah, I like it when you get all dressed up," Jeff added:

"Honey, I'm not all dressed up," she said, smiling tightly and wishing with all her heart that he was old enough that she could kick him under the table without him yelling, "Hey, whadya do that for?"

"But that's your special new shirt," he persisted. "That's dressed up."

She glanced through her lowered lashes to see if this might possibly be lost on Rex. It wasn't. "Drink your milk, Jeff."

"And you smell good, too," added Ryan magnanimously. "I like perfume."

"Me, too," said Jeff.

She met Rex's amused gaze across the table.

"Me, too," he said.

Jennifer loved her children, but there were times when she thought they should have come with seals over their mouths that said Break At Your Own Risk. The most frustrating thing was that even when she got them alone during the ride to camp, she couldn't explain to them what they had done wrong. How did you delicately explain to a four- and a six-year-old that it was sometimes wrong to be polite and tell the truth? You didn't. She would just have to tread very carefully in the future if she wanted to avoid giving Rex any wrong ideas. But then, she already knew that, didn't she?

She'd left Rex loading the furniture on his pickup while she dropped the boys off at camp, and returned to find the job almost done.

"I held off on the crib and high chair," he said as they stood together in the now nearly empty living room. "They look like they're in real good shape. You sure you want to get rid of them?"

"I'm sure," she replied, running her finger over the grooves in the back of the high chair. Both pieces were handcrafted reproductions that had taken her and Jack months to find. "The crib had a canopy," she said impulsively. "I didn't use it for the boys, but I always hoped that maybe someday I'd have a girl and... I'm sure," she said again, dropping her hand to her side. "This house is too small to save everything."

Rex nodded and hoisted the chair to one shoulder. "You're the boss."

"Can I help with that?"

"Get the door," he grunted.

Noting that the back of his shirt was already wet with sweat, Jennifer tossed a couple of ice cubes into a glass, filled the glass with orange juice and had it waiting when he walked back through the door.

"You didn't have to go to any trouble," Rex told her as he accepted the frosty glass, pleased beyond reason that she had. When you were used to taking care of all your own needs, something as minor as a cold drink you didn't have to ask for meant a lot. "I have a thermos of water in the truck."

"Save it for later. I'm sure you're going to need it. I can't believe it's this hot so early in the morning...and it's only June."

Rex wiped his face with the dark blue bandanna tucked in his back pocket before tipping his head back to take a long swallow of juice. "It's going to get worse, too. Haven't you heard about the disappearing ozone layer?"

"I've heard. I've also heard this is supposed to be a record hot summer." She wrinkled her nose in a way that hit him hard. "I don't think I can live through a heat wave."

"You lived through one before. Remember that last summer I was home?"

Her face got all smoothed out and serious. "I remember."

"Remember that song you were always singing?"

"Hotel California."

"Right, that's it. How did it go?"

She sang a few lines as off-key as she had back then.

He grinned. "Yeah, that's it. I can't believe I couldn't think of it. That damn song stuck in my mind for years." Just like you did, he thought, looking at her. Only you never did come unstuck. *Oh, Jen.*

"Remember the day you got your foot caught in the weeds by the edge of the lake?" he asked.

She nodded, half smiling. "And you dove under to get it loose."

"While you screamed your head off."

"I thought it was a water snake."

"And when I finally got you free, you took off like a shot."

"And you chased me."

"And caught you."

She tossed her head, a nervous gesture, but Rex was looking past the nervousness. Her long hair sparkled like gold in the sunlight coming through the front windows and it plummeted him back twelve years, to a beach buried deep in his memory....

"Got ya," he said as his fingers closed around her ankle and brought her down on top of him in the sand. He twisted, pinning her under him, employing a little too much force until he realized she wasn't struggling.

"Looks that way," she said, smiling up at him. "The question is, Lovell, now that you've got me, what are you going to do with me?"

He knew what he wanted to do with her. He'd known since the first day he walked onto the beach and found her there all alone. He knew in more detail each time he touched her under the guise of teaching her to swim. But this sudden metamorphosis from shy student to laughing, teasing female had him off balance.

"I don't know," he muttered. "What am I going to do with you, Jen . . . ?"

The same question rang inside him now.

"Jenny—"

"Anyway," she said, cutting him off as if she knew exactly where his thoughts had taken him and didn't want to go there. "I really appreciate your helping me with this." She glanced around. "It already looks better in here, don't you think? With a fresh coat of paint, I guarantee you won't recognize the place."

"Paint can cover a multitude of sins," he said. "I can vouch for that."

"Mmm," replied Jennifer distractedly. "I picked out new wallpaper for the kitchen, and I had thought I'd pick up the blue in it for the walls in here, but now I'm thinking yellow. Lemon yellow . . . no, a little lighter. . . . Daffodil." She glanced anxiously at Rex, as if to see if the subject had been safely changed. "What do you think?"

"How about Ivory Bisque?"

She squinted at the walls consideringly. "That's like cream, right?"

"Cream, white." He shrugged. "Whatever, I've got about a dozen gallons of it over at my place. I'm using it on all the interior walls," he explained when she glanced at him quizzically. "I've got more than enough to do this room, too."

"Thanks, that's very sweet, but I really think I need color in here."

Rex shrugged again and bent to put his back to the folded crib and lift it. "I can't help you with that."

Color was definitely not his area of expertise. Not unless it was exploding in the sky above him, packed with dynamite and smelling like gunpowder. And even then he couldn't make it last. No matter how hard he worked, how spectacular the display, it always faded back into blackness.

It required a little creative rearranging of the items on his pickup, but he would be able to make it in one trip after all, Rex decided. Which was nice, since he really hadn't felt like driving all the way to Providence twice in one morning. Not even if it was for a good cause.

"What's this?" Jennifer asked from behind him.

"Oh...damn." He glared at the old rocker she was pointing to. "I had to take that off the truck in order to slide the crib on. Now where the hell am I going to fit it?"

"This isn't mine," she said.

"No." He shoved aside a box of dishes. "It's mine. Or rather, it belonged to my mother. This isn't going to work."

Hot and irritated, he pulled the bandanna from his pocket and knotted it around his head to keep the sweat out of his eyes, then went back to shoving things around, trying to free up enough square inches to accommodate the chair.

He heard Jenny talking behind him. "I think it's an antique. Early American. Looks like the original finish, too. Did you mother ever say where she got it?"

"No," he snapped. "She just sat in it. Out on the porch every summer, in front of the fireplace all winter. Sat and rocked. Whenever I think of her, I picture her sitting in this damn chair." He reached for it and got that same picture now, prompting a small, reluctant smile. "She loved the foolish old thing. For a while I even thought maybe I'd hang on to it—just this one thing..." He shook his head to clear it. "Hell, what do I need with a rocking chair?"

"I could use it."

He turned his head to look at her, the chair poised and ready to go on the truck. "What?"

"I said if you're getting rid of it, I can use it."

His mouth quirked. "I thought you were trying to clean out."

"Only stuff I don't want or have duplicates of. I don't have even one rocking chair and, well, I'd sort of like one. Maybe I'll put it out on the deck for the summer like your mother used to."

He placed it to the side of the driveway. "You want it? It's all yours."

"I didn't mean for you to give it to me," she said hastily.

He grimaced, impatient to get going. "I thought you just said you wanted it."

"I do. But not for free. I mean, if you sold the rocker along with all this other stuff, you would be paid for it, so I'll pay you instead. What do you want for it?"

Rex froze in the act of closing the tailgate. "What did you say?"

He must look as close to exploding as he felt, Rex thought, because she seemed to lean away from him, her expression concerned and confused.

"I only said that you should be paid what you would be paid if you sold the rocker along with—"

"Oh, so that's it," he cut in, slamming the tailgate so hard, everything inside rattled. "That's why I'm doing this. To scare up a few bucks. I couldn't simply feel like doing you a favor—you just naturally assume I'm working my own angle."

"Rex, there's nothing wrong with—"

"There's everything wrong with it," he shouted. "There's something wrong when people always think the worst of you and ascribe ulterior motives to everything you do. But what's most wrong this time, is that you're the one who thought it."

He stalked to the passenger side of the truck and yanked open the door. "Get in."

"Why?"

"Because you're coming with me," he said.

She shook her head. Rex hated the wary look she aimed at him, but more so he hated what she thought of him.

"No, Rex, I have work to do and..." She was edging back toward the house as she spoke.

He didn't move. "Run and I'll catch you," he said softly. "Just like last time."

For a few seconds their gazes locked and held, then she made a face that made it clear that one, she wasn't scared of him, and two, she was being put upon in the extreme. Only then did she come flouncing toward him.

"Fine, you want me to come with you, I'll come."

"That's what I want," he said, slamming the passenger door behind her and glaring at her through the open window. "I may not have any way to prove to the rest of this lousy town that they're wrong about me, but I can damn well prove it to you."

Phoenix House was a women's shelter located in an old warehouse in a not very picturesque part of Providence. It didn't matter because the women and children who lived there were seeking refuge, not atmosphere—a safe place where they didn't have to worry about dodging someone else's moods, or fists.

For their sake, the exact address was kept a closely guarded secret, and Rex had had to go through a series of contacts and checks before it was revealed to him. Even now he had to stop a few blocks away and call to ensure that someone would be downstairs to allow him entry.

From the start of his dealings with the Catholic nuns who ran Phoenix House, he had understood that he was especially suspect simply by virtue of the fact that he was a man. The nuns had learned the hard way that a man seeking the woman and child who had fled from him could be extremely crafty, saying and doing whatever it took to get his hands on them.

The cautious treatment didn't bother Rex or offend him. This was suspicion he could understand, rooted as it was in the hard cold reality of the bruised faces and cowered gazes he'd seen on the women and children at the shelter. And not merely the product of rumor and old wives' tales you could never live down.

He didn't bother to tell Jenny where they were going. Partly because during the long silent drive there, his anger had dissipated some. And also because it was hard to find words to explain it to her without making it sound as if he were painting himself to be some sort of saint. He wasn't, not by a long shot. But he also wasn't the lowlife everyone in Pleasure seemed to think he was. *Everyone,* he thought grimly.

Without being asked, Jenny pitched in to carry some of the lighter things up to the shelter on the second floor of the warehouse. Inside, the place was cheerfully bleak. The sisters had done what they could with what they had, but it was still a warehouse, and a few donated plants and kids' drawings tacked up on the brick walls didn't change that.

Rough interior walls had been erected to provide some degree of privacy, but he'd noticed that the residents still seemed to gather in the big room at the front, watching television, the kids playing with secondhand toys. Hoping for safety in numbers maybe.

Jenny didn't say anything to him, but a couple of times when they passed on the stairs she smiled, a really special smile, and perversely that made him feel worse, as though he'd backed her into thinking well of him. At one point he saw her talking with Sister Ann, who ran the place. Good, he thought. Sister Ann could do a whole lot better job of explaining what this was about than he ever could.

When they had unloaded everything and returned to the truck, he started the engine and gunned the motor without saying anything. Maybe if he drove fast enough he could make it all the way to Pleasure without talking.

No such luck.

"Rex," said Jenny, placing her hand on his arm. "Don't go yet. Not before you give me a chance to say I'm sorry."

"There's nothing to be sorry about," he replied, avoiding her gaze. It just felt too intense to confront.

"Yes, there is. I jumped to the wrong conclusion about you and you had every right to be angry."

"Forget it. It was hot and I was ticked off because the chair wouldn't fit. I shouldn't have taken it out on you."

"It just never occurred to me that you were giving those things to a women's shelter."

"There's no reason it should have. Look, Jenny," he said, finally looking at her as he stretched his arm along the seat, "I can't sit here and come off like Saint Rex. The truth is, the only reason it occurred to me to bring it here is that I saw a piece about this place in the paper a while back. If I hadn't, I might have sold the junk I had to get rid of...but never yours," he added emphatically. "I never would have sold your stuff and pocketed the cash."

"I should have known that," she said, wincing.

"Yeah. You should have."

"I'm sorry," she said again. "And I think it's wonderful what you've done for these people."

"Nothing wonderful about getting rid of some old junk."

"Sister Ann told me about the carpentry work."

"A few walls. It took me two afternoons. Big deal."

"It is for them. God, Rex, it's just so sad in there. Some of those women and children are running for their lives."

He nodded. "Most of them are, one way or another. And most of them walked away from their old lives with nothing but the clothes on their backs. When they finally leave here, they need everything—furniture, dishes, even toothbrushes, for Pete's sake."

"It makes me realize how lucky I am," she said softly. "And I know what I'm going to do from now on with the clothes and toys the kids outgrow."

"Good. These folks can use whatever they get."

"I just can't get it out of my mind," she said. "Those poor babies."

"I know what you mean. You see that kind of pain and—I don't know—despair, just once, and it stays with you."

"I especially keep thinking of those two little girls off in the corner. Did you notice them?"

"The ones with the mother who looked about seventeen?" he said, his expression grim. "I noticed."

"She was so pretty, and at least she was reading to the kids. Some of the mothers in there looked..."

"Beaten," he offered. "In more ways than one."

Jennifer shuddered. "God, Rex, what kind of man could do something like that to his own family?"

"I don't know," he said, and jerked the shift into first. "Let's get out of here."

For the entire ride home he kept his gaze focused on the road ahead, as if navigating the light midday traffic required all his attention, while all the while her question replayed in his head.

What kind of man could do something like that to his own family?

Actually Rex had an opinion as to what kind of man could strike a woman or a child. No man at all, as far as he was concerned. Only an animal, worse than a coward. The problem with Jenny's question was that it led him to a larger one he had no complete answer for. What kind of man could destroy his own family?

His own father, for one. He could say that unequivocally because he understood that there were many ways to destroy a family. You didn't have to shout or raise your fists; all you had to do was walk away in the middle of the night. That's it. But again, what kind of man could do a thing like that?

He had no answer for that, no definition. Only a fear, deep down in the darkest place inside him, that maybe all the old wives' tales were right after all. That no matter how much he chafed at hearing it, maybe he was that kind of man.

Chapter Seven

He couldn't stay away from her.

He should, he knew that for a fact, and yet he couldn't do it. For a lot of reasons, old and new, and some Rex would rather not think about because they had their roots in a part of himself he'd closed off a long time ago.

All these reasons had been pushing and pulling inside him since the moment he turned around and saw Jennifer standing behind him in line at Hindley's Market. For the most part he'd had the sense and the strength to ignore them, until one reason, more simple and overwhelming than all the rest combined, had done him in and made it impossible for him to stay away.

Jenny had worn perfume for him.

Just thinking about it made him smile like a happy idiot. She hadn't wanted him to know. That had been obvious from the way she'd blushed when the boys had innocently let the cat out of the bag. It wasn't every day their mother wore perfume and her special new shirt, as Jeff had referred to it. She'd done it for him and there was only one reason a woman wore perfume for a man.

She might not want it or like it, but the fact is that Jenny was interested. That meant that all bets were off. And that he was doomed.

In the days following their trip to Phoenix House, he seized every opportunity to see her. He went to the beach when he knew she and the boys would be there, he brought her mail to her when he was the first to check their adjacent mailboxes, which he made sure he always was, he dropped in after dinner to thank her for the bone, which she herself had saved for Bear this time.

Once he'd arrived in time to hear her swearing at the old gas stove and had offered to take a look at it for her. When you're made the man of the house at a very young age, with not much money for outside help, you learn to perform a variety of useful tasks. Rex was never so glad for the experience as he was when he got the pilot light working again and Jenny beamed at him as if he'd done something only several degrees shy of walking on water.

A few days later, he'd helped her wallpaper the kitchen, savoring the chance to hang around for an entire day.

When there were no legitimate reasons for seeing her, he invented them, sometimes resorting to walking over to her place at dusk to fetch Bear when he could easily summon him home with a whistle—and both he and Jennifer knew it.

As telling as his compulsion to see Jenny was, the way her face brightened whenever he appeared confirmed she felt the same for him. It had been the same tonight when he showed up at her door at sunset with the sparklers he'd promised the boys a few days ago. Her blue eyes warmed, her smile coming as naturally as breathing and almost making his heart stop as he stood on the deck and drank in the sight of her as if it had been years rather than hours since he'd seen her last. No *Playboy* centerfold had ever looked as sexy or desirable as Jenny looked to him in cut-off jeans and an old black T-shirt, her hair in a ponytail. Her long legs were tan and smooth and bare and so distracting that he burned himself lighting a sparkler because he was looking at them instead of at what he was doing.

He loved bringing her mail and seeing her full of morning energy, and he loved working throughout the day knowing she was only a stone's throw away, picturing her bent over her desk or stenciling pale seashells on the bathroom walls. But more than anything else, he liked seeing her at this time of day, relaxed and mellow, as if there was nothing in the world more important than watching her sons paint fiery circles in the air with sparklers.

He liked to think that he had something to do with her mood, as well. Thinking that gave him a good feeling, an elusive sort of good feeling. Like the airy rush of pleasure that sometimes comes out of nowhere and runs along your spine, but if you think about it too hard or try to hang on to it, disappears completely.

"Ryan, don't run with a sparkler in your hand," Jennifer called out from her seat beside Rex on the deck steps as Ryan ran in circles around a tree at the other side of the gravel drive.

"Half the fun of sparklers is running with them," Rex pointed out quietly.

"Well, then they'll have to settle for having the other half of the fun of them."

"You mean the fun of throwing them in the air and watching them fall?"

"Don't you dare tell them about that."

"Give them another year or so and I won't have to. It's something you just come to naturally."

"I didn't. I never threw a sparkler in my life."

"That's because you lack the testosterone necessary to undertake such a high-risk maneuver."

"That sounds like pure macho bull to me."

She snickered as she said it, but snickered with such affection that Rex decided that pure macho bull was her favorite kind. He stretched his legs out in front of him contentedly and watched Ryan running around the tree again.

Jennifer sighed. "Ryan, I told you not to run."

"I'm not running. I'm chasing."

"Chasing what?"

"My sparkler."

"Can't argue with that logic," Rex told her, chuckling. "How about if you compromise and let him chase it over here on the drive where he won't trip over any tree roots or anything?"

Jenny agreed just as both boys' sparklers burned out. They came trotting toward Rex for another.

"Last one," Jenny reminded them as Rex flicked his lighter.

They both groaned in dismay.

"I mean it," she said in a tone that even he understood was final. "It's already way past your bedtime."

"But I wanted a camp fire," Ryan protested.

"You can dream about one," she responded.

"But if we dream about it," said Jeff, "then Rex won't be there to read it for us." She had finally given up trying to enforce the "Mr. Lovell" rule of manners.

Rex met her quizzical glance with a sheepish smile. "I did tell them I would read their fortunes in the next camp fire we built."

"Rex, I've heard of fortune-telling, but reading a camp fire?"

"All Gypsies can do it," Jeff explained on his behalf. "Just like they can read your hand and the leaves in a cup."

"Tea leaves," Rex explained.

Ryan nodded vigorously. "Rex can even answer a question for you with a spoon and water."

"It's an old Gypsy tradition," he told her. "You just balance the spoon on the edge of a cup and let the water drip.... Forget it, it's no big deal."

"It's awesome," Jeff said. "I'm going to be an astronaut when I'm twenty-one. Ryan's just going to ride a horse when he's fourteen."

"You see, you count the drips and ..." He halted a second time, shrugging uneasily under her amused regard. "Really, it's no big deal."

"It sounds fascinating."

"Just something my Rom grandmother taught me. The kids and I got talking about Gypsy traditions one day and I showed them a few."

"Rex knows more than anybody about the stars and dogs and all kinds of great stuff," Jeff informed her.

"Yeah," agreed Ryan. "More than a Ninja Turtle even."

"That much?" Jennifer queried, smiling broadly at him. "Rex is truly an amazing man."

"And I learned it all from my grandmother, who was a *shuvani*—that's Gypsy for very wise woman. Just like your mother, and if she says it's past bedtime, it is."

"But we still have a whole box of sparklers," Jeff protested.

"We'll save them for another night," Rex promised.

"Tomorrow night," Jeff said instantly.

"All right with me," Rex said, more than pleased by the prospect of spending another lazy night sitting close beside Jennifer under a sky full of stars.

She shook her head. "You won't be here tomorrow night," she reminded the boys. "Tomorrow is the day Grandma and Grandpa are taking you to the ball game." She turned to Rex. "They bought tickets to see the Red Sox in Boston and they want to make a weekend out of it . . . dinner afterwards, Sunday brunch—the works."

"Sounds like fun," Rex said, smiling even as he contemplated unhappily how long a weekend here alone was going to feel.

The reminder of the game shelved the fireworks issue for the time being and after the final sparklers of the night, the boys insisted Rex go along to tuck them in. Back downstairs, he turned at the back door to say good-night to Jennifer and found himself standing face-to-face and all too close to her.

It wasn't the first time. Actually it happened all too often, usually by chance, sometimes by design. He couldn't resist the temptation of standing close enough to her to torment himself with the awareness that just by leaning forward and bending his head he could do what he spent so much time daydreaming about doing. Brushing his mouth across hers, feeling her soft lips heat and part as the two of them melted against each other in a kiss that ended with them on the floor or the sofa or the grass down by the brook.

At least that's the way it always happened in his daydreams, and part of Rex was convinced that if he succumbed and touched her one of these times, it would happen very much like that in real life. He thought about that now as he gazed into her wide blue eyes and felt desire begin pulsing down low inside him. She didn't back away and neither did he. It was as if they were playing a very adult version of the game of Chicken. One of these days, he thought, neither one of them was going to blink in time.

But not tonight. Letting go of his breath, he smiled. "I'll leave the rest of those sparklers here for you."

"Oh, no. We wouldn't light them without you. I mean, I'm sure the boys would rather do them when you're around."

"Okay. Maybe some night next week."

"Sure."

Maybe even Sunday night, he thought, but managed not to say. "So have fun at the game."

"Oh, I'm not going," she said. "This is a grandparent thing. Besides, I can use a few hours to myself, to work."

She wasn't going with them. The knowledge shot through Rex, igniting all his nerve endings so that he felt as if one gigantic sparkler had been set off inside him. She was going to be here. All weekend. All alone.

"In that case," he said, "how about having dinner with me tomorrow night?"

The prospect of having dinner with Rex forced Jennifer to confront a question nearly as old as femininity itself— what to wear. She didn't want to go all out, as if she thought it was a real date, and then have him saunter over in jeans and a work shirt with visions of Pizza Hut in his head. On the other hand, she didn't want to dress too casually on the off chance that *he* considered this a real date. Then it would appear that she didn't consider him worth dressing up for.

Throughout the day on Saturday, she tried to work. She'd sit at her desk for a while, then change her mind about what to wear and hurry to the closet to make sure it was clean and ironed. In the end she settled for a black cotton sundress, simple and classy enough for a nice restaurant and yet not entirely out of place at a burger joint on a hot summer night.

At the last minute she added a gold chain and big hoop earrings and switched from flat sandals to heeled ones, and was enormously glad she had when Rex showed up wearing a dark blazer over a white cotton shirt and dress slacks and—to her amazement—a tie.

What did all this mean? she wondered as she let him in, feeling his hungry gaze slide over her bare shoulders to the vee in the bodice of her dress. His attire, not his staring. She knew what that stare meant. It means that if she were smart, she'd plead a headache and stay home.

Rolfe's, a few miles south of Pleasure, was one of the poshest restaurants in Rhode Island and, aside from the country club, the last place she expected Rex to bring her. The dining room was formally decorated, with Victorian-inspired murals and crystal chandeliers and a tuxedo-clad quartet ensconced by the dance floor. An old Sinatra tune drifted across the room.

A white-jacketed waiter took their order and poured a sample of the wine Rex had selected for him to taste. He nodded, a wry, almost imperceptible smile on his lips.

"I probably should have had you do that," he said when the waiter had filled both glasses and left. "But I figured that kind of macho bull was probably de rigueur here."

Jennifer grinned at him and took a sip of her wine. "It's perfect."

"That was a good year for the Dallas Cowboys," he said, nodding at the bottle, "so I figured how bad could the wine be?"

"Sounds like pretty sound reasoning to me."

She took another sip and smiled at him across the table. Rex tugged at the knot on his tie.

"Would you like to dance?" he asked.

"I'm probably a little rusty."

"I'll pretend not to notice."

"Maybe later."

Another sip. At this rate she'd be tipsy before the appetizers arrived.

"You're sure you don't want to dance?" he asked.

"I'm sure," Jennifer replied, glancing at the couples on the dance floor. Was that the fox trot? Now she knew she wasn't ready to dance. Not unless she got a lot tipsier or the band decided to play something that wasn't older than she was. She turned back to find Rex watching her with a concerned frown.

"It's very nice here," she suddenly felt compelled to say.

He glanced around as if for the first time. "Fancy."

"Yes. Very. Tell me something, Rex," she said, leaning forward, "why did you bring me here?"

He shrugged. "For dinner."

"But why here? There are dozens of places to have dinner that are less . . . *fancy.* This doesn't strike me as your kind of place."

"It's not. I figured it was yours, though. The truth is I was trying to impress the hell out of you. Did it work?"

"Who wouldn't be impressed by all this? Especially when she's used to picking up Happy Meals at the drive-thru. One thing's for sure," she added drily. "It will impress the hell out of my mother when I tell her about it."

"Swell. Now maybe she'll think of me as a child snatcher with good taste."

On that sobering note they both reached for their wine, then glanced awkwardly toward the dance floor. Thank heavens for the fox trot. At that instant, Jennifer would gladly swap being impressed for being comfortable. Somehow the easiness that had grown between Rex and her over the past week or so had disappeared, leaving behind only the underlying tension. It was something about this place, she thought, searching for some way to restore balance between them.

"So..."

"I..."

They both stopped at once.

"You first," Rex said.

"I just wanted to tell you that I took your advice about bringing Jeff to visit Jack's grave," she said. "The three of us went after camp a couple of days ago."

"How did it go?"

"Fine. Actually, it went great...or at least as great as something like that can be. They both asked a lot of questions about dying and about who else was buried there. I think they liked seeing that there are so many of Jack's relatives around him."

Rex nodded.

"Jeff made this planter out of Popsicle sticks at camp," she continued, "and we dug up some violets to put in it and he left it there for his dad. When we were leaving, he asked me if we could come back and water the flowers someday and I told him we could come back anytime he wanted, and he just broke into this huge smile." She laced her fingers on the table in front of her. "Maybe it's naive to think that the solution could possibly be that simple, but going there seemed to change things for Jeff, change something inside him, I mean. I can't explain it really, but I felt it, and I saw it in his smile when he looked back. I've got my fingers crossed."

"Maybe it isn't the whole solution. But it might be a start for him." Rex pushed his hand across the white linen tablecloth until his fingertips butted hers. "And how was it for you?" he asked softly.

Jennifer kept her eyes focused on their hands. "It was good for me, too. I thought it would be...painful, and it was, but it also felt good to be there with the boys. It was easier to talk to them about Jack, and when I read the names of all those other McVeighs to them, I suddenly had this sense that Jack is where he belongs now, a sense of...I don't know, rightness. Maybe we all needed one last chance to say goodbye."

She looked up and met Rex's gaze, his eyes were narrowed and thoughtful. He slid his finger along one of hers.

"You have very soft skin," he said. "Softer than anything I've ever touched. Turn your hand over for me, Jenny. Your left hand."

She did as he said and he slid his under it.

"Shall I read your palm?" he asked.

Jennifer smiled, feeling the light touch of his fingers in distracting ripples the whole length of her arm. "If you like, I guess. I should warn you though. I don't really believe in any of that."

He smiled, a small, not to be trusted smile. "Of course not. Me, either. Not really."

He gently took her left hand and turned it again, so that he was staring at the back of it.

"Why the left hand?" she asked, not sure if it was his touch she found so unsettling, or the sudden fear that maybe he could read things there that she'd rather not have him know.

"Because it's closer to your heart," he explained, meeting her eyes briefly. "Also the Rom believe that the left hand shows what was intended in your life, what you were born with, as we say. The right shows what you've made of yourself."

He slowly traced the outline of her hand and between her fingers. She had no idea there would be so much touching involved in this.

"The shape of the hand is inherited," he said, "and impossible to alter to any degree. Your fingers and palm are well balanced, about equal in length."

"Is that good?"

"None of this is black and white. Some things are an advantage, some a disadvantage. What matters is knowing what our advantages are and using them. Now for you, this is definitely a plus. It means you have good judgment and good instincts. You should trust them above all else."

"What else do you see?" Jennifer asked, caught up in it now.

"I see that you've painted your nails since last night," he teased. "But my grandmother never got around to telling me what that might mean."

"Just as well," she muttered.

"Let's take another look at your palm."

Jennifer let him turn her hand over and hold it cradled in his as he studied it.

"Do you actually read the lines themselves?" she inquired.

"The lines, the shape, the Mounts—those are the rises here at the bases of your fingers and thumb," he said, showing them to her. "The lines themselves reveal character, the habits you encourage."

"Like eating potato chips in bed?"

He looked up, interest flickering in his dark gold eyes. "We don't get quite that specific. I was using the word *habit* in a more general sense. For instance, a surgeon's hands will be creased differently than a brick layer's. As for a fondness for potato chips, that could either indicate a lack of willpower, or a highly sensuous nature."

"Oh, I like that one better. Is that me?"

"I'll let you know when I get that far. *Dukkerin* takes time."

"Dukkerin?"

"Fortune-telling. Now hold still."

"That tickles."

"Mmm . . . ticklish palm. Indicates tremendous sensitivity and potential for great fame and fortune."

"Really?"

"No, but that's what everyone hopes to hear so I thought we'd get it over with. Now this is interesting." He followed a deep narrow line that circled the base of her thumb to her wrist. "This is your life line. It's very long and unblemished. That means a long, healthy life."

"Of poverty and obscurity."

He smiled. "Not necessarily. There is some middle ground. This is the line of the head," he continued, indicating the line that crossed her palm just above the life line. "It shows good judgment, which we already covered, and also a great degree of creativity and energy. But see here, where it's connected to the line of life? That could mean a problem with self-confidence. You sometimes let people push you around instead of following your own instincts."

"You really see that?" she asked, feeling his observation hit home uncomfortably.

Rex nodded. "This tiny branch here means that something has happened or could happen to change that though. Or force you to change."

"Jack's getting killed," she said softly. "That changed me." She straightened and eyed him accusingly. "But you already knew that."

"I never said this was an exact science. All sorts of things come into play in a reading. My grandmother used to say that you can't read someone's palm without first looking into their eyes." He leaned forward slightly, as if unconsciously drawn closer to her. His eyes caressed her face. "Would you like to me tell you what I see when I look in your eyes, Jenny?" he asked softly.

Jennifer took a deep breath, both eager and scared to death to hear what he had to say. She was spared by the waiter arriving with their appetizers. Once he'd left, there was a short silence while Rex watched her closely, as if still waiting for permission to say what he had to say. Which, knowing Rex, might be anything. It was like standing blindfolded at the edge of a cliff. How could she know whether or not it was safe to jump if she couldn't see what was waiting for her down there?

She couldn't. Realizing that Jennifer deliberately broke the silence by reaching for her fork. Rex smiled sardonically as he followed suit, and the rest of the dinner passed smoothly enough. They both talked about their work, and about music and movies and all the other safe topics that any new acquaintances might discuss on a first date.

But this wasn't a first date, and they weren't new acquaintances. The past hung in the air between them as hauntingly as the unfinished palm reading. It was there each time their eyes met and clung and whenever their hands brushed, and it was definitely there when Rex deliberately caressed the small of her back as he helped her into the truck. By the time they reached her back door, Jennifer was worried about much more than whether or not he would try to kiss her good-night.

On a gut level, she understood that there would be no good-night kisses for her and Rex. No teasing, no making out and probably no more pseudodates. They were beyond that. With every glance, every breath, he made her aware that he wanted from her now the same thing he told her he wanted that first night on the deck. All or nothing.

"Thanks for dinner, Rex," she said in a remarkably casual voice, considering that her insides were tied in knots. "I had fun."

"So did I," he said, following her until she stopped and turned, her back to the door.

She found her key in her purse and paused before fitting it into the lock. "It feels strange to be doing this without the boys arguing over whose turn it is to unlock the door. In fact, the whole day felt strange, like it didn't belong in my life somehow. All that silence and free time... I keep waiting for someone to call *Mommy.*"

"That's not going to happen tonight, so you can relax."

Relax? Didn't he know there was safety in having the boys with her all the time? Her own tow-headed, blue-eyed, sticky-fingered suit of armor. But not tonight. Tonight there would be no squabbles to settle, no sudden interruptions, no convenient excuses.

She unlocked the door. "Well, thanks again."

"Not so fast," Rex said, catching her hand. "I never finished reading your palm."

"Are you kidding? You've already told me I have great instincts and creativity. I think I'll quit while I'm ahead."

He held on to her hand, rubbing it in a way that seemed to her to have nothing to do with reading her palm. "But I was just getting to the best part."

"The best part?" she echoed, utterly distracted by his touch.

"It's right here. The Mount of Venus."

He caressed the soft rise at the base of her thumb. Funny, she'd had the distinct impression the Mount of

Venus was located somewhat more intimately. Maybe that was the *Mound of Venus,* she thought, her face heating.

"See how it's raised and well-defined," he said. "That indicates a very passionate nature. But it's also soft, which means your sensuality hasn't been fully developed. Maybe you've never had the opportunity to explore that side of yourself. Or maybe you're afraid to."

"And maybe you make all this up as you go along, to suit your purposes."

"I might if I had to. But with you, I don't have to. It's all there, Jenny. The passion and the hunger and the uncertainty. I'm just an interpreter."

"Well, your interpretation is getting a little intense for me," she grumbled. "Whatever happened to *you'll meet a tall dark stranger and live happily ever after?*"

"You already have," he said, tightening his grip as she tried to pull away. "Shall I make you happy, Jenny?"

"I thought you were supposed to answer questions, not ask them."

"All right. Next question."

His eyes held hers.

Jennifer shook her head.

"I don't have one."

"Yes, you do, Jenny. You're wondering if I'm going to try to make love to you tonight. The answer is yes, I am. The reading's over. Now I have a question— I'm wondering if you're going to let me."

Chapter Eight

Jennifer couldn't breathe.

He was right, the idea of making love with him had been tucked away at the back of her mind all evening. All day, too, for that matter, and even before. She supposed it was inevitable...considering their history. But while she'd half expected that his attentions were less than honorable, she hadn't expected him to announce them so bluntly ahead of time.

She should have, she realized now, when it was too late.

His unwavering gaze held her prisoner as she struggled to control the storm of conflicting thoughts and desires breaking inside her.

"Damn," he muttered suddenly. "I should never have taken you to that place tonight."

"Why not? Dinner was wonderful, Rex, and..."

He cut her off with a shake of his head, his expression tight with frustration. "It was a farce. *This* is a farce," he added, jerking the tie loose. "A game. I thought I could play it, but I can't. You're standing there looking like you've got the weight of the world on your shoulders and I can't help wondering what the hell is going through your mind. Are you trying to come up with a reason to tell me no? Or an excuse to tell me yes?

"Maybe," he persisted in a harsh tone, "you're trying to convince yourself that your mother and everyone else is wrong about me. That maybe you've been wrong, too. That maybe a suit coat and tie and the money to buy a bottle of French wine make a difference."

His accusations sliced close enough to make Jennifer sweat.

"Because they don't," he snarled as she stood there in silence. Raising his hands, he planted one on the door on each side of her head and leaned closer. "Nothing's changed. Least of all me. We're right back where we were twelve years ago, Jenny. I want you. You want me. Now what do you want to do about it?"

What did she want? If she wasn't feeling so overwhelmed by him, Jennifer would have laughed. How could she possibly explain to him what she wanted? How she wanted to run *and* stay—wanted to go on hiding behind her Good Mommy persona *and* set free the lonely woman trapped inside her...how she wanted safety *and* she wanted him.

She wanted him badly. She wanted him to hold her and do to her all the things she'd imagined and longed for...ached for. She wanted him in a way that was absolutely mad. And inevitable. Inevitable. The word came from nowhere and blew through her with the sweet power of truth.

This was meant to happen. Like the lines on her palm, it wasn't right or wrong, black or white. It was simply a moment in time for her to seize, or let pass. Oh, God, she thought, feeling more alive and excited at that instant than she had in years; she didn't want to let this slip away as so much else had.

Just this once she didn't want to be cautious, think logically and go alone to her empty bed. This night was special, stolen from her real life, a bonus, like an extra image caught between shots on a roll of film. Tonight belonged to her alone, to do what *she* wanted, to grab on to with both hands.

All or nothing. Everything or nothing at all. It would be pure folly to think that what she felt with Rex could ever be everything she needed in her life. But tonight it was all she wanted.

"What's it going to be, Jenny?" Rex prodded, his voice low and controlled, a vivid counterpoint to the tightly wired energy radiating from him. He was still looming over her, still without touching her with anything but the heat of his body. "Say the word and I'm out of here. If I stay, you're mine."

"Yes," she whispered, "that's what I want. For tonight, that's what I want."

Almost before the words were out, his mouth came down on hers, hot and demanding, his kisses rushing her senses with a sudden explosion of pent-up desire... hers, his. It was a fusion of lust that had been building for weeks now, and maybe much longer.

He took her head in his hands, shoving his fingers through her hair as he held her still for the fevered exploration of his tongue.

For a moment, the sheer power of his assault left Jennifer reeling and rocky. Then his hands slid down over her bare shoulders and arms, and the rough heat of his callused hands against her softer flesh filled her with a heady feeling of erotic femininity.

She was no longer quivering with sensation alone, but with hunger. She was starving for this, desperate for it.

Reaching for his tie, she jerked it free of his collar and dropped it to the deck, then went for the top button of his shirt. Her movements were every bit as frantic as the caresses he was pressing along the back of her thighs, urging her impossibly closer, arousing her as sharply as if there were no barriers of clothing between them.

As if stunned by the sudden violence of her desire, Rex hesitated for a second, rearing back to look at her with eyes that glittered like gold. For only a second. Then his chest rammed hard against her once more and his hands were moving again on her legs, shoving the full skirt of her dress higher, pulling her closer, deep into the vee of his spread thighs.

They were both winded now, their breath coming in broken pants that blended and tumbled over one another in the darkness. In her haste to feel more of him, Jennifer ripped a button from his shirt and didn't care. This was all so unlike her, and she didn't care about that, either. This was pure animal heat, desire slamming against desire, needs being aroused as quickly as they were filled, dragging them both closer to an inferno of pleasure beyond words, beyond thought, beyond reason.

With the last button freed, his shirt fell open and Jennifer spread her fingers through the wiry hair on his chest, relishing the slick heat of his skin, the hard ridges of bone and muscle. Rex grunted with pleasure, adding to hers, as well. Then, hooking his fingers beneath her shoulder straps and looking directly into her eyes, he slowly peeled the top of her dress down, baring her breasts.

Still holding her gaze, he rubbed his chest back and forth against them, caressing her that way until her breasts throbbed with pleasure. She arched her neck, crying out with excitement. Only then did he lower his eyes to gaze at her.

Groaning softly with delight, he scraped his thumbs across her nipples. Jennifer's knees buckled and when he lowered his head and drew one rosy peak into his mouth, she felt everything inside melt into a hot, molten need too strong to be delayed or toyed with.

Her desperation was contagious. The moment Rex felt her fingernails bite into his shoulders, he straightened and lifted her dress in front. His hand plunged beneath, sliding inside her panties and finding her wet and ready. It blew the top off what remained of his self-control.

Jennifer felt rather than heard his husky, fractured pleas and urging. It was plenty eloquent enough. Her body responded instinctively. Eagerly she reached to open his belt buckle, then his zipper, freeing him so that he was hot and moist in her hands.

Planting himself more firmly, Rex gripped her fanny and lifted her.

And in that instant Jennifer understood that he meant to take her right then, right there. Far from being shocked, she gloried in it, in this roaring desire neither of them could control or resist, and which left them at each other's mercy. They clung to each other, both after the same thing, pleasure and release and that headlong tumble into mindlessness.

For Jennifer, the rest of creation seemed to come to a dead, silent stop around them as he entered her with one hard thrust. She cried out loud from the soul-wrenching impact, feeling a remembered tightening begin down low inside her. Holding her tightly, Rex found her mouth with his and used the rhythmic movements of his tongue to double the power of the sensations racing through her.

Jennifer gripped his shoulders, clenching him as tightly as she could with her body as his hips rocked her higher and higher, closer to the edge. She climaxed almost instantly, with a fervor that left her shattered and dazed and able to manage only a weak smile when seconds later she felt Rex's grip tighten spasmodically and heard his soft cry of satisfaction echo her own.

She was still breathing hard when he lowered her to her feet. Her legs wobbled, making her grateful for the support of his strong arms around her.

When she was steadier, he caught her face between his hands and kissed her lips, then grinned at her. "Were you planning to invite me in?"

"I guess I better. Before the neighbors complain to the police about a woman screaming over here."

"I'm your closest neighbor, and I'm definitely not complaining. I like your screams only slightly less than your moans."

"Please, stop," she said, burying her face in her hands. "I've never been like this before."

"Then I'd say it's about time," Rex retorted, reaching past her to open the door. "Inside, Jenny."

They moved into the kitchen, Rex shutting and locking the door behind them. When she automatically reached for the light, he caught her hand. "No. No lights. Not yet. As much as I want to see every sweet inch of your body, I'm not sure you're ready for that. Show me your bedroom, Jenny."

Her heartbeat had gradually slowed. Now, as she heard the seductive intent in his command, it began pounding once again. He reached for her hand and held it as she led him through the moonlit living room to her bedroom.

Inside the door, she hesitated, nervously pulling on the top of her sundress. She was suddenly glad he hadn't let her turn on the light a minute ago. Somehow their disheveled and loosened state of undress seemed more suggestive and erotic than total nudity.

"Hold on," he said, pulling her hands to her sides. "You're going the wrong way with that." She could hear the amusement in his voice, feel the curve of his lips as he moved closer and pressed them to her throat in gentle kisses as he lowered her zipper and removed her dress. "There. That's much closer to what I had in mind. Now these."

He peeled her panties off, taking her sandals along with them and flinging them over his shoulder. "Much better. Perfect, in fact," he murmured, running one hand over her hips and belly even as he used his other to rid himself of his shirt and pants.

When they were both naked, he pulled her into his arms, sealing her body to the hard length of his. Jennifer could feel his arousal cradled against her, so hot she'd swear it would leave a mark there forever. He kissed her, hard, then pushed her down onto the bed with a single word. Jennifer couldn't decide if it was a command, a request or a promise, and was beyond caring.

"Again," he said.

In the long hours of sleeplessness that followed, Jennifer learned more about herself than she'd thought there was to know. She had been married and she had loved her husband, but until tonight she had only scratched the surface of what it meant to give and receive pleasure. Rex led her through the dark secrets of intimacy, a world of excruciatingly slow delight, of moans and whispers, of bruising caresses and insatiable hunger.

Jennifer thought she had felt it all, given all she had to give, taken as much as she could stand, when he slid lower and gently pushed her knees wide.

Kneeling between them, he looked up at her and lightly caressed her tender breasts, slowly sliding his hand down until his fingers touched her intimately, opening her in a way that signaled his intent and started every nerve ending in her body vibrating with anticipation and uncertainty.

"I wanted to do this the last time," he said, his husky tone a different sort of caress, "but I was afraid."

Amazement joined all the other feelings inside Jennifer. "You? Afraid? Back then I thought you were the most reckless, most outrageous person I knew. I never thought you could be afraid of anything."

"That's what I wanted you to think. What I wanted everyone to think. But I was afraid that night. Afraid you'd stop me," he murmured, his head slowly lowering as Jennifer's stomach muscles clenched. "Afraid you wouldn't. So I held back. And I've been hungry for the taste of you ever since."

He buried his face in her as her nails bit into his back. The softness and the sting combined to bring Rex a fierce, long overdue pleasure. He could feel her natural resistance to this deepest intimacy weaken and give way and that brought him even greater joy.

He could also feel her fatigue. Poor Jenny. He'd bet anything this night had been much more than she bargained for. And still he felt he had cherished her less and given her less pleasure than she deserved. And so he relentlessly drove her on to this final pinnacle, nibbling, bathing her with his tongue, teaching her what it meant to be drowned in pleasure, to be steeped in sensation, to be sated.

Afterward, she fell asleep curled by his side, and for a while Rex hoped he might sleep, as well. Maybe it would be different with Jenny. Maybe his demons wouldn't find him here.

No such luck.

The feeling came on him stealthily, at first no more than an elusive itch between his shoulder blades. Then it wrapped around his chest, burning a path straight through him at the core. Is that where your conscience is located? he wondered.

And still he hoped to fight it. He wanted to. God knows he wanted to. He wanted this time to be different from the one-night stands of years past and the brief, desire-driven relationships he could never seem to hold together. He wanted it to be different because *Jenny* was different, and the way he felt about her was different. And *he* wanted to be different, too. For Jenny.

The restless feeling inside didn't much care what he wanted. It grew steadily.

Maybe if he got a breath of fresh air. A drink of water.

Just leaving the bed brought him some relief. He purposely stepped over his pants, knowing that if he got dressed he'd keep on going right through the kitchen and out of there. And you didn't do things like that to a woman like Jenny. Not unless you wanted things to be over, once and for all. Even he, with his vast inexperience with women like her, knew that much.

Her kind of woman expected you to be able to stay in the damn bed beside her for a few hours after making love to her. And she expected you to be there in the morning. She expected a lot of things, he thought, wishing to hell he'd grabbed his cigarettes off the table by her bed.

He was about to go back for them when his foot slammed into what felt like a cement mixer. Close, he

thought, as he bent down with a pained oath to shove aside
a yellow metal dump truck belonging to Ryan. A few steps
later his foot landed on a small GI armed with what felt
like a bayonet. He swore again. Hell, you needed a recon-
naissance map to negotiate this place in the dark. Not like
in his house where everything was safe and barren, and
getting more so with each passing day.

Deciding he needed the water more than a cigarette, he
headed straight for the kitchen. There was enough moonlight coming through the window over the sink for him to
find a glass and fill it. It wasn't until he'd taken his first
gulp that he noticed the decal on the bottom. The figure of
a black bat stared back at him, silhouetted against the
moon so that it glowed eerily. Damn, even the glasses here
weren't what he was used to.

The awareness of how different Jenny's home was from
his suddenly grabbed hold of him, like something that had
been chasing him for days and wasn't about to let go
without a fight. It was all real simple; this was a home, his
place wasn't. For the first time, he considered the irony in
how hard Jenny was working to put down roots here for
her children, while he spent his days methodically eradicating all traces of his own.

The result of her efforts was right here in front of him,
in the ruffled lace curtains on the window, the new towel
rack shaped like a butler with one arm extended and the
kids' drawings hanging on the front of the refrigerator.
There was nothing remotely like any of it in his house.
He'd done what he'd set out to do, created a clean palette,
a world without blemishes or mistakes. Or color. He didn't
care what the paint can said; it was white. As white as
show. White as ice. So white that he sometimes looked
around and shivered even on a sweltering hot day.

He set the half-full glass in the sink. Water wasn't going to wash away the feeling lodged in his gut. And a cigarette wasn't going to fix it, either. He knew that now. Hell, he'd always known it, he'd just been horny enough to let himself forget it for a while. No matter how right tonight had felt, it was wrong.

The itch between his shoulder blades had been a small reminder, as had the dump truck and toy soldier, but it had taken their damn black bat decal to make it all come together for him. Rex didn't belong here. Not tonight. Not tomorrow. Not ever.

Rex stared to turn, then stopped suddenly and gripped the counter with both hands, stricken by the belated realization that on top of everything else, he'd broken his own cardinal rule tonight. In making love to Jenny, he'd done something he never, ever did.

With a look of remorse, he glanced over his shoulder toward the bedroom where she slept peacefully and, for the first time since he'd put it there hours ago, thought about the condom in his wallet.

Jenny woke and with her eyes still closed, stretched her legs across the double bed. After nearly three years of sleeping alone, she ought to expect to find the space beside her empty. But she didn't. Not this morning. Somehow, even asleep, her body had hummed with awareness of Rex and what had happened last night. And so it was a shock when her legs encountered only cool empty sheets.

She opened her eyes and sat up. The fact that she was naked and a little sore here and there gave instant testimony that she hadn't dreamed the whole thing... again. No, this time it had really happened and, amazingly, she wasn't at all sorry.

She'd done exactly as she pleased last night, reached out with both hands and seized the moment, fully expecting that when she regained her senses this morning she would be choking on regrets. Somehow, in the desperate madness that had possessed her last night, she had convinced herself that it would be worth it.

Now she would never know, because there wasn't a single regret or second thought or recrimination in her entire, satisfied body. She wasn't sure at precisely what moment during the long night she had known that there wouldn't be any, only that at some point their eyes had met, and without a word being exchanged, promises were offered and accepted and an understanding reached that what they felt for each other could never be explored, or contained, in a single night.

And she recalled being very glad that no words were spoken. Words came too easily in the moonlight. Rex's eyes hadn't lied. She knew that as surely as she knew what was in her own heart.

So where was he?

Even before she had her robe knotted, she'd figured it out. She vaguely recalled that as she drifted off to sleep last night he'd said something about getting his truck out of her driveway at dawn, lest they become the talk of the neighborhood. Jennifer grinned. Very chivalrous of him, but, she was afraid, ultimately a waste of time. A pickup truck would be a whole lot easier to hide than the stars in her eyes.

Humming happily, she put on a pot of coffee and went to shower and brush her teeth. She was dressed in shorts and a T-shirt and the coffee had already finished dripping, but Rex had not yet reappeared. She contemplated surprising him with a big breakfast, then thought of a surprise she was certain he would enjoy much more. Set-

tling for some hurriedly defrosted blueberry muffins piled
in a napkin-lined basket, she transferred the coffee to a
thermal pot and swapped her oversize T-shirt for a sleeve-
less one that laced up the front, before heading for Rex's
house.

She was across the brook and nearly at his back steps
before she noticed that the truck wasn't parked in his
driveway, either. Maybe he'd gone to get the paper, or had
to run out for dog food, or to pick up ingredients to surprise her with breakfast. But even as she tossed off possibilities like grenades lobbed at an unseen enemy, the truth
began to pound inside Jennifer.

Maybe it was the fact that the shades were all tightly
pulled or that Bear's food and water dishes weren't in their
customary spot on the porch. Maybe it was just that her
instincts were every bit as good as Rex had said they were.
Whatever the reason, in that instant she knew that he
hadn't gone to pick up the paper or a dozen eggs. He was
just gone.

As if a strong wind had swept her here from her house
and now had suddenly fallen absolutely still, Jennifer
stopped moving. She wafted briefly, feeling sort of like a
small boat carried much too far out to sea, then she lowered herself to a boulder a short distance from his door and
wondered how she could have been so wrong.

Coffee dripping from the thermos spout splashed in the
dirt at her feet. She absently swiped at it with one sandal-
clad foot, wincing as she caught sight of the toenails which
she had spent an hour yesterday covering with two perfect
coats of Sizzling Scarlett. What an idiot.

She had been sizzling, all right. Probably the most un-
forgettably sizzling one-night stand Rex Lovell had ever
had. Make that two one-night stands, she thought miser-

ably, suddenly hurling the muffins, basket and all, into the woods beside her.

So much for her big surprise, and for unspoken promises, and for following her instincts. In fact, the only bright spot in this whole wretched mess she'd made for herself, was the fact that the boys wouldn't be home for hours yet. She hated for them to see her cry.

Chapter Nine

The boys didn't return home until that evening, after side trips to Bunker Hill, the top of the Prudential Center and Grandpa's favorite Boston steak house. That gave Jennifer ample time to accept the fact that Rex had made love to her and then taken off without a word of apology or explanation. So why couldn't she accept it?

It wasn't as though she didn't have experience in this area. This was, taunted a small voice inside, just like last time. Except, she thought miserably, that last time Rex had tried to contact her afterward and she was the one who had all but gone into hibernation to avoid him. The possibility that this whole thing had been a carefully plotted act of retaliation hit her hard. It also made a mockery of her desperate, steadily waning hope that at any minute, Rex was going to call to say he'd been called away on an emergency or to offer some other explanation for his disappearance.

Slowly, but surely, the minutes had ticked their way into an hour, then several, and still the hot summer air remained a frustratingly silent wall around her. It was cause for celebration when she finally heard the sound of tires on the gravel drive and in spite of her own common sense she hurried to the door, hoping in vain to see Rex's pickup truck pulling up outside instead of her father's Lincoln.

She stood in the doorway, forcing back tears that should have been used up hours ago, as the boys spilled from the car laden with Red Sox pennants and T-shirts and what looked to Jennifer like one of every other souvenir Boston had to offer. Bending down, she gave them each a big hug, happy all the way to her soul that they were back with her. Now life could go on the way it should.

They chattered nonstop, about the game, the hotel room, the life-size cows they got to pose on, outside the steak house. Their words ran together so that Jennifer, who volleyed her smiles and nods between the two of them, felt as if she were piecing together an abstract verbal puzzle. But at least this was a kind of puzzle she was used to.

"...Spilled his strawberry slush on the man in front of us and he..."

"...A big bed, bigger than yours even, and our own TV."

"...Up so high you can see everything, even the Boston Hopper."

"You mean Harbor."

"I guess."

It went on and on, as her parents, looking almost as glad the weekend was over as Jennifer felt, collapsed into chairs at the kitchen table.

"And," Ryan announced, as if unveiling the pièce de résistance, "I even saved part of my hot dog for Bear."

He proceeded to pull something vaguely resembling a half a hot dog from the pocket of his shorts.

"Ryan," gasped her mother as Jennifer laughed and shook her head in response to his generous offer to let her hold it. "Have you had that in your pocket since yesterday?"

"I guess," he said again. It was a nice, nonincriminating sort of response—one of Ryan's favorites lately.

"That's disgusting," her mother told him. "You'll get deathly sick if you eat that. Now go and throw it away right this minute."

"I'm not going to eat it," he protested. "It's for Bear. Can I go give it to him now, Mom? Can I?"

Jennifer bit her lip. She'd been so absorbed in her own feelings, she hadn't thought yet of how last night was going to affect the boys. Of course, there was the distinct possibility that Rex was gone for good. But what if he did eventually return? What then?

"Can I, huh, Mom?"

"No."

"But, Mom..."

"Ryan, you can't go over there now, because Bear isn't there. They're gone."

"Gone where?"

"I don't know actually," she said, scooping up some of the debris they had dropped on the kitchen floor and turning away to organize it on the kitchen counter far more neatly than she ordinarily would have. "Back to their real home, I suppose."

"But this is their real home," Jeff argued. "At least for the whole rest of the summer. Rex even said so."

"Well, maybe Rex doesn't know everything after all," Jennifer snapped. "I just know that they're not there now." The disappointment on Ryan's small face melted through her own misery. "Why don't you put the hot dog in the refrigerator and you can give it to Bear the next time you see him?"

"But when will that be?"

She curled her fingers into her palms. "I don't know for sure. Maybe a few days." Maybe never.

Still looking disappointed, he moved toward the refrigerator to do as she suggested.

Feeling her mother's gaze zero in on her and cling, Jennifer purposely continued to fuss with the mess on the counter.

Her mother moved to stand beside her. "Are you all right, Jennifer?" she asked.

"Fine."

"You look a little . . . tired."

"I took an antihistamine a while ago. Allergy, I guess."

The answer pleased her mother. She liked a nice tidy problem that she knew how to deal with. "There, you see? I knew you had allergies. Didn't I tell you that, Jim?"

Her father nodded agreeably.

"What did you take?" she asked Jennifer.

"Mom, I don't know. Whatever I had in the medicine cabinet."

"Well, that's no way to treat an allergy. Just take a shot in the dark. My heavens, Jennifer, haven't you learned anything at all from me? Some antihistamines are better than others. You really should read the ingredients or better yet, talk to Stanley at the pharmacy. He knows—"

"I will," Jennifer promised. "I'll talk to him tomorrow . . . while the kids are at camp."

"I hope you at least checked the expiration date."

"Oh, I did."

"Because if you didn't—"

"Mom, I said I checked it."

"Well, all right. No need to get huffy."

"I'm sorry," Jennifer replied, forcing a smile. "I didn't mean to be."

"Maybe whatever you took disagrees with your system and that's why you're so on edge and—"

"Mom," she interjected warningly. "I'm fine. And I really appreciate you taking the kids for the weekend. It sounds as if they had a ball. You spoil them."

"To make up for all the time you kept them away from us."

Somehow Jennifer managed to hold the smile in place.

"I hope you were able to get some work done while they were gone."

"Oh, I did," Jennifer lied. "Scads."

"Good." Her mother glanced out the window, a sparkle of satisfaction in her eyes. "So, he's gone."

He's gone, he's gone, he's gone. The same two little words that had underscored the beat of Jennifer's heart all day. Now, hearing them, she blinked, her gaze purposely blank. "Who?"

"Him," her mother retorted impatiently, thrusting her chin in the direction of the brook and beyond. "That Lovell character. You see? I was right about him, too."

"How's that?"

"I predicted he wouldn't hang around long. Not that it took any special insight," she added, with a small laugh. "His kind never does, you know. Here today and gone tomorrow. Just like I said. All you had to do was stay out of his way and he'd be gone before you knew it. So I was right."

"You sure were," Jennifer agreed softly. "All I had to do was stay out of his way." She stepped around her mother and shoved open the screen door. "I think I'll get the rest of the kids' stuff from the car."

She reached the back of the car before realizing she didn't have a key to the trunk. She was eyeing the house reluctantly, thinking how much she didn't feel like continuing that conversation with her mother, when, like an angel of mercy, her father ambled out, swinging the keys.

"I guess you need these," he said.

"Thanks, Dad. I'm afraid I'm a little foggy tonight."

"Sure, I know, the antihistamine."

Their eyes met, Jennifer's sheepish, his as gentle and understanding as always. The strength and longevity of his marriage was testimony to his tolerant, compassionate nature.

"I, ah . . ." Jennifer paused, her eyes filling.

Her father's hand curled around the back of her neck. "I know. It's not easy, this business of being alone."

"Today, nothing feels easy. It feels like nothing will ever be easy again."

"But you know that it will," he said quietly, not pressing for answers or explanations. Jennifer knew that if she wanted to talk, he'd listen. And if she didn't, well, that was all right, too.

"I guess," she said, kicking the gravel at her feet.

"So that's where Ryan gets it," he observed and they both laughed. "You know, Jennifer, it was good having the kids to ourselves for a couple of days. It brought back a lot of memories for your mother and me. Good memories."

She smiled. "I'm glad."

"I was remembering that time we went to the big Fourth of July parade and we spent the whole morning looking for a pink sparkle balloon for you. Remember?"

She nodded.

"We found dozens of pink ones and dozens of sparkle ones, but no pink sparkle ones. Then, finally, when the parade was nearly over, we found one."

"And I let go of the string before we got back to the car," Jennifer recalled, her expression rueful.

"So back we went, but before we got back as far as the fellow selling those balloons, you saw a red one and insisted you wanted it instead. When we got to the car, your mother lambasted me for letting you grab the first thing you saw, and I guess she was right." He shrugged, looking a little sheepish himself suddenly. "I'm not sure what the point of all that was."

"I am," Jennifer said, giving him a quick hug. "Thanks, Dad."

"I love you, sweetheart. And I know you must get lonely. But you're young and talented and beautiful. There'll be another man for you—the right man. Don't you settle for less."

"I won't." She smiled at him. "No more red balloons, I promise."

"That's my girl. Now what do you say we get the rest of this stuff in the house so your old man can go home and sleep for about a month or so? I'm not as young as I used to be, you know."

"Mom's sad."

"How do you know?"

Jeff looked at his younger brother with disgust. "I just do, that's all."

They were sitting down by the brook... their own side of the brook. They had been forbidden to cross it. Not that there was much reason to, with Bear gone away.

It had been four days now since they got back from Boston and found out that Rex and Bear had left. Jeff wasn't sure whom he missed the most, Rex or Bear. Ryan said he missed Bear more than anything. Every day he took the stupid hot dog from the refrigerator and walked down to the brook to see if Rex's truck was back yet.

Mom kept telling him the hot dog was going to go bad from being held in his sweaty hands and sure enough, it had gotten all moldy and yukky and Mom said he had to throw it away and he screamed and cried so hard that she finally said go ahead and keep it and what did she care if the damn dog got sick.

That was the first time Jeff could remember her saying damn about anything, especially something as great as Bear, and it was just one more way he knew that she was sad. The only reason Ryan didn't know it, too, was on account of he was only four and a dork.

"You know how come she's so sad?" he asked Ryan now.

Ryan shook his head. "Cause I broked the lamp?"

"No, that just made her mad. Good and mad," he added, thinking of how she'd shouted at Ryan last night when he got his foot caught in the cord and pulled over the lamp next to his bed. She usually never shouted at them. That was the second time he heard her say "damn."

"She's sad," he informed Ryan, "on account of how Rex and Bear went away. I think she misses them."

"I miss them, too. 'Specially Bear. And I don't care what Mom says, I'm saving him the hot dog."

"Ryan, it's green. Even dogs don't like stuff that's green."

"Bear will, you'll see."

"Anyway, that's not even what's important."

"I think it's 'portant."

"That's because you're just a kid and you don't know."

"Do you know?"

"Sure. I know that Mom gets up extra early and looks out the window over there at Rex's house and that's when she looks most sad of all. And I know a way to make her stop being sad all the time and grouchy and stuff."

"What way?"

"I'm going to go find Rex and tell him he's gotta come back."

Ryan brightened. "And bring Bear?"

"Of course he'll bring Bear, dummy."

"Where will we find him?"

"Not we. Just me. You gotta stay here and take care of Mom and stuff."

"I want to come."

"Well, you can't. And if you try and tag along you'll just spoil everything and then you'll never get to see Bear again probably."

"Not ever?"

"Not ever even once."

Ryan gulped, and tears came from his eyes.

"Don't be a crybaby," ordered Jeff. "I told you I'd find him for you."

"But how will you know where to look?"

"Remember the day Mom took us back to see the fancy mailbox and she told us how that road out back circles around over way behind Rex's house?"

"I guess."

"Well, that's how come I know where to go. I'll just cut through the woods on the other side to that road, then I'll go along that road the way Grandpa did when he took us to Boston. That's near where Rex's other house is. Then I'll just ask somebody which house is his."

"Oh."

"Your part is to stay here and not tell Mom. That's real important, cause if she finds out she'll try and stop us."

"How come?"

"I don't know. Cause that's what moms do. So you can't tell."

"Okay," said Ryan, shaking his head.

"Not for anything."

"Okay."

"Swear?"

He nodded. "I swear."

"Spit and swear?"

They both spit on their fingers and pressed them together, saying "Spit and swear" at the same time.

Then they gave each other a high five and Jeff licked his lips as he peered into the woods across the brook for a minute before taking off.

Ryan stood at the edge of the brook and watched him go. When he was gone, Ryan kicked stones into the water for a while, then used a stick to poke the mud for a while longer before he got sick of just sitting there waiting. He wondered if he had time to run home and go to the bathroom and grab his hot dog from the refrigerator before Jeff got back with Bear.

"Where's your brother?"

Ryan stopped at the door and turned back to Jennifer, who sat working at her desk in a corner of the kitchen. Control center, she called it, though these days she didn't feel in control of anything, not even her own emotions. Especially her own emotions. From minute to minute she never knew if she was going to feel more sad, frustrated or just plain mad as hell. Only that whatever she felt, it was all because of Rex Lovell.

"What?" Ryan countered.

"Your brother. You know—short skinny kid, looks a lot like you. Where is he?"

"I don't know."

"What do you mean you don't know?" she asked, pushing the papers in front of her aside. "You were together at the brook, weren't you?"

Ryan nodded vigorously.

"And you came home to use the bathroom?"

More nodding.

"So is Jeff still down there?"

His small shoulders shot upward. "I dunno."

An uneasy feeling curled in the pit of her stomach. "Ryan McVeigh, did your brother go across that brook after I warned the two of you not to?"

"I dunno."

Jennifer glared at him. "I'll deal with you later... after I take care of Jeff."

She hurried down to the brook, calling Jeff's name from the time she left the deck. When there was no response, the uneasiness inside began to turn to something colder and sharper. It wasn't like Jeff not to answer, or to disobey or to venture off alone for that matter. True, she'd seen many encouraging signs of increasing confidence in him during the past few weeks, but not all *that* encouraging.

She stepped across the brook without a thought of how this might look to Rex if he had suddenly returned. At the moment she didn't care about appearances or pride or what Rex Lovell thought about anything. She only cared about finding Jeff.

Taking the hill that lay between Rex's house and the brook at a full run, she reached the top half expecting to find Jeff on the porch playing with Bear. What she saw instead sent her heart crashing. The window shades were still tightly drawn, the driveway empty, and Jeff wasn't in sight anywhere.

She turned as she heard Ryan trot alongside. "Ryan, listen to me. Where was Jeff when you left him?"

"I dunno."

"Stop saying that," she shouted, dropping to her knees as she gripped his arms tightly. "Think. When you came in to go to the bathroom, where was Jeff?"

He stared back at her, eyes wide with alarm.

She immediately loosened her hold, rubbing his small arms reassuringly. "Honey, Mommy's not angry with you. I just want to find Jeff as fast as I can. Will you help me?"

"I guess."

She grit her teeth. "Where was Jeff the last time you saw him?"

"Back there." He gestured in the general area of the brook.

"On this side? Or on our side?"

"Not this side," he said, shaking his head. "You said not to come here, remember?"

"I remember. Okay, so he was on our side of the brook."

"I guess."

Her chest tightened suddenly. "Was there anyone else around? A stranger? Anyone at all?"

He shook his head again. "Nope. Just Jeff and me."

"And you don't have any idea where Jeff might have gone?"

He shook his head.

Jennifer stood and gazed around in a full circle, calling Jeff's name again and again. She heard the frantic edge creeping into her voice and she hated it. Stay calm, she told herself. Stay calm and in control. Grabbing onto Ryan's hand, she pulled him along as she retraced her steps across the brook, then plunged through the heavily overgrown woods, heading first in one direction, then another. This wasn't getting her anywhere. And with each passing second, with each step she took farther from the safety of her own backyard, her fear grew.

Where was he? God, where could he be? All the time she was calling his name out loud, she was praying just as loudly on the inside. Please, God, please just let him be all right.

Their closest neighbors on the other side were the Randalls, a friendly couple with three teenage children. Jane Randall was sitting in the backyard with her daughter Kristen when Jennifer approached.

"Hi, Jennifer," she called. "Lose somebody?"

"I hope not," Jennifer replied. "It's Jeff. You haven't seen him this afternoon have you?"

Jane Randall got out of her lawn chair, sobering instantly as she read the deep concern on Jennifer's face. She shook her head. "No, neither of your little guys ever comes over this far."

"I know," Jennifer said. "That's why I'm so worried. He never just wanders off like this."

"Now, now, all kids wander away sooner or later. My Kristen over there scared the life out of me at the beach one day when she was five, wandered off looking for shells and ended up nearly a mile away. I'm sure he'll—"

"Yes, me, too," Jennifer broke in impatiently. "Thanks.... If you do see him will you call..."

"Of course, but I'll do better than that. We're just sitting here wasting time. Kris and I will help you look for him."

The three of them, with Ryan in tow, searched for nearly a half hour, covering more ground than Jennifer believed Jeff could possibly have covered. They fanned out and searched the area between their houses and the road, then crossed the brook and looked on the other side again. At

Jane's suggestion Jennifer even returned home and checked the cellar, under the beds, any nook and cranny where Jeff might have curled up and fallen asleep.

It was Jane who finally gave voice to an idea Jennifer didn't even want to think about.

"Jennifer, I hate to say it, but I don't think he's around here. You don't suppose he would have crossed the road and headed toward the lake, do you?"

"No," Jennifer cried. "Absolutely not." Clamping her cupped hands to her face, she added, "Oh, God, I don't know what to think right now. Where could he be? What am I going to do?"

Jane took hold of her arm and steered her firmly in the direction of the house. Her tone was just as sure and unwavering as her grip. "I'll tell you what we're going to do—we're going to call Chief Haggard. Let him get a few men out here to help us look and we'll find Jeff in no time flat."

After calling the police, Jennifer called her mother, who promptly summoned her father from the golf course and had him phone an old buddy on the state police force. Within a half hour, there were cars overflowing her driveway and people streaming in and out of the house.

Pleasure was a very small town, and when word spread that Jeff McVeigh was missing, nearly everyone turned out to help look for him. Jennifer was finally persuaded that it was best for her to wait at home in case the police needed to touch base with her quickly, but she paced like a caged animal, making pot after pot of coffee even after the diner in town had sent out an urn and a supply of doughnuts to fuel the search. She needed to keep busy.

The day wore on until she glanced at the clock and realized that Jeff had now been missing for nearly six hours. Another couple of hours and it would be full dark. The thought of him out there somewhere, alone and terrified, made her shiver violently in spite of the continuing heat.

For the first time in her life Jennifer understood what real fear was. What she'd felt at the time of Jack's death had been grief, deep and pervasive enough to make every bone in her body ache and make the future seem like a black cloud that would never lift. But always, beneath her sadness, had been a sense that the worst had happened and that if she hung on long enough she would survive.

This was different. It was gut-wrenching, sickening, deafening. It crawled through her insides like a relentless army of the worst insects she could imagine. It filled her head, making it impossible to think of anything but her little boy and every gruesome, heartbreaking headline she had ever read about a missing child.

And so she paced, because to sit still would be to go crazy, and she made deal after deal with God. Promising what she would give up or do or never do again if only he would let Jeff be found safe. She had paused by the window to stare out over the trees, willing the sun not to set, when she heard the familiar roar of a truck engine across the brook.

She had barely registered the fact that Rex was back, when he was coming at her across the yard, vaulting over the deck rail and charging into her house without knocking as if he had every right in the world to do so.

"I beg your pardon," she heard her mother say.

Rex ignored her, ignored everyone gathered in the kitchen, his gaze skimming over them with undisguised impatience as he searched for and found Jennifer.

"What the hell is going on here?" he demanded.

Chapter Ten

Jennifer had both daydreams and nightmares of this moment, her first face-to-face meeting with Rex since waking up and finding him gone. She pictured herself being cool and disdainful, or righteously, brilliantly angry.

Instead, what she felt was a deep-down relief, as if he were some sort of white knight there to make everything better. Staring up at him, she couldn't help remembering how solid his chest had felt beneath her cheek, how strong his arms were, and from out of nowhere there came an intense desire to collapse against him. It was ridiculous, but it was also an urge so primordial, she had to wrap her arms around herself tightly to keep from reaching out to him.

"Answer me, Jenny," he said. "I asked you what's going on here?" He suddenly glanced around the room, and Jennifer swore that his deep bronze skin paled a bit. "Where are the boys?"

"It's Jeff," she said, finally feeling capable of speaking. "He's missing."

Rex's eyes narrowed so that there was only a glint of gold visible between the mesh of his long black lashes. "What do you mean, he's missing? Where is he?"

"That's the point of saying he's missing," her mother chimed in tartly. "We don't know where he is."

He flicked her with the briefest look of reproach before turning his full attention to Jennifer.

"Tell me what happened, Jenny," he said stepping closer so that they might have been alone there for all she could see around his tall frame and broad shoulders. His soft tone made his words no less a command, and Jennifer heard herself repeating what she had been saying all day.

He listened attentively to every word, even her rambling asides and desperate uttering of fears and regrets. At one point he pulled a neatly folded blue bandanna from his jeans pocket and gently wiped the tears from her face with it before handing it to her.

"I'm just so afraid he went down to the lake alone and...and..." Her thought was choked off as she pressed her lips together so tightly, she tasted blood. "I've been trying to teach him to swim, but he's still not...he's not..."

"Shh." Rex touched her cheek with his hand. "Don't think about that now. You're sure Jeff was still down at the brook when Ryan came back to the house to go to the bathroom?"

"I think so. It's hard to be absolutely sure of anything where Ryan is concerned. Even he's acting weird. I think he's scared."

"Of course he's scared," her mother said from behind Rex. "Why wouldn't he be? His brother is missing . . . my poor little Jeff, God only knows what's happened to him. Why, right this minute he could be—"

"Stop." Rex's tone brought the room to absolute silence. "Standing around here speculating about what *might* have happened isn't going to help matters. And it's only going to make it worse for Jenny."

Her mother's lips twitched at the familiar way he referred to Jennifer, but she wisely kept them sealed.

"What I want to know is—" He broke off as a war whoop sounded from the loft where Ryan was being entertained by Kris Randall.

A few seconds later, Ryan charged into the kitchen, shouting, "Bear's back...he's back. Bear's back, Mom." He came to a skidding halt in front of her, his eyes glittering like turquoise ice. "Did you see him, Mom? He's right outside. I'm gonna get his hot dog and—"

"Whoa, hold on, pal," said Rex. Reaching down, he corralled Ryan as he skittered toward the refrigerator. "I know Bear will be happy to see you, too, but first I need to ask you a few questions about your brother."

Ryan's eyes widened. "Jeff?" He glanced around as if bewildered. "Where's Jeff?"

Frowning, Jennifer crouched down beside Rex. "Honey, you know we can't find Jeff. We've been looking for him for hours."

"Yeah, but that was before," countered Ryan.

"Before what, Ryan?" Rex asked.

"Before you and Bear came back. Jeff is with you guys, right?" He looked around again, his soft face perplexed. "Isn't he with you guys?"

"What makes you think Jeff is with Bear and me?"

"'Cause that's what he said. He said he was going to find you and tell you to come back so Mommy would stop being sad all the time."

Rex's startled gaze shot to meet Jennifer's. She quickly averted her own to Ryan.

"Ryan, why didn't you tell me this before now?"

"Because Jeff said not to. He made me swear. Swear *and* spit." His bottom lip trembled. "He said he'd go get Rex and Bear and I'd stay and take care of Mommy. I wanted Bear to come back and now I want Jeff to come back, too."

Jennifer pulled him into a tight hug. "Jeff's going to come back, honey. But you've got to help by telling us everything you know about which way he went to find Rex and Bear, okay?"

Ryan nodded earnestly as Jennifer released him. "He said he was going to go by the fancy mailbox to the road Grandpa took us to Boston on and then he would just ask somebody where Rex's house was."

"Oh my God," Jennifer moaned, devastated by the childlike innocence of the plan. She pictured Jeff on the twisting highway that led out of town, approaching strangers, maybe getting into the car with someone if they promised to bring him where he wanted to go. And all because he wanted to stop her from being sad.

She straightened, clenching her hands in front of her. What had she done?

"Don't look like that," Rex ordered, his voice rough and low, intended for her ears only. "This isn't your fault."

"Isn't it?" she snapped.

"No. And as long as Jeff was headed the way I think he was, he was moving away from the lake. There's that to be thankful for."

"Right," she retorted, her voice rising sharply. "I should be thankful that my six-year-old son is alone out there in the woods, when it's nearly pitch-dark, or maybe he's wandering down the highway or maybe…maybe…''

"Cut it out, Jenny. That's not going to help. Those woods are pretty thick in places, with no real paths to speak of. Unless I miss my guess, Jeff is wandering around in circles out there." He hunkered down to talk to Ryan again. "Listen, pal, you have to tell me exactly where Jeff went when he took off. You did watch him go, right?"

Ryan nodded.

"Did he go up and around my house? Or did he follow the brook?"

"He went up around your house," replied Ryan.

Rex grinned. "Good job, Ryan. Now you do as Jeff said and stay here and look after your mom."

"Where are you going?"

"Bear and I are going to go look for your brother." He stood and faced Jennifer. "And I'm going to bring him home, safe and sound. At least I can promise you that much, Jenny."

Rex left Jenny's kitchen wishing that he felt a fraction as confident as he'd tried to appear. Grabbing a heavy-duty flashlight from the cab of his truck, he swung his narrowed gaze across the thickly wooded landscape. That was a lot of woods to cover. And a very little boy. The phrase "needle in a haystack" ran like a taunt through his head. And the rapidly setting sun didn't do anything to alleviate the pressure that resulted.

The fact was that he had no idea if he would be able to find Jeff and no right to promise Jenny that he would. Hell, with his track record he had no right to make Jenny any promises at all. He only knew that if it was humanly possible to bring that kid back to his mother, he wasn't going to quit until he'd done it.

At the moment, most of the searchers were still working on the lake side of the street. No doubt when they got
word of Ryan's revelations they would be coming in behind him, but for now, it was just him and Bear.

He quickly covered the path that skirted his house and
led into the low hills beyond. They walked this way often,
and Rex knew even before he reached it, the exact point at
which the path forked. When he got there, he paused.
Okay, I'm a six-year-old kid, he thought, which way would
I go?

He recalled what Ryan had said about the LeBlancs'
mailbox and how Jenny had recently brought the boys
there to visit. If Ryan was right and that was Jeff's first
landmark, he would have had to have gone right when he
reached this point. He just hoped Jeff knew that.

The heavy growth of branches overhead made it necessary to use the flashlight right from the start. He swung it
back and forth as he walked, scanning from side to side of
the path. A few times he called Jeff's name, with no response other than the eager lifting of Bear's ears each time
he heard the familiar name.

For a long time he saw no sign that anyone had passed
this way recently. The first time he did see something, he
hesitated only a second, then dismissed it. Then, at the
next crook in the path, it was there again and his heart
hammered an extra beat.

What he saw was a broken twig, close to the edge of the
path. Coming to a full halt, he examined it closely, touching the exposed inner pulp and determining that it was a
fresh break.

Which didn't necessarily mean anything. It certainly
wasn't proof that Jeff remembered the conversation they'd
had a while back about the traditional manner in which
Gypsies use twigs and stones to mark the way for those

following along behind. A broken twig indicates a turn was taken and also points the correct direction. A small pile of stones dead center of the path means to go straight ahead.

Had he missed a snapped twig back at the first fork? Or had Jeff only begun to leave markers later, when the woods thickened all around him? Or was this whole thing wishful thinking on his part?

Rex kept going a while longer before he made up his mind for sure. Just as the path came to an abrupt end, disappearing into a long stretch of low-lying brush, he saw before him a small, very deliberate pile of stones. Without it, he might not have noticed how the adjacent brush was slightly tramped down where someone small had forged straight ahead.

With a small grunt of satisfaction, he crouched down and took a good look at the carefully built pile. So the little guy had remembered about the markers, and he was doing a hell of a job of leaving them. That was one smart, gutsy little kid. Jack's son, all right, he thought with a surge of affection that filled his chest and throat.

Over the past few days Rex had confronted a lot of truths about himself and his feelings. Now he was hit with one more. He hadn't just fallen in love with Jenny, he'd fallen in love with her children, as well.

Ah, hell, he muttered, rubbing his hand across his face. Could things get any worse? He couldn't ignore this and hope it would go away. No, now he was definitely going to have to do something to fix things. But what? He was right back where he'd been for days now, trapped between what he wanted and what was right. He straightened abruptly. All that would have to wait until later. Right now he had to apply all his attention to finding Jeff.

He accelerated his pace until he was covering ground at a slow trot, using his flashlight and watching carefully for the next marker. And still in the end it was Bear who actually sniffed Jeff out first. He let out a rapid series of excited barks and when Rex caught up, he was licking Jeff's face with wild abandon.

Jeff, who had fallen asleep on a grassy patch of earth, sat up slowly, rubbing his eyes, then breaking into a face-splitting grin when he saw who it was who was attacking him so lovingly.

"Bear," he shouted. "Rex! I found you."

Rex laughed as he went down on the ground beside him. He felt happy, and very grateful to a God he hadn't turned to in a long time. He had turned to Him in the past hour though, over and over again, and He had come through for Rex. That bore consideration. Later.

"Yeah, you found us all right," he said, starting out tousling Jeff's hair and ending up clutching his small head to his chest for as long as Bear would permit Jeff to be free of him.

"I knew I could do it," Jeff exclaimed excitedly. "I knew it. For a while I thought maybe I was lost, 'cause I kept walking and walking. But I left markers almost the whole way, just like you said, Rex."

"I found them."

"So I did right?"

"You did great, Jeff," Rex told him, the tremor near his heart barely audible in his words. "A-1. The best."

Jeff's smiled faded. "Except for one thing."

"What's that?"

"I ripped my new Red Sox shirt. Do you think my mom will be real mad?"

Rex smiled at him. "No, Jeff, somehow I don't think your mom is going to be mad at all."

Jennifer couldn't explain why she trusted Rex to find Jeff when the local police and dozens of volunteers hadn't been successful. She only knew that she did. In some instinctive way that defied common sense, never mind explanation, she believed in him.

And so she was the least surprised of anyone when late that night he walked into the backyard carrying an exhausted, slightly scratched and very dirty Jeff.

The search had shifted to that side of the road by then, and the news that he'd been found was quickly relayed back to the house. Jenny knew without being told who had found him, and she, along with almost everyone else who'd turned out to help, was waiting to meet them with jubilant cheers and applause.

She clung to Jeff for a long, teary hug that ended with her telling him that she would buy him a new Red Sox shirt, a hundred Red Sox shirts, and then, in universal maternal fashion, telling him that he was never, ever, for any reason and as long as he lived, to go off like that again.

That established, he was commandeered by his grandparents on both sides and his many aunts and uncles, along with assorted friends and neighbors. At first he seemed a little taken aback by the crowd, but after realizing he wasn't in Big Trouble after all, he gradually warmed to the limelight. The happy ending established a partylike atmosphere that prevailed even as people said goodbye and left with their car horns blaring.

Jenny did her best to thank everyone there personally, and it was only when things started to quiet down and only close family remained that she realized she hadn't formally thanked the one man most responsible. She hurriedly searched the yard and house without finding Rex.

"Oh, he left right after he brought Jeff back," her mother explained when she asked if anyone had seen him. Her eyes narrowed suspiciously as she added, "Why?"

"Because I just realized I never actually thanked him for finding Jeff."

"Humph," said her mother. "If you ask me it was the least the man could do since he was the cause of this whole thing. Imagine, filling their little heads with all that Gypsy nonsense."

"Mother! That Gypsy *nonsense* is what helped him find Jeff in the first place."

"And Jeff wanting to go off after him and that damn dog of his is what started all this in the first place. Next thing you know Jeff will be wanting a gold earring like his friend Rex. Then what will you do?"

"I don't know," Jennifer retorted hotly. "But right now I plan to go over there and thank him properly. Can you hang around a while longer to keep an eye on the boys?"

"Jennifer, really, I don't think it's very wise for you—"

"Victoria," her father said simply. It was enough.

"Of course we'll stay," her mother told her.

Jennifer could tell that Rex was sitting on the back porch from the pinpoint red glow of his cigarette. As she approached, she saw him stand and walk to the top of the steps. She stopped safely at the bottom and looked up at him. And instantly felt all the glib remarks she'd prepared on the way over evaporate.

"Hi."

"Hi," he replied. After a few seconds, he added, "Sounds like things have finally quieted down over there."

"They have. It turned out to be the biggest party I've thrown in years."

"All's well that ends well, I guess. You found Jeff *and* repaid your social obligations for the next few years or so."

Jennifer shook her head. "I don't think I'll ever be able to repay all those people. You can't imagine how much it helped just knowing that so many folks cared and were out there looking for him. It made me feel like I was really home at last.''

"Yeah," he said, the heavy cynicism in his tone reminding Jennifer that his own feelings about the town weren't so warm. And with good reason. Even tonight, instead of being lauded as the hero he was, he'd been ignored . . . or blamed.

"Actually, that's why I'm here—I didn't have a chance to really thank you for finding Jeff."

"I don't want you to thank me, Jenny."

It hadn't been a good week for Jennifer. And for hours now, fear and tension and exhaustion had been pushing her closer to some emotional danger point. Suddenly she was there.

"What the hell is that supposed to mean?" she demanded.

Rex's brows shot up. "Just that. I don't want you thinking that you need to thank me for helping you with something like that."

"Oh, I'll just bet you don't," she drawled.

"What the hell is that supposed to mean?"

They were both as poised and wired with energy as two prizefighters facing each other at the start of a bout.

"It means," Jennifer countered, "that I'm sure you don't want me to *thank* you for your help. Shall I fall into the trap and ask what you do want from me in payment."

"I hadn't thought of being paid at all. Although I'd be mighty interested to hear what you're willing to offer me."

"Nothing. Do you hear me?"

"I think all of Pleasure hears you."

"Nothing," she repeated with less volume, but no loss of emphasis. "Not a single thing. I'm not going to waste another thought or tear or minute on you, Rex Lovell. And

I certainly am not going to let you charm me into jumping into bed with you again. I made that mistake once already."

"Twice, actually, but who's counting?"

"See? There you go again."

"There I go again where?" he asked, his voice alarmingly calm as he moved down to the next step.

"Saying things!"

He took another step closer. "What kind of things?"

"The kind of things you shouldn't say. Things that I don't want to hear."

"Why not, Jenny?"

"Because they remind me of things I don't want to think about."

"And maybe because they make you feel things you don't want to feel?"

"Maybe they're things I can't afford to feel, and that's all the more reason not to talk about them."

"But since we already are talking about it—making love that is—is it really such a bad idea, Jenny?"

"It's not making love when only one person's heart is involved," she retorted, shooting his own words back at him. "And yes, it's a bad idea, a horrible idea. It was a mistake last time—*both* times—and it would be an even bigger mistake to let it happen again...no matter how you make me feel when we're together," she added, her voice dropping of its own accord to a dismayingly wistful note.

"Make that how we both feel when we're together."

"Ha!"

He tipped his head to the side. "You don't think I'm feeling the same thing you are right now?"

"I *know* you're not. You couldn't possibly be or else..."

"Or else what, Jenny?"

She lifted her chin, gazing at a point over his shoulder in stubborn silence.

"Or else," he suggested, "I wouldn't have taken off the way I did and stayed away for days?"

"Oh?" she countered, eyes innocently wide. "Were you away?"

"Cut it out. You know damn well I was away. And why."

"Rex, at the risk of denting that ego of yours, I have to point out that I hardly have the time, or the interest, to keep track of all your comings and goings, much less try to fathom them."

"Bull. I needed time to think, Jenny."

"Bull. You were scared you'd bitten off more than you bargained for and so you ran."

"I thought you didn't think about it?"

Jennifer shrugged. "It didn't take a lot of thought to figure that out. Either you were scared or you decided a one-night stand would pay me back for what happened twelve years ago." His expression hardened, prompting Jennifer to take a step backward. "Either way, I don't feel like talking about it."

Rex grabbed her arm. "How about the truth? Do you feel like talking about the truth?"

Jennifer didn't reply, but she didn't try to pull away, either.

"The other night had nothing to do with paying you back for what happened twelve years ago, and I think deep down you know that. And I think you know that you've got me feeling a lot of things I'm not used to feeling. And wanting things I never thought I'd want...maybe because never before have I felt like there was a real chance I could have them."

"What sort of things?" she asked in a near whisper.

His shoulders lifted awkwardly. "I don't know....
Things... You, kids, glasses with black bat decals on the
bottom."

"What?" she gasped.

"Forget it. Look, this isn't easy for me, none of it. I'm
not used to feeling..." He shrugged again. "I'm not the
kind of man who can just get down on one knee and
promise you a lifetime of picket fences and station wag-
ons."

"What?" she gasped again, more loudly.

"I need time, Jenny. Time to work this through my own
way. If it comes to that, I'll have to do it my own way. But
right now, I don't even know enough about these feelings
to know for sure where they're headed and—"

"Don't you see?" she interrupted. "That's just it. I
don't know where this is headed, either, and I need to.
Maybe it wouldn't matter to another woman, a different
kind of woman, one without two kids to consider. But Jeff
and Ryan need all the stability and security they can get,
and they need a mom who feels safe and secure, too.

"I'm working hard on being that kind of mother," she
went on, "and I know I don't need a man around to make
it happen. But I also don't need a man who makes me feel
all torn up and out of control all the time, so that my little
boy thinks he has to do something to rescue me. No matter what we feel for each other... physically, for me, for
now, this is wrong."

"It doesn't have to be. I could try harder. You could
loosen your standards."

"Maybe...if it were only me at risk. But I have the boys
to think of."

"The boys like me."

"Of course they do. They think you're daring and exciting...and so do I. It's so easy to be tempted.... It's like

that damn red balloon all over again. Only this time," she vowed, "I won't let it happen."

"What red balloon? What are you talking about?"

"You. You're the wrong man, Rex."

"In what way specifically?"

"In every way," she said miserably. "You're too reckless and too independent and used to answering to no one but yourself... and you said it yourself, you like it that way."

"Is that all?"

"And...and...you wear an earring, for heaven's sake."

Before she realized what he intended, he reached up and jerked the gold earring off with such force Jennifer knew it had to hurt. He fired it into the woods, his expression one of granite determination. "Is that better?"

"Yes, I mean no.... Oh, Rex..."

"Not good enough? All right, how about this?"

As quickly as he'd dealt with the earring he reached for her and pulled her against him. With his arm around her waist, one strong hand at the back of her neck, she wasn't going anywhere. And when his mouth found hers, she wasn't sure she wanted to.

He parted her lips with his tongue and pushed inside, clearly bent on possessing her and bending her to his will. For Jennifer, there was something inherently thrilling in the fact that his feelings for her could drive him to such hunger. He framed her face with his hands and kissed her as if he would never get enough.

Then, slowly, the heat and fury of the kiss began to melt into something softer and infinitely more devastating to Jennifer's will to resist. Desire, sharp and sweet, began to uncurl inside her.

When he finally lifted his head, he was smiling grimly. "Come one, Jenny," he said softly, "give it a chance. Give me a chance. We're so good together, and the kids like me. For now, can't that be enough?''

It took every shred of willpower Jennifer possessed to pull away from him and, remembering the decision she'd made in a much saner, safer moment, give him the only answer possible.

''No.''

Chapter Eleven

After Jenny left, Rex worked through the night, painting one of the remaining upstairs' bedrooms. There were plenty of other things he could do, but painting suited his mood, repetitive enough not to interfere with his thoughts and physical enough so that he might eventually be able to turn off those thoughts and self-recriminations and fall asleep.

One irrevocable truth filled his head: Jenny didn't want him. At least not in the way that counted. The way he suddenly, for the first time in his life, wanted to be wanted. And he couldn't understand why. He'd fixed her stove, hauled her junk away, found her son when he was lost. Didn't that show that in spite of whatever else he was, he was dependable? Didn't it count for anything?

Apparently not. Because when Jenny measured him on whatever yardstick was used to measure a man's "rightness," a caliper he had no experience with or understanding of, she still found him lacking. Too risky. A threat.

Part of him had wanted to grab her as she walked away from him earlier and shout, "You're wrong. I can be the kind of man you need, the kind of man you and the boys can count on." But another, more deeply rooted part of him had been afraid maybe she was right, and so he'd just stood and watched her go.

Worn out, physically and emotionally, he finally went to bed and got a couple of hours' sleep. Unfortunately it wasn't in one chunk, but rather in restless bits and pieces of fifteen minutes or a half hour here and there, interrupted by a lot of tossing and turning and second-guessing. Maybe he should have pressed Jenny harder last night.

When he held her in his arms, he had no doubt that she wanted the same thing he wanted, and just as badly. Maybe he shouldn't have been so honest about his feelings and instead simply told her what he knew she wanted to hear... what every woman wants to hear. That he would love her and be there for her forever, no matter what. Who knows? Maybe he could be. He wanted to be, that much was certain. And maybe... maybe...

Feeling as if he were going to explode from thinking about it, he vaulted from bed at dawn and staggered downstairs to make coffee. From force of long habit, he opened the back door and looked around, expecting to see Bear at his heels, executing his usual morning stretch before heading outside. But the dog was nowhere in sight.

Frowning, Rex gave a short whistle, then called out, "Let's go, Bear, rise and shine."

In all the years they'd been together, it was something he'd never before had to do. Whether it was 10:00 a.m. or 2:00 a.m., if Rex got up, Bear was always right there by his side, raring to do whatever Rex wanted to do... as long as he got his morning biscuit first. It was a routine, a tradition, such as the after-dinner walk and the Milk-Bone at bedtime. Suddenly Rex realized how intricately Bear was woven into the fabric of his life.

Feeling the muscles around his heart tighten, he started up the stairs, calling Bear's name again with no response. *Poor fellow really is getting old,* he thought in an effort not to think about the obvious. *Now he needs a personal wake-up call. Next thing you know, I'll have to haul him up and down the stairs.*

He found Bear lying in his usual spot between his bed and the wall. His eyes were closed, and above his head the thin curtains Rex had left hanging blew gently in the morning breeze. Usually, even when he was asleep, Bear's nose would twitch in response to even the mildest breeze, but not now. It was as still as the rest of him, and Rex knew before he'd reached him that he was gone.

The pain that followed was so real, it forced a low moan from Rex as he sank to his knees by Bear's side and instinctively reached out to touch him. It was awkward trying to hoist the heavy, lifeless body onto his lap, but once he got him there, Rex held on to him tightly, lowering his head to rest on Bear's thick side, the feel and texture and smell of him all heartbreakingly familiar.

The thought came to him from out of the blue—had he remembered to give him his damn Milk-Bone last night? Or had he been too wrapped up in his own problems? God, had he even remembered to let him out before turning in? He must have, he decided, or Bear would have woken him with a gentle thrust of his cold wet nose. God knows he'd done that often enough, tactfully reminding Rex that he'd forgotten to fill his food dish or replenish his water or simply say good morning. Rex laughed bitterly. Maybe Jenny was right about him. Since he hadn't done such a bang-up job seeing to a dog's needs, what on earth made him think he should be trusted around people?

Pulling Bear closer, he pet him with long, sure strokes, the way he'd petted him so often, the way he liked to be petted best. Memories of all the other things Bear loved came crashing in on him: playing Frisbee on the beach, having his stomach rubbed, chewing on the rawhide laces of Rex's work boots so that they snapped when he pulled on them. How many times had Rex yelled at him for doing that? And how much would he give if Bear could wake up and do it again right now?

High on the list of things Bear had loved were Jeff and Ryan. Rex's fingers encountered a burr buried in the thick fur, and he carefully worked it loose, thinking Bear had probably picked it up last night as he went charging through brush and thickets in search of Jeff. He'd been like his old self last night, full of energy, no wheezing or dragging behind. Maybe, thought Rex, it was all the activity that had done him in. If so, he couldn't object. He liked to think of old Bear going out with one last burst of glory, and he suspected that Bear would have wanted it that way, too.

His hand fell still on Bear's neck as he suddenly struggled for control. Damn, he couldn't even remember the last time he'd cried. He hadn't given in to tears in the third grade when Kenny Munson had accused him of stealing his pencil case and called him a no-good Gypsy, nor in the fifth grade when a similar accusation had led to him throwing a punch at a much bigger seventh-grader and then getting ambushed and beat up after school. That had been the start of his personal "get-tough" program and the last time he'd ever lost a fight of any kind to anyone.

He hadn't cried when his mother died, although for months afterward he'd walked around feeling as though he wanted to. He'd told himself that if he hadn't been willing to stick around for her, or even return home for her funeral, he didn't deserve to shed any tears.

Ever since, he'd felt he owed her something. Coming here had been as much to make things right with her memory as for Bear. He guessed he'd finally done that, he thought now. Sometimes he looked around at night and thought how proud his mother would be if she could see how the old place was shaping up. At those times he missed her more than ever, and still he had never cried. Not until now.

After a long time, he left Bear where he was and walked down to the beach, swimming until his lungs and every muscle in his body throbbed and ached. He threw himself down on the sand and lay there until he was dry and breathing normally, and then he steeled himself for what had to be done.

Back at the house, he carried Bear downstairs and laid him in a corner of the porch while he went for the shovel. It hadn't been easy for Rex to decide where to bury him. As happy as Bear had been here, it went against Rex's grain to leave him in a place he didn't have much love for and would never be coming back to once the house was sold. But he also didn't like the idea of burying him in the backyard of his apartment. Based on his past history, he could move out of there on a minute's notice.

In the end it was thoughts of Jeff and Ryan that led him to choose a shady spot down by the brook for Bear's final resting place. He wouldn't be coming back, it was true, but they'd be around, and he knew Bear would like that. He'd barely put the shovel into the ground when he stopped short, jarred by the sudden realization that someone was going to have to break the news to the kids. Who? He'd let Jenny make that call, he decided. And with the kids still at camp, this would be the perfect time to talk to her about it. Jamming the shovel into the soil, he went to find her.

"Rex," she said when she answered his knock. Her instinctive smile flickered and faded as she pushed open the screen door and saw his expression. "What is it? What's the matter?"

"Bear," he said. He ran his tongue over his dry lips, looking off to the side, wishing his sunglasses hid more than his eyes. "He's...uh, he died last night, Jenny."

"Oh, Rex, no. I'm so sorry."

"Yeah, well..." he said hurriedly. "I knew it didn't look good. I told you that."

"I know you did," she said softly. "But it's still a terrible shock. I know how—"

"Anyway," he interrupted. "I just wanted to let you know before the boys got home from camp. I don't know how you want to handle it, whether you want to be the one to tell them, or you want me to do it or what."

"No, I'll tell them. I think that would be easier all the way around. But they'll probably want to talk to you about it anyway."

He nodded. "Sure. No problem."

"Rex, I..."

She reached out to him, but he quickly stepped away. "I really have to go," he said. "I have to, you know... I have things to do."

"Have you taken care of things, I mean, have you buried Bear yet?" she asked softly.

He shook his head.

"Would you mind if the boys and I were there when you did?" she asked.

The request caught Rex off guard. "You want to be there with me?"

"Of course. We loved Bear and we...we care about you, too. People who care about each other ought to be together at times like this."

"I didn't think..." He paused and shrugged. "Sure, why not?"

"I also think it might help the boys if they had a chance to say a prayer and say goodbye to him."

"A prayer. I hadn't thought of that. I was just going to dig a hole and..."

Jennifer saw his broad shoulders tremble and it tore at her heart. "I understand. You're pretty upset. But if I know Jeff and Ryan, they'll want the utmost pomp and circumstance."

"I'm no good at pomp and circumstance," he said in a tone that struck Jennifer as more defensive than defiant.

"Don't worry, they are. Just tell me what time you want us to come over."

"I don't know. Whenever they get home I guess. Maybe after lunch. Around two?"

"Fine."

"I'll see you then," he said, turning away, then hesitating. "You know, it's not that I didn't care or want to do this right. It's—this isn't easy for me."

Jennifer stepped onto the deck beside him. "I know that, Rex, believe me."

"Yeah, I guess you would know." He looked at her, his eyes shielded behind the dark lenses so that only the grim line of his mouth betrayed his sorrow. "Not that I'm comparing this to what happened to Jack. I mean, Jack was a man, your husband. And Bear..." He shrugged. "Bear was just a dog, I guess, but you know, sometimes it didn't feel that way to me. Bear was...well, he was all I had."

Jennifer's eyes filled with tears, but Rex left without giving her a chance to offer any comfort or understanding.

By the time she saw him later that afternoon, the vulnerability he'd revealed earlier was tightly under wraps. He was kind to the boys, but somber, stoic, the image of a man who was in control of his emotions, and who had a job to do and wanted to get it over with as quickly as possible.

Unfortunately the boys had other ideas. For Jennifer, the hardest part had been telling Jeff and Ryan. They had been stunned and bewildered at first, then had sobbed uncontrollably as the permanence of what had happened sunk in. Even Jeff had curled up in her arms in a way he usually insisted he was too big for these days. She was glad Rex had arranged for them to come over a little later. It gave them more time to adjust to the idea that they wouldn't be seeing Bear anymore.

No one had felt like eating lunch, but they used the time to make plans for their part in Bear's memorial service. At the last minute, she hastily changed from her cutoff jeans into a white skirt and led the boys across the brook to where Rex was waiting.

Bear was lying on the ground by Rex's side and the sight of him so still brought on more tears from the boys. Rex was wonderful, crouching down to talk with them in a deep, sure voice that made Jennifer feel better even though she couldn't make out his exact words.

"He'll be with my daddy now, won't he?" asked Ryan.

"I believe he will, Ryan," Rex replied.

"Me, too," said Jeff. "I believe it. And my dad likes dogs. He'll take good care of Bear. You'll see...."

A smile barely lifted the corners of Rex's mouth. "I'm sure he will, Jeff. Maybe they'll take care of each other."

That brought a pleased smile to Jeff's face.

"If you want," said Rex, "you can go on over and tell him goodbye. You don't need to be afraid or feel funny about it. It's just like he was asleep, that's all."

"'Cept he won't wake up?" asked Ryan.

"That's right. This time he won't be waking up again."

The boys moved together, tentatively, toward Bear.

Straightening, Rex turned to her.

"What's that?" he asked, nodding at the sheet folded in her hand.

"It's an old Pound Puppy sheet of Ryan's. We thought that if you didn't have something special you wanted to wrap Bear in, maybe you wouldn't mind..."

"I don't," he said. "Have anything special that is. What's a Pound Puppy?"

"It's a stuffed animal, a big, sad-looking dog who supposedly comes from the pound."

His mouth twisted with affection. "That sounds like Bear."

"It's one of Ryan's favorite toys."

"Doesn't he want to hang on to that, then?" He nodded at the sheet again.

Jennifer shook her head. "He wants Bear to have it. He also drew a picture to leave with him, and Jeff would like to leave his softie."

He frowned. "Do you think that's wise? I mean, aren't you afraid he might change his mind and—" He broke off at the firm shake of her head.

"Not this time. He wants to leave it here with Bear, and I think we should let him. Jeff's changed, Rex. Just the fact that he set off on his own yesterday to do something he thought would make me happy is proof of that."

"Too bad it didn't work, huh?"

"Rex, it's not a question of—"

She was interrupted by Ryan coming up behind Rex. "We said goodbye to Bear," he announced.

"Good," Rex responded. "Then I guess we ought to get on with it."

He already had the hole begun. While he finished digging, Jennifer and the boys did their best to wrap Bear in the sheet. Rex came over to help, and then gently laid him in the deep hole he'd prepared.

"Your mom tells me you two have something you want to leave with Bear, is that right?" he asked.

The boys both nodded. Ryan held out his drawing first. "I made this for him. It's a picture of me and Jeff and Bear and popcorn. Bear likes popcorn," he added a little guiltily.

Rex helped him put it on top of Bear. Next Jeff stepped forward with the tattered piece of softie clutched in his hand.

"I want to give Bear this," he said.

"Okay, Jeff. Come on over and put it in," said Rex.

For just a second as he gripped the scrap more tightly than ever, Jennifer thought he might change his mind. Then, his small mouth set with grim determination, he leaned forward and dropped it into the grave. Afterward, they all bowed their heads while Jennifer said a prayer out loud.

"Now what, Mommy?" asked Ryan when the moment of silence she suggested was barely past.

"I can handle the rest by myself," Rex offered, glancing at her.

Jennifer shook her head. "We'll stay. This is hard enough on you without having to be alone while you do it.

Besides, we brought some violets to plant on top of his grave after you . . . cover him up.''

Rex worked quickly, his face expressionless even as tears slid down the cheeks of everyone else present. Only the tightly drawn cords in his throat told Jennifer how badly Bear's death had ripped him up inside. When the soft earth was finally tramped into place around the clusters of purple and white violets, the boys headed toward home. Jennifer lagged behind to talk with Rex.

''Are you going to be okay?'' she asked.

''Sure. I have plenty to keep me busy.''

''Busy's not always the same as okay.''

''I'll survive, Jenny.''

''I know you will, but no matter how tough you try to act, Rex, I also know you're hurting inside, and I know how that feels. If I can help, I want to. How would you like to come over and have dinner with us? No big deal, just hamburgers on the grill and—''

''Why?''

''Why? Because you have to eat dinner anyway, so why not—''

''I mean why are you inviting me?''

''Oh.'' She shrugged. ''Because you're a friend, of course, and a neighbor.''

''Come off it, Jenny. I'm selling this place just as soon as I can unload it. So much for us being neighbors. And I don't want to be your friend.''

''All right then, maybe I'm inviting you just because I feel like being nice to you. Is that a crime?''

''No. It's just that last night you seemed convinced that I was the wrong man for you, the last man in the universe you wanted anything to do with.''

She squirmed in place. ''I didn't say that exactly.''

"Well, that's how it sounded. Anyway, I'm just wondering if something happened overnight to change your mind, if maybe you decided to give me a chance after all—"

"Rex, please, why can't we—"

"Or," he continued, overriding her effort to speak, "if you're just offering to feed me because my dog died."

"Rex . . ."

For the second time that day he abruptly moved out of reach when Jennifer went to touch him. His aloofness silenced her.

"Because if that's all this is," he continued, "then I think it would be a whole lot smarter, and less painful in the end, if I just ate alone."

Let him eat alone, Jennifer thought more than once over the next several days. He could eat and sleep and do everything else alone for as long as he lived for all she cared. As soon as she thought it, she invariably felt a stab of guilt.

If Rex had been harsh in refusing her dinner invitation the other day, he had a good excuse. He'd been very upset by Bear's death, and still was, judging from the sounds of hammering and sawing that came from his place pretty much around-the-clock. Certainly he wasn't getting a whole lot of sleep these days. But then, neither was she, and the reason had nothing to do with the noise he was making.

Standing in the dark kitchen at night, staring through the trees at the light coming from his house, listening to the almost frantic rhythm of hammer hitting metal, Jennifer recalled the long sleepless nights she'd suffered through after Jack died. She would scrub floors, clean closets and polish woodwork until her nails split and her skin was puckered, all in an attempt to keep from remembering. It had never worked for her, and she suspected it wasn't working for Rex, either.

As Rex himself had pointed out, Bear was only a dog, but he had still been the only emotional attachment Rex seemed to have had to anyone or anything. Even in her darkest moments, she'd had the boys. Rex had no one, she thought, aching for him.

Heck, even she missed having Bear hanging around the back door waiting for the kids, looking for a piece of cookie or whatever else she had to offer. He was a lovable old lug and she could imagine how Rex must be feeling.

Still, as much as he was no doubt missing Bear, something told Jennifer it was more than simple grief that had Rex going night and day to finish work on the house. He was obviously eager to get away from Pleasure. And from her. That fact brought Jennifer a stab of disappointment that was totally irrational, considering the fact that she'd already made up her mind there was no place for Rex in her life.

She'd tried to explain that to him the other night, but had ended up feeling as if nothing had really been settled, for either of them. Some things weren't so easily explained or dismissed. The fact is that they were a part of each other's past which they had both thought safely behind them. It was sheer coincidence that they had ended up back in town at the same time and living right next door to each other. But coincidence or not, it had happened.

Thanks to Bear and the kids, their lives had become entangled once more. More than entangled, she acknowledged ruefully. They had made love, and that had stirred something inside Rex as surely as it had inside her. Maybe things would be different now if he had stayed around that morning after, she mused. If they'd had a chance to talk and share their feelings, then maybe...

Maybe what? she thought, shaking off her wistful mood. Rex had taken off the way he had because that's what he always did, and to contemplate anything else was simply wishful thinking on her part. Deep down, she knew that no amount of talking or wishing could change the fact that chemistry aside, she and Rex were as mismatched a pair as a woolen mitten and a bikini bottom.

That's what she had really been trying to say the other night, not so much that he was the wrong man, but that he was wrong for her, that they were wrong for each other. Of course when she'd told him, rejecting his request that she give things a chance on his "live for the moment" terms, she'd had no idea that very shortly he would be suffering another emotional blow. The fact that she'd had no way of knowing Bear's fate at the time didn't make her feel any better about it. Almost as if she'd kicked him when he was down.

She knew well enough how miserable Rex must be feeling right now, and how absolutely alone. She'd felt that way herself in the past. She'd felt that way just the other night when Jeff was missing. Even surrounded by family and friends she'd felt a desperate aloneness that no amount of kindness or reassurance had been able to break through. Until Rex had come, that is.

He'd walked into her house, and she'd instantaneously felt calmer and more hopeful. He'd promised her he would find Jeff, and she had believed him. And then he'd done it. He'd brought Jeff home and made her world whole again. She only wished she could do the same for him now.

Chapter Twelve

Friday was grocery shopping day for Jennifer and the boys. Jeff's doctor had stressed the importance of routine in a child's life, and she did her best to curb her spontaneous side and stick to one.

On Mondays they visited the library, Sunday afternoons were spent at Grandma and Grandpa McVeigh's and Fridays they stocked up on Froot Loops and peanut butter for the week. It was as much of a schedule as Jennifer could handle.

This week however, Friday also happened to be the Fourth of July, and so on Wednesday afternoon she and the boys piled into the car for the trek to town. Her grocery basket was even more crowded than usual with picnic supplies for the holiday. On Friday evening nearly everyone in Pleasure would gather at the grassy field between the lake and town for the annual Independence Day celebration. They would bring picnics and blankets, sharing both so that it turned into one big potluck affair. There would be a concert by the high school band, followed at sunset by a fireworks display totally out of proportion to the size of the town.

This was the biggest event of the year in Pleasure, a matter of tradition and collective pride. When the mayor had suggested downsizing the display a few years back, in deference to budgetary restrictions, there had been an instantaneous and very emotional protest. The people had spoken; the idea was shelved. Pleasure would rather give up its mayor than its fireworks.

Jennifer had been telling the kids about the celebration for weeks, and she wasn't sure who was looking forward to it more, them or her. Would Rex be there? she wondered as she tossed a large bag of potato chips and some dip mix into her basket. Perhaps he might show up out of professional curiosity if nothing else. No, probably not, she decided, trying not to think about why that prospect, like so much else lately, left her with a vaguely hollow feeling. Rex had never had much regard for the town and its traditions, and the fact that they hadn't seen fit to select him, a native, to handle the fireworks display, must have only reaffirmed his belief that the feeling was mutual.

Once the groceries were loaded into the back of the car, cold foods packed in the small cooler she'd learned to bring along, the three of them headed for the ice-cream shop a block away for the cones she'd promised her sons.

"Don't dawdle, Ryan," she urged, as he slowed to peruse every discarded Popsicle stick and ant hill they passed. "Cooler or no, I don't want to leave the groceries in the car too long."

He picked up the pace for a minute or so, only to come to a complete halt in front of the pet shop.

"Look, Mommy, look," he called after her, his voice high-pitched with excitement.

With a glance at her watch, Jennifer reluctantly walked a few steps back to join him and Jeff, who also had his face plastered to the window.

"It's Pound Puppies," Ryan exclaimed. "Bunches of them."

They were indeed puppies, and several, three at least, were bunched together in a sleepy heap in one corner of the box. Two more were wide-awake, scampering over each other and their sleeping siblings, chasing after a small rawhide toy as if it were the grand prize in the game they were playing.

"Look at his ears," Jeff said to no one in particular. "They flop everywhere."

"Hey, they're biting each other," said Ryan.

"They're just playing," Jennifer explained.

"You tell us not to bite."

"That's right. But you're not puppies."

"I wish I had a puppy," he returned with great conviction.

Jennifer decided to let that one slide.

They stood watching the playful puppies for a few minutes longer, she as captivated as the kids by their antics. They were, without a doubt, the cutest little dogs she'd ever seen. Especially the frisky pair. Finally she stepped away from the window.

"Okay, guys, who wants ice cream?"

"Not me," Ryan cried, grabbing onto her arm. "I want a dog instead."

"Me, too," Jeff added.

"Absolutely not," she told them in her best mean mother voice.

Ryan wasn't impressed. "But I want one."

"Please, Mommy, please," pleaded Jeff.

"No."

"Why?"

Because I said so, she thought. Instead, with a sigh of strained patience, she said, "Because a puppy is not something you just walk into the store and buy on the spur of the moment."

"Why?"

She should definitely have gone with "Because I said so."

"Because," she told them, "you just don't. A dog is something you have to think about and plan for."

"I did think about it," Jeff told her earnestly. "Lots of times."

Ryan nodded. "Me, too."

"And also because a dog is a lot of work. He has to be walked and brushed and—"

"That's not work," Jeff interjected. "I'll love doing all that."

Yeah, right, she thought.

"He has to have a special place to sleep and special food and..."

"I'll feed him," Ryan announced. "I fed Bear real good."

And that, Jennifer realized suddenly, is what this was really all about. Both boys missed Bear terribly. In the weeks they'd been here, he had become a very big part of their lives and there was now a giant hole where he had been. She had no doubt that one of the frisky little black-and-white fur balls in the window would go a long way toward filling that hole. But it would also bring a whole new set of problems and complications to her life. Did she really need to be house-breaking a puppy with her deadline looming ever closer?

No, she definitely did not. Maybe they could think about getting a pet of some sort in the fall, when they had time to make arrangements beforehand.

But then again, why couldn't they just buy a dog? The puppies in the window needed a home, and the boys needed a friend. So what if it wasn't the practical or prudent or *routine* thing to do? That word again. But the truth was that *routine,* along with most of the other tried-and-true medical theories she'd used on Jeff, hadn't done him half as much good as a little Gypsy magic had. And there was certainly nothing practical or prudent about that.

She glanced from the puppies to her sons. They knew her well and could sense that she was weakening. Instead of nagging or whining, they peered up at her, their eager, imploring faces a wall she had no chance of getting around.

"Let me get this straight," she said as sternly as she could manage. "You're asking me to just walk in there and buy one of those puppies and take him home with us today? Right this minute?"

They nodded solemnly.

"A puppy who's going to chew our slippers and cry and keep us awake all night and probably end up sleeping in our beds?"

"Can we, Mommy?" asked Jeff.

She grinned at them. "Why not?"

It took only a second for them to realize that meant "yes." Whooping with joy, they scurried after her as she headed for the shop entrance.

Mr. Jasper, the pet-shop owner who'd been selling puppies and parakeets since Jennifer used to stand with her nose pressed to the glass outside, was so thrilled to be selling one of the litter that had arrived only that morning, that he threw in a two-compartment food dish and a week's supply of puppy food. The boys lobbied for a rubber newspaper and squeaky toy, along with a box of biscuits and some absolutely essential chocolate doggy kisses. Jennifer added a collar and leash to the growing pile on the counter.

The puppies were a cross between a poodle and a Lhasa apso. They were, he assured Jennifer, a perfect dog for children.

"You're sure?" she asked, frowning slightly. "Aren't some of those small dogs supposed to be high-strung? The boys can be a little rough and I don't want a dog who'll snap at them."

He shook his head with the full weight of his years of experience. "There won't be any snapping, you'll see. The crossbreeding gives them a good temperament. Don't get me wrong. A purebred is a purebred, if that's what you're looking for. Lots of people are—they turn their noses up at anything less. You want a bigger dog," he said with a wave of his arms toward the row of cages at the back of the store, "I've got 'em. You want a purebred, I've got them, too.

"But I've been in this business more years than you've been alive, and I say there's more to a dog than a certificate from the Kennel Club. Keep your blue ribbons—give me a dog with less pedigree and more heart any day. How does that saying go? They try harder.

"And that's the situation you've got yourself here," he continued. "They're hardy little imps, perfect for a couple of boys. Plus," he said, his eyes twinkling at Jennifer, "these breeds don't shed."

"Not at all?" she countered, thinking of how she was still finding wisps of dog hair from Bear and he had rarely made it through the back door.

Mr. Jasper shook his head. "Not a bit. I guarantee it. Along with their health, of course." He went on to explain which shots the puppies had already been given and when they should be taken to the vet for the next ones.

"So all that's left," he finally said, reaching to lower the inside of the showcase window, "is to take your pick. And you really can't go wrong. Every one of them is a sweetheart. Yes, sir," he continued, holding them up one at a time, scratching behind each tiny set of ears with genuine affection, "you're going to be happy with your new family member. And that's what you're getting, make no mistake about it. A dog is a member of the family. It'll worm its way into your heart in no time—always there when you come home, tail-a-wagging to beat the band, never moody or grumpy. Even when you're down to your last penny, without a friend in the world, you'll still have a pal you can count on here."

His words lingered in Jennifer's head as the boys debated which puppy they should make their own. They took turns holding them as they compared the spots on one's bottom to the black-tipped ears of another. Mr. Jasper was right, a dog was like a member of the family. She couldn't help thinking how much more important that must be when it's also your only family. The way it had been with Rex and Bear.

The idea came to her slowly, and at first she did her best to dismiss it. It was crazy, impulsive and more importantly, not her decision to make. Every advice column she'd ever read stated in no uncertain terms that pets should not be given as unsolicited gifts. Besides, suggested her common sense, it might be too soon for Rex to think about another dog. She should probably ask him first, and she should also probably wait a few weeks.

Except that at the pace he was working, he might not be here in a few weeks.

"I think we've got a winner here."

Still torn with indecision, she looked up in response to Mr. Jasper's words.

"I'm sorry, Mr. Jasper, I'm afraid you caught me daydreaming. What did you say?"

"I said I think the boys have picked themselves a new dog. And a pretty little lady, she is," he added, holding her aloft like a proud father.

Jennifer smiled and stroked the puppy's silky head. "She's adorable. Isn't she one of the two live wires who were chasing each other around in there a while ago?"

"She sure is. Is she the one you'll be taking?"

Jennifer looked at the boys, who nodded excitedly, and then happened to glance back at the window, where the other frisky pup was up on her hind legs, straining to see where her friend had disappeared to. Maybe she was just imagining that the little dog's expression was forlorn, but it touched off the memory of another pair of sad eyes she'd looked into recently. How often did you get a chance to cheer up two sad sacks at once?

"Actually," she said, facing the shopkeeper with a rueful smile as she pointed toward the second puppy. "I'm going to take both of them."

She was doing the right thing, she told herself over and over on the short walk from her house to Rex's. The thoughtful thing. The compassionate thing. Besides, nothing ventured, nothing gained.

If she'd left the second puppy in the store, it would have remained lonesome and so would Rex. This way she could at least say she'd tried, and if Rex really didn't want the dog—which was unimaginable once he took a look at it—

all he had to do was say so. She'd already decided that if
that were the case, she would keep it. Two kids; two puppies. It sort of balanced everything out. My God, she must
be losing her mind.

They had skipped the ice cream and gone straight home
from the pet shop to get Mikki settled into her new home,
a corner of the kitchen. The name Mikki had been selected after much debate. It was a shortened, feminized
version of the name of the kids' number one hero, Mi-
chelangelo...the Ninja Turtle, not the painter.

When they had filled her dish with food and water and
surrounded her with enough blankets, hot-water-bottles
and toys for ten dogs, they gathered up her sister, along
with a complete matching set of canine essentials, and
headed for Rex's house. The boys trotted ahead, giddy
with anticipation. Apprehensive was a better word for
what Jennifer was feeling. Also known as cold feet.

Suddenly what had seemed like such a good idea in the
pet shop seemed a whole lot less brilliant. In fact it seemed
a little ridiculous, and if not for the boys, she would have
turned back. As they climbed the slope to his house, she
almost began to hope for a reprieve, that maybe Rex
wouldn't be home. But his truck was parked in the drive
and the whir of an electric drill overriding rock music
blared from somewhere inside the house. Considering the
racket, it was understandable that their knock went un-
answered.

"Maybe we should come back another time," Jennifer
suggested brightly.

The boys looked crestfallen.

"Knock harder," ordered Jeff.

"Like this," added Ryan, banging his curled fist against
the door. The kid packed a punch. First the glass rattled
and then the door swung open by itself.

Jennifer grabbed Ryan as he stepped forward.

"Where do you think you're going?"

He looked over his shoulder at her matter-of-factly. "To find Rex. We came to give him the dog, didn't we?"

There was no denying that. Following her son into the kitchen, Jennifer called Rex's name, but the only response was more music and drilling. She knew now that it was coming from the second floor and that there was no way Rex was going to hear them unless he shut the music off.

"Come on," she said to Jeff and Ryan, adding under her breath, "we might as well get this over with."

With them at her heels, she led the way through the first floor to the staircase. She was amazed at the transformation that had taken place in the short time since she'd last been here. The very impressive results of Rex's almost nonstop labor were obvious around her.

The walls and ceilings were all freshly painted and had a soft finish; the elaborate old woodwork wore a glossier version of the same shade. Ivory Bisque, as she recalled. The recessed bookcases in the living room, as well as the oak stair treads and banister had all been recently stained and lacquered. Everything was shiny and immaculate.

"Don't touch anything," she warned the boys.

"I can't climb the stairs unless I hold on," complained Ryan.

"Let me see your hands," she ordered. Finding them marginally clean, she said, "All right, but hold on lightly."

Even the light switches and electrical plates were new, noted Jennifer. And white. One thing hadn't changed since her first impression of the house. It was cleaner and fresher now than that night, but it still had no personality. If anything, it had even less than before. As if eradicating its essence had been part of Rex's mission. This was like walking through a hospital ward or some eerie future world without color or texture. A stark contrast to her own house, which had so much color and texture, she found herself stuffing it into closets and under beds.

She gave the puppy inside the carrier a rueful glance. "I don't know, kiddo. Somehow this doesn't strike me as your kind of place."

Following the noise to a corner bedroom, she found Rex standing on a stepladder installing a ceiling fan. Jennifer placed the carrier with the puppy on the floor outside the door and motioned for the boys to do the same with the rest of the evidence.

"This way it will be more of a surprise," she explained in a whisper.

They grinned, liking the sound of that. As they entered the room, Rex caught sight of them and turned off the drill, climbing down from the ladder to silence the radio, as well.

"Hello, Jenny.... Hi, guys," he said, his slightly wary expression doing nothing to alleviate her uncertainty about being there.

How could a man look so absolutely wonderful and horrible at the same time? It was good just seeing him again, feeling the small tremor of excitement he always caused in her. But objectively speaking, he looked awful. His face was drawn and tired, his eyes hooded and both his whiskers and clothes looked as though they'd been with him for a few days.

With the boys like two ticking time bombs at her side, Jennifer smiled and said, "Hi, Rex. I'm sorry for interrupting your work, but from the sounds of things it would be hard not to these days."

His wide mouth tipped downward. "Am I making too much noise?"

"No, not at all," she replied hastily. "I wasn't complaining, just commenting. You've been working pretty hard."

He shrugged. "I had a lot to do."

"But not anymore it seems. The house looks great, Rex."

"Thanks. I'm getting there."

She noticed the open beer can and box of Twinkies on a nearby chair and shot him a wry look. "I hope that's not dinner."

Rex shrugged. "Could be. Dinner, breakfast. I've sort of let things run together."

"Ahh," she observed teasingly as she gathered her courage. "Things here are even worse than I thought. Good thing we came," she said to the boys.

They were both giggling and squirming impatiently.

"Why did you come?" asked Rex.

Ryan couldn't stand it any longer. "We brought you a surprise," he shouted.

Rex managed a smile. "Let me guess, you brought me dinner." He glanced at Jennifer. "If Muhammad won't go to the mountain . . ."

"Sorry, Muhammad," she shot back, "this mountain doesn't do take-out. No, we brought you a real surprise."

Rex frowned quizzically as she nodded at the boys and they dashed into the hallway, reappearing a second later each holding one end of the plastic dog carrier.

"Surprise," they shouted in unison.

"Surprise," Jennifer echoed weakly.

Sure enough, Rex looked surprised. Stunned even. Then the lines in his forehead smoothed out a little as he said, "Oh, I get it. You got a new puppy. That's great, guys."

Jeff and Ryan laughed and spoke over each other, trying to explain until Jennifer cut in.

"Yes and no," she said. "We did get a puppy, it's true."

By now they had let the dog out of the cage, and instantly there was more chaos than a five-pound ball of fur ought to be able to cause. Laughing, Rex scooped her up and cradled her against his chest.

"She's a lively one, all right, and real cute."

"I'm so glad you think so," Jennifer said in a rush, "because this one is yours."

He froze and pinned Jennifer with twin gold daggers. "What did you say?"

"I said she's yours," Jennifer repeated quickly. "You see, while we were buying our new puppy, we decided to get you one, too."

Silence. At least as much silence as was possible with two little boys and a brand-new puppy in the room. Though the silence was contained in the six or so feet of electrified space stretching between her and Rex, to Jennifer it still felt thick enough to choke on.

"Yep," Rex said, his smile too tight to fool anyone over the age of six, "she's a real lively one, all right. In fact, I think maybe she needs to run around outside for a while and burn off some of that energy. You guys think you can handle that?"

They agreed eagerly, proudly showing Rex her new leash and waiting as he attached it, then taking off at a gallop, the little dog's favorite pace.

When they were alone, true silence filled the room. She'd always wondered how silence could be deafening. Now she knew. Her ears hurt and her nerves were wound so tightly that when he finally spoke, she jumped.

"I just have one question," he said softly.

Too softly actually, but even so, surely she could handle *one* question.

"Have you entirely lost your mind?" he asked.

Good question, thought Jennifer.

"What makes you ask that?" she said.

Rex glared at her in disbelief. "What makes me ask that? What made you show up on my doorstep... no, not even my doorstep, in my damn bedroom, with a damn dog?"

"I thought it might help, that's why."

"Help what?"

She swallowed. "Cheer you up."

"Cheer me up?" He stepped closer, much closer. "Do I look cheerful to you?"

"As long as you asked," she said, her temper gradually edging aside any remorse she might have felt. "You look like hell."

"There's a good reason for that. I haven't had a full night's sleep in a week, I've got a near-lethal combination of caffeine and Budweiser running through my veins, and I've got a crazy lady living next door who thinks that having a puppy take a leak on the wood floor I just broke my back refinishing will cheer me the hell up."

"That is not what I thought at all."

"Of course not. Excuse me, but it's obvious you just didn't bother to think."

"I did so think. And what I thought was that I was doing the right thing. The *compassionate* thing."

"Oh, this I've got to hear." He grabbed his beer, plopped himself down in the only chair in the room and hitched his feet on a rung of the ladder. "Go ahead, shoot."

"I thought that since you had a dog and that dog..."

"Died," he said emphatically when she hesitated.

"Yes, died, and that since you were obviously taking that very hard, I thought that perhaps a new dog might take your mind off Bear and give you something else to think about besides ... Oh, I don't know, maybe it was a rotten idea.''

"No maybe about it." He took a swig of beer. "First of all, Bear wasn't a dog. He was a ... a ... he was just Bear. And I never went out and got him and went through any of that housebreaking crap. He sort of found me and stuck. For weeks after he showed up at the warehouse, I kept telling him to get lost, but Bear had his own agenda, so after a while, I accepted it. He was just there. I didn't go looking for a dog then, and I'm not looking for a replacement for one now. But if I were looking," he added, hitching his thumb toward the window through which drifted a blend of laughter and yapping, "that walking dust mop out there wouldn't be it."

"There's no need to be nasty."

"Just calling it like I see it."

"For your information, I never intended for her to be a replacement for Bear. That would be impossible. She has her own style and personality."

"Isn't that what they used to say about leisure suits?"

"Look, if you don't want the damn dog, just say so."

"I don't want the damn dog."

"Fine. We'll keep her ourselves. The boys already love her, which is something you obviously wouldn't understand." At the doorway, she glanced back. "Just for the record, I hope you overdose on Twinkies and throw up on your precious wood floor."

She heard the chair scrape across the floor. "Jenny, wait..." A pause and then, "Please."

Against her better judgment, she stopped and turned to face him as he came after her. Despite its ample width and bright walls, the hallway suddenly felt like very close quarters.

"I'm sorry," he said. "I guess maybe I'm acting like an ingrate."

"No maybe about it."

His mouth twisted into a grim smile. "Bringing me the dog was a sweet thing for you and the kids to do. The fact is, I'm not so good a handling people doing sweet things for me."

"Here's a perfect chance for you to get some practice."

He shook his head, the smile slipping away. "I can't, Jenny. I wouldn't be any good at taking care of that puppy."

"You did fine taking care of Bear."

"Bear took care of himself. He pretty much had to," he said, a note of self-recrimination in his tone. "The last thing I need is a puppy depending on me all the time."

"Well, you need something," she told him.

His jaw tensed. "No. I don't. I don't need anything or anyone."

"And you like it that way, right?" Jennifer countered, her sharp tone hiding the sharper pain that his words had sent shooting through her.

"Let's say I'm used to it being that way. What I'm not used to is worrying and thinking and caring about someone else. Caring so much that when you lose it, it hurts so bad, it messes up everything in your life."

"Are you talking about Bear?" she asked, suspecting, hoping, otherwise.

He shifted his gaze away from hers. "What else? Look, I've got work to do."

"What about the puppy?" she dared to ask.

"Do the puppy and me both a big favor and take it with you, okay?"

She nodded and turned again to leave. If he hadn't stopped her when she'd stormed out of the room a minute ago, she would have flounced right past the next open door without a second glance. But now she did happen to glance that way, and what she saw stopped her in her tracks.

She looked back at Rex and his trapped expression immediately banished any possibility that she might be mistaken. Even leaning against the hallway wall, his hands thrust carelessly in his jeans pockets, he had an air of the proverbial kid caught raiding the cookie jar.

"Rex, that's my crib and high chair in there."

"Yeah," he said, "I guess it is."

"But we brought them to the shelter."

"They must have got left on the truck that day, so I stuck them in there until..." He broke off in the face of the slow, insistent shaking of her head.

"No way," she said. "We unloaded that whole truck. Nothing was left. How did you get them back?"

He sighed. "I sort of traded for them," he admitted, meeting her gaze as if it took effort to do so.

"Traded?"

"Right, I bought a new crib and high chair for the shelter and swapped them for yours. I told Sister Ann they had sentimental value."

"Why?"

"How should I know?" he countered with exasperation. "They're your things. Part of your family history. I don't know anything about any of that, I just remembered the look on your face that day when we put them in the truck and I figured they must mean something to you."

"They do," she admitted softly. "I was too quick to get rid of them and I... I've regretted it since. But that's not what I meant. I meant why did you do it?"

"I don't know," he replied, his words rough and low-pitched.

"But you must have had a reason and—"

"I don't know," he said again, a note of desperation creeping into his tone. "And I don't want to know. So just leave it at that."

Chapter Thirteen

"Well, girls, it looks like it's just you and me," Jennifer said to the two new members of the family when she finally succeeded in getting the boys to sleep.

They'd been running on high since arriving home with the puppies and had resisted going to bed long after their usual bedtime. Jennifer hadn't insisted. It wasn't every day a kid welcomed a new puppy into the family. Make that two new puppies.

Jeff and Ryan had been bewildered by Rex's rejection of Foxy, as the second puppy was now officially known. Jennifer had explained that he still felt too sad about Bear to have another dog come live with him. One thing the kids hadn't been bothered by however, was the end result. Two puppies of their own! Or as Jeff had put it, twins!

She shook her head as she gazed into the big cardboard box that would be their nighttime quarters until they learned to climb out of it. Which, based on the aptitude and creativity they'd demonstrated so far, would be two days maximum.

They were both rascals and truthfully, more bother and just plain maintenance than she'd bargained for. More than once as she swung the mop across the kitchen floor and shuttled back and forth to the trash can with wet newspapers, Jennifer had thought, "So this is why you shouldn't buy a puppy on impulse." Still, when she considered how happy the boys were, she didn't regret her decision.

The fact is, she sort of liked having them there herself. And she still thought Rex was making a mistake by not wanting Foxy. In fact, she wasn't convinced he didn't want her. After promising to drop off the crib and high chair first chance he got, he'd followed Jennifer outside and helped catch the puppy, who had by that time given both her new collar and the kids the slip. She was fast and crafty and they had all ended up with mud-stained knees and were laughing so hard it hurt, by the time Rex finally plucked the puppy from underneath a blueberry bush.

Holding her against his chest, he'd tousled her silky fur and grinned at her with grudging admiration. And before plopping her back into her carrier, he'd given her one final squeeze. Not, in Jennifer's estimation, the tactics of a man who wasn't interested.

Actually, now that she thought about it, his behavior toward Foxy was a lot like his behavior toward her. He kept saying "no" and acting "yes." Jennifer surmised she'd come closer than Rex would care to have her know the other night when she'd accused him of taking off after making love to her because he was afraid. Hadn't he confessed to almost that exact thing earlier when he said he wasn't used to caring for someone else, to worrying about them, and ultimately losing them? He'd claimed he was referring to Bear, but then and now she had a feeling there was much more to it.

It would be simple to dismiss Rex as a man of his times and say he was afraid of the *C* word, *commitment,* unwilling to give of himself, living only for the day, the hour, the minute. It would be simple, but it would be wrong. Certainly that was his reputation and he seemed to accept it, embrace it even. But there were too many things about him that just didn't mesh with that characterization.

If anything, she decided, thinking back over the past few weeks, Rex was a man trying desperately to connect to someone or something. She thought of how willing he was to spend time with Jeff and Ryan, who sometimes pushed her own patience to the limit, and of his work with the women's shelter and of the reason he'd returned to town in the first place, to make Bear's last summer a happy one.

And finally there was the way he had made love to her. Jennifer was no expert on one-night stands, but she knew in her heart that no matter what followed, while it was happening it was no one-night stand. There had been lust and passion to be sure, but there had also been tenderness and promises made with hearts rather than words. She and Rex had touched on more than a physical level that night, she was certain she wasn't mistaken about that. And while that had thrilled her, for some reason it had scared the hell out of Rex. Scared him enough that he took off before having to face up to it, or her.

Even then he hadn't stayed away, as he would have if he had truly been after nothing more than another notch on his bedpost. After all, he'd already gotten that, she thought, wincing. He had come back and he'd helped her at one of the most frightening moments of her life, helped her find Jeff when no one else had been able to.

In return, she recalled shamefully, he'd gotten accusations and recriminations. But had he shrugged at that and told her to kiss off, as any "love 'em and leave 'em" type worth his salt would have? No, instead he'd asked her to give him another chance to try to be what she wanted, another chance to love her and bring her more pleasure than she had ever before felt. And she had foolishly said no to all that.

It had seemed her only choice at the time. She'd been so sure that Rex didn't want any part of a real commitment, that she'd been blind to the obvious. Rex wasn't so much opposed to committing himself as he was afraid to do it only to be rejected as he had been so often in his life. It was as if he wanted a guarantee before he was willing to commit his heart and soul to anyone. Which was utterly ridiculous, since love, like life, didn't come with any guarantees. She of all people understood that.

As if it were a pivoting searchlight, the truth of that brilliant insight shifted suddenly and shone full force on Jennifer herself. My God, she thought, here I am analyzing Rex and I'm just as guilty as he is. How superior she'd felt about the way she had handled their lovemaking. Now she could see that she'd been just as scared by it as he'd been. True, she hadn't run away afterward, at least not physically, but then, Rex had spared her the trouble by doing it first. The bottom line was so much the same, it made her shake her head in wonder at the tricks the mind can play on itself.

She had been so sure they had exchanged silent promises that night, and so willing to condemn Rex for reneging on them. But the truth is that she wasn't looking for promises, she was looking for the same thing Rex was— guarantees. And no man could provide her with that.

She'd learned that the hard way. After all, in contrast to Rex, Jack had been exactly the right man for her, and that had ended. He had been her husband, her lover and friend, the father of her children. What loss could ever possibly be worse than the one she had already suffered, and survived?

No, she realized, and the answer brought her both peace and renewed hope. If she kept waiting around for iron-clad guarantees, she would never take a chance and lose, but she would also never win. And she could use a win, she thought. From out of nowhere, she remembered what Mr. Jasper had said: "Give me a dog with less pedigree and more heart any day." Yes, thought Jennifer. A man with heart, that's what she needed. That's what Rex was.

The boys could use a win, too. They needed a man in their lives, she thought as she had so frequently in the past year. With a small jolt of satisfaction she amended that. They needed *Rex* in their lives. They needed him because somehow, in some way, he was able to reach Jeff and Ryan in a way none of their uncles or other relatives seemed able to. Maybe that was because of the special relationship he had shared with Jack. Jennifer only knew that she needed him for much the same reason.

Passion and her kids' happiness... what more could a woman ask for? she thought. Unless maybe it was a night alone with the man she loved. The thought came automatically from somewhere deep inside her, and it took a minute for the rest of her to catch up and adjust. *The man she loved.* Yes, she thought joyfully, that's exactly what Rex was. Now she had to find the perfect, *private* moment to tell him so, and to tell him that she was willing to give him another chance, a million chances, and ask if he were willing to do the same.

Jennifer glanced at her watch, thankful it wasn't too late at night to phone the McVeighs and praying they were still interested in having the boys for a sleep-over tomorrow night. And hoping that she would be able to persuade Jeff and Ryan that they would love to spend the night before the Fourth camping out in their grandparents' backyard.

When Rex opened the door to her at about eight-thirty the next evening, he glanced around warily before saying anything.

"Are you alone?" he finally asked.

"Unless you count the anchovies on your half of the pizza," Jennifer retorted, indicating the box in her hands.

"How come?"

"Because I remembered you like anchovies and I don't."

"I mean how come you're alone?"

"The kids are spending the night at the McVeighs, sleeping out in the backyard with their cousins for a big pre-Fourth of July bash."

"And the new arrivals?"

"Mikki and Foxy are home sleeping off a Popsicle hangover. Ryan left a half-eaten one on the steps," she explained, "and the rest is history."

"Foxy?" he countered, his lip curling with distaste. "That's what you named it?"

"What's wrong with that name?"

"Nothing. Actually it's a fitting name. It just reinforces my decision. I couldn't picture myself hanging out with a dog that looks like it was conceived in a broom closet, never mind actually calling out 'Here, Foxy' in public."

"Well, I promise that if you accept the anchovies you won't have to call them anything."

He followed her pointed glance at the pizza box, hesitating as if reluctant to let her inside. Did he think she'd planted a bomb in it, for pity's sake? wondered Jennifer. She shifted awkwardly from one foot to the other. She'd expected this to get difficult when the moment arrived to say what she had to say, but she had expected to at least get past his doorstep with no problem.

"I thought you didn't do take-out food," he said at last.

"I don't usually. Tell me, does the expression 'Never look a gift horse in the mouth' mean anything to you?"

"I suppose it means that if I want to eat I'd better stop acting like a jerk and invite you in."

"Smart man," she said, stepping inside as he held the door open for her.

She had no trouble finding room for the pizza on the newly installed counter. The counters were completely bare and, like everything else in the kitchen, they were a gleaming, never-touched-by-human-hands white.

"I feel like I should be wearing a surgical mask," Jennifer said dryly.

Rex glanced around, as if seeing the room for the first time. "I guess it is a little . . . bright."

"No, Rex," she said, "this is white. Very white. Bright is something else entirely. Butterflies are bright, Santa Claus's suit is bright, kites are bright. Hospitals are white."

"I wanted it plain. It seems to me that the people who live in a house ought to make it what they want it to be, not what some decorator or real-estate agent thinks a home ought to look like. Like your place," he added, his tone earnest. "Toys and stuff all over the place. You wouldn't see anything like that in a magazine. It's a real home."

"Thank you," she returned sweetly. "I'll try to take that as a compliment rather than an indictment of my housekeeping skills."

"Your skills are just fine," Rex shot back, holding her gaze. "All of them."

Jennifer warmed and let her gaze drift awkwardly to the tile floor at her feet. White tile.

"How come you changed your policy on take-out food?" he asked, in reality asking much more.

"Actually, I've changed my policy on a lot of things," she said quietly, lifting her gaze to meet his. If she hoped to find encouragement there, she was disappointed. The expression in his dark gold eyes was cautious, and the way he was standing with his arms crossed and hip cocked made it clear he was waiting to hear her out.

"You made me a proposition the other night," she said, and saw his eyebrows arch in response. "When you asked me to give things another chance with us, to meet you halfway."

"Oh, that. I thought you were talking about a different sort of 'proposition.' Lately I've been thinking and dreaming about propositioning you so often, that for a second there I wondered if I'd slipped over the edge and gone and done it."

"No," she said, thrilled to hear he'd been thinking such things, too. "But this would be a whole lot easier for me if you would."

"I have no intention of making this easy. For either of us. Not this time."

Jennifer looked at him in surprise.

"I could touch you right now, kiss you, move you up those stairs to my bed with almost no effort at all." In spite of his words, his voice was filled not with passion, but tension. When Jennifer's face colored, he swore impatiently. "Damn it, Jenny, that's nothing to be embarrassed about, it's just a fact. We're so hot for each other,

I can do everything but taste it whenever we're together. And so can you."

She shrugged, unable to deny it and not really wanting to. Even if this wasn't going according to the script she'd rehearsed, isn't this what she had come here for tonight? To be totally honest? And if things went the way she wanted them to, to make love with him?

"That would be the easiest way out of this for both of us," he continued, as if reading her mind. Smiling wryly, he said, "Sex is like buying a puppy. It feels so damn good when you're doing it that the hard, complicated part—and the regrets—come later."

"I don't regret buying those puppies," she said defiantly. "And I don't intend to regret coming here tonight. Regardless of what happens."

"I don't have any intention of regretting tonight, either. That's why I want to get everything straight from the start. No giving into impulse like last time."

"Last time was great."

"It was more than great. It was better than anything I've ever felt before. I'm still greedy enough to want more this time. I want things clear enough between us that I don't have to wake up in the middle of the night with a guilty conscience."

"You won't," Jennifer told him, instinctively moving closer, reaching up to touch his face with her hand. "That's what I wanted to tell you. You asked me to take you on your own terms and I refused. I've done a great deal of thinking since then, and I'm willing now to do that... be with you on your terms."

He grabbed her wrists, stilling her hands on his whiskered cheeks. "How can you even be sure what my terms are?"

"One day at a time, wasn't that it? No commitments, no obligations, nothing to make you feel guilty or feel like running away."

"How the hell can you agree to something like that?" he demanded roughly.

In spite of the anger in his question, Jennifer saw that excitement now burned alongside of the suspicion in his eyes, and it gave her the courage to speak the truth.

"Because I love you," she replied. "And that makes me willing to do a lot of things I hadn't planned on doing."

He groaned softly, and for just a few seconds his grip on her wrists turned caressing. Then his expression hardened once more.

"What about the kids?" he asked. "Where do they fit into all this?"

"With me—where they'll always fit in. It will be good for Jeff and Ryan to have you around, whether it's for a week or the rest of the summer or longer. But I'll make it clear to them from the start that you're a friend, not a permanent fixture."

"A friend?" he echoed, eyes narrowed.

"A friend to them. What's between us is private. I guess that's something else you should know up front. Nights like tonight will be few and far between. And I'll always be pretty straitlaced around the boys. I won't flaunt our intimacy in front of them. No matter how much I loved any man, I couldn't do that."

"You can't do any of this," said Rex flatly. "Either you sincerely believe what you're saying...and are misguided. Or you've got one hell of an ulterior motive."

"I admit I have hopes about the way things will turn out," she snapped as she pulled away, bristling. "That's not the same as having an ulterior motive."

"What sorts of hopes?"

"Hope that things will be so good that you'll never want to leave, that in time you'll trust me never to hurt you the way I know you've been hurt in the past, hope that there might come a day when you trust me completely, when you won't be afraid to make promises and commitments because you'll know I won't ever let you down."

Rex's jaw went rigid except for a muscle that ticked at the left side of his mouth.

Afraid she'd said too much, Jennifer quickly added, "But I understand why that's impossible now and that it might always be that way for us. I have my eyes wide open, Rex. You'll have total freedom to walk away whenever you want. But I'll never send you away again."

"God, Jenny," he groaned, dragging his fingers through his hair, standing for a minute with head hung, his palms pressed tightly to his forehead. "You've got it all wrong."

A light-headed, queasy feeling washed over Jennifer. Could she have been wrong about his feelings? Misunderstood something—make that everything—that he'd said to her? Impossible. Yet something was clearly eating at him. She'd laid everything on the line and now she braced herself to have it thrown back in her face.

"What do I have wrong, Rex? I know you don't want to be tied down. You told me yourself that you're not ready to make any commitments, that you have to do this your way. Now I'm agreeing to do it your way. I'm doing it all your way, damn it, telling you that you can always count on me when you're just about telling me the exact opposite and—"

"That's it," he growled, reaching out to take her by the shoulders and holding her in front of him as if afraid she might bolt. "That's what you've got all wrong.

"Ah, Jenny," he said, his voice trembling as much as the hand he lifted to touch her cheek and stroke the hair back from her face. "Don't you see? I'm not afraid that you'll hurt me or let me down. It's never been that. I'm afraid that I'll be the one to let you down. That I'll end up hurting you... you and the boys."

The realization that he was more concerned about her and Jeff and Ryan than himself brought Jennifer a rush of tenderness.

"Anybody could hurt us," she argued. "What happened to Jack is proof of that. There's no way we can't see into the future. But I'm willing now to take that risk. Risks are part of life—and I want to start living, really living, again. You make me feel alive, Rex. I want to feel that way again... for as long as it lasts."

"It's not just that," he said, disentangling himself from her embrace. His chest lifted with a deep, shuddering breath and he avoided looking her in the eye. "I never talked about this to anyone before. Hell, I hate even thinking about it. It's true what I said about being afraid I'll let you down, but what I'm most afraid of is facing the truth about myself, and maybe finding out that I'm more like my father than I ever wanted to be.

"Maybe," he continued, the undercurrent of pain in his voice making Jennifer's heart ache, "maybe I really am the kind of man that everyone in this town has always accused me of being, and that I always denied.... Maybe I am a Gypsy at heart as well as in blood. The truth is, Jenny, I want to stay here with you more than I've ever wanted anything in my life. But in the beginning my father wanted to stay, too. He told me that himself. Then one day, he woke up and knew he had move on. It was like a fire in his blood, he told me, and said there was no fighting a fire like that."

He swung tormented eyes to Jennifer. "What if that same fire is burning in me?"

"Rex, that's crazy."

"Is it?" he shot back. "I'm not so sure. And I've never stayed in one place long enough to find out. What if I stay here with you and one day I wake up, like he did, and know that I have to go?"

"Then you can go," she said simply. The serenity she'd found while working this out alone earlier was stronger than ever now that she understood why Rex really feared involvement. "I don't know anything about your parents' marriage," she continued. "But I do know in my heart that if that day ever comes when you feel you have to go, it will be because there's something lacking in our relationship, and not because of the genetic makeup of the blood in your veins."

He looked at her in silence for a long time. Jennifer resisted the urge to argue or cajole. This was too important. It was an understanding he had to come to the same way she did, on his own.

"What if you're wrong?" he asked her finally. "What would that be like for you? I saw how hurt and upset you were when I took off without any reason or explanation after we'd been together for only one night. How much worse would it be for you after a month? Or a year? Or two?"

"I don't know," she replied calmly. "And I'm willing to bet I won't ever have to find out."

"How can you be that sure of me when I'm not at all sure of myself?" he demanded.

"Because I know you, and I trust you, and I love you...which is more than you can say right now. As much as you deny it, I think you've bought into all the myths about Gypsies as much as anyone. Maybe more. If for no other reason, you ought to stick around so I can raise your consciousness along with my mother's."

He gazed at her, amazement slowly lifting the harsh, weary lines of his face and a wry smile tugging the corners of his beautiful mouth upward. "You're really willing to take that big a chance on me?"

"I'm more than willing," she said, stepping closer so that their bodies were touching even though their hands remained at their sides. The temptation incited by the light contact was excruciating. "I'm ready. How about you, Lovell?"

His smile turned wicked as with a swift movement of his hands he bracketed her hips and tilted them into his. "You tell me, wise ass."

"Ahh, that definitely feels ready to me."

"Then there's only one..." He paused, losing track of his words as his hands searched for and found a way under the loose-fitting blouse she was wearing. "One problem."

He lifted her bra and cupped her breasts as Jennifer moaned and arched against him. "What...problem...is...that?" she murmured.

"Me." His mouth toyed with hers, nibbling at the corners before straying to the side of her throat. "I've been working all day."

"I understand. You're too tired for...this."

"Not as long as I'm still breathing," he growled, proving his point with a long, hard, deep kiss that left them both breathless. "But I've been fighting with a damn piece of ceiling molding most of the afternoon...sawing," he said, circling her breasts with his fingertips, the contrast of his light touch and callused skin maddeningly arousing. "I've been sanding, trying to get the curves exactly right." As he spoke he ran his hands over her curves, down to her hip, then up again. "God," he breathed against her hair, "you are the softest damn woman."

"Mmm. Rex, not that I don't find this discussion . . . fascinating . . . but would you mind getting to the point?"

"The point is that I'm probably not too pleasant to be close to right about now."

"You got that wrong," she whispered, pressing closer still.

"Just the same, I'd feel better after a shower."

"All right. Just make it quick."

"I'll do better than that," he countered, lifting her into his arms. "I'll let you help."

The shower turned into a foray into a steamy world of pure sensation. With no doubts or misgivings between them, they played beneath the warm spray without restriction or reservation. Their soap-slicked bodies rubbed together, their hands explored and learned, their mouths came together for slow, wet kisses and pressed soft exclamations of delight into each others' damp flesh.

Soon they were each anticipating the other's desire . . . where . . . how much . . . how hard . . . growing so attuned to the precise pleasure points of the other's body that sensation became sweetly sharp, desire irresistible—a heated wave pushing them forward. They had joined together in every way except the ultimate. When Jennifer couldn't wait any longer and reached to draw Rex inside, he stopped her and turned off the water.

" ̅ant to protect you this time," he explained in a ̅e ̅ ̅oice. "I can't do that if we finish here."

 ̅f ̅ ̅y moved to his room and made dripping wet love, laughing afterward and rousing themselves reluctantly to put dry sheets on the bed and then making love again until they were totally helpless, lost in each other's power, offering each other anything and everything and in return finding everything they needed to be whole.

Later, they lay together, letting the warm night breeze move over them. Jennifer moved against him, tipping her head higher on his shoulder to see his face only to discover she was too weary to open her eyes.

"I wanted to ask you something," she said sleepily. "But I can't remember what...."

"Go to sleep and ask me in the morning," he said, his chuckle rumbling beneath her ear.

"But it was about the morning... about waking up alone. I don't want to wake up alone."

Rex lifted his head to look down at her. "You won't, Jenny. I promise."

Chapter Fourteen

Rex awoke before Jenny, amazed to see daylight outside his bedroom window. More amazing still was that he'd slept through the entire night with no demons coming to call, no elusive fear driving him from his own bed, no regrets or self-recriminations.

He lay very still, not even turning to look at Jenny, although the sweet, even tempo of her breathing on the back of his neck filled him with the urge to watch her sleep. He knew he would find that as fascinating and compelling as he did everything else about her. The mere knowledge that she was so close and so naked filled him with even more urgent, hard-to-resist urges. The only thing that kept him still was the thought that perhaps his demons and fears were also sleeping late this morning and that if he moved too suddenly they would all come crashing in on him.

Chiding himself for being ridiculous, he finally rolled over and smiled at the sight of Jenny curled up close beside him. She slept with her hands pressed together and tucked under her chin. Her cheek, like the soft swell of breast visible above the sheet, was pink, either from sleep or, he thought regretfully, from his whiskers. Whisker burn or no, however, she reminded him of a picture of a golden-haired angel he'd once seen, all pink and white and innocence. If he'd had any doubt that Jenny was sincere in everything she'd said last night, they would have ended now.

She'd said she loved him. At the time he'd been too overwhelmed and too torn between what he wanted and what he thought was right, to savor that simple fact properly. But not now. Jenny loved him.

The realization swelled up inside him, like every good thing that had ever happened in his life all rolled into one. This was the thing he'd wanted most and longest and never thought he could have. For him, Jenny was like the shiny red bike in the toy-store window when you're a kid, perfect in every detail and so expensive you knew you didn't have a chance of seeing it under the tree on Christmas morning. That didn't stop you from dreaming about it, though. Just like he'd never stopped dreaming about Jenny.

God, she was beautiful. And she was his . . . she wanted to be his . . . wanted him. She'd said so, he reassured himself, trying to ignore the threads of doubts that were stretching weblike across his mind. He didn't want to get caught in them, not this morning. But the doubts wouldn't be so easily pushed aside. He didn't doubt that Jenny loved him. This question uncurling in his gut was about something more subtle and insidious. He wondered if she understood all that loving him entailed.

The answer to that fell like the crack of a whip. She couldn't understand, not possibly, not in a million years.

To understand, she would have to have grown up in this house instead of where she had. He suddenly recalled the name of the street that Jenny's folks lived on, Candy Cane Lane. He shook his head. Candy Cane Lane, like something out of a damn fairy tale.

How could a woman from Candy Cane Lane know about the ugliness that could be directed at you simply because some people didn't care for your last name or the life-style of your ancestors? Jenny might love him, but there's no way she could know what she was up against, no way she was tough enough to take what might come her way if she let their relationship become known in this town.

That was a bridge they hadn't even approached crossing last night, he realized suddenly. Jenny had mentioned that she intended to be discreet around the kids and he wholeheartedly supported that decision. But just how far would that policy of discretion extend? To include her parents? Her in-laws, the illustrious McVeigh family of which he was the acknowledged black sheep? The whole town? Would all their meetings be secret, time cut out of and squeezed into the rest of her life?

The bitch of it all was that he couldn't really blame her if she did decide to handle things in that furtive way. There were people in Pleasure who wouldn't be pleased to hear that he and Jenny were seeing each other. Her folks for starters, but there were plenty of others besides, others who wouldn't be so kind or polite in letting Jenny know they disapproved. True, Jenny was well liked around here, but would that be enough to stop people's animosity toward him from rubbing off on her? And the boys? Or would the good folks of Pleasure be so shocked to think that a nice woman like Jenny could see something in him, that it would make matters even worse?

Rex folded his arms under his head and stared at the ceiling. She'd said she wanted to take it one day at a time, and he was determined to try to do that. But if the coming days brought the same kinds of whispers and snickers he'd grown accustomed to, could Jenny take it? Could he? It was one thing when he was the one being attacked. For the most part he'd learned to take criticism from where it came and react accordingly. Most often that meant just walking away.

That was easier these days than it had been when he was a kid. There comes a point, he'd discovered, when winning one more fist fight, breaking one more jaw, making one more idiot eat his words, just isn't worth the effort. But even twelve years ago he'd found the strength to walk away when he thought that was what was best for Jenny. He'd taken off after the first time they'd made love to spare her from making choices and decisions she wasn't ready to make at eighteen.

She wasn't eighteen any longer, but he was still prepared to do what was best for her and Jeff and Ryan. He loved her enough to walk away if he had to. The question was, did Jenny love him enough to face whatever came if he stayed?

A slight rustling of the covers beside him drew Rex's attention and he tried to wipe all trace of what he'd been thinking from his expression before turning to face Jenny.

"You're here," she said, reaching out to stroke her fingers over the length of his chest with the lazy satisfaction of a cat.

"You don't sound surprised."

"I'm not. You promised, remember?"

"I remember. I remember everything about last night," he added, his tone growing husky as he caught her hand and drew it to his mouth to paint lavish kisses in her palm.

Jenny arched with pleasure and turned the full force of her smile on him. "I remember, too, every word, every touch...every whimper." Her eyes sparkled like blue-gray ice. "So this time don't you dare try telling me that we didn't make love...or that your heart wasn't involved."

He stopped kissing her. "I never said that."

"Yes, you did. That night out on my deck, right after I got back. You said that we hadn't made love that night in your car, that we'd screwed."

Rex winced. "If I recall correctly, I was feeling pretty angry and frustrated at the time."

"You also said that to make love, it takes two hearts, and that there was only one heart involved that night in the car."

"Right," he said, emotions he'd tried to bury in the past stirring inside of him. "Mine."

Jenny frowned as if confused. "What did you say?"

"The same thing I said on your deck, that there was only one heart involved that first night—mine."

"But I thought you were referring to my heart, that you were trying to let me know just how unaffected you were by me...by what had happened."

"Oh, Jenny," he said, laughing roughly as he rolled her onto her back and pressed against her. "When it comes to you, unaffected is one thing I have never, ever been. Not then...." He nudged her thighs apart and found his place between them. "Not now. I love you, Jenny. I always have. I always will."

Her eyes ablaze with love, Jenny's only reply was to reach for him, pulling his head down, her mouth opening to meet his in a kiss of soul-searing sensuality. Desire swirled to life in his blood, pooling like liquid heat down low in his body, starting a slow, instinctive rocking of his hips against hers.

The sound of an explosion somewhere outside intruded long before he was ready to stop kissing her. It was rolling and distant, but far too familiar for Rex to ignore.

"Is it my imagination," Jenny asked when he jerked his head up to listen, "or did the earth move when you kissed me?"

"It wasn't your imagination," he told her, knowing even before the second rumbling series of blasts had ended what had caused them. "What you hear is fireworks going off."

Jennifer sat up and watched in bewilderment as he rolled from bed and grabbed a pair of jeans from a chair. "Fireworks? At this hour of the morning?"

"That's right. I've heard that sound often enough to know. I told that jackass Haggard that this would happen if they left them out there in the field with only some canvas thrown over them. The sun pouring down on them all day, not to mention the fact that they were stacked right out there where any idiot walking by had access to them."

"You think someone set them off accidently?"

"If someone set them off, I don't think it was any accident. But there are other things that could have caused them to go off. If they got wet somehow and then sat there in the heat, a chemical reaction could have taken place that would ignite them suddenly."

"You talked to Carl Haggard about all this?"

"Wasn't much of a talk, at least on his part."

"What did he say?"

Rex had his shirt on now and was impatiently working his way down the buttons. He stopped briefly to look at Jenny, his smile tight. "He told me to mind my own business."

As he picked up his boots, Jenny sprang to her knees in the center of the bed. "Where are you going?"

"Out to the field. I might be able to help."

"I want to come. God, I hope they keep the boys away from there."

"You'd do better going to see about them."

She'd grabbed one of his shirts and pulled it on as she got to her feet. "I want to be with you," she insisted.

Even with the shirt hanging off her shoulders and the sleeves trailing below her hands, she managed a show of defiance Rex knew better than to tangle with when he was in a hurry.

"Then find the rest of your clothes and let's go," he told her.

By the time they made their way through the rapidly growing crowd to the general area of the field, Pleasure's sole fire truck was already on the scene, along with trucks from several neighboring towns. They all had their hoses going full force on the smoldering, blackened heap that was all that was left of what was to have been the focal point of tonight's celebration. Rex saw evidence that chemical extinguishers had also been used and his best guess was that the situation was under control.

Not that anyone asked for his opinion or his help. When he finally reached the police line surrounding the scene and identified himself to one officer as a pyrotechnician, making it clear he was willing to help if he could, a local policeman quickly joined them.

"You want to help, Lovell?" he said. "Is that what I heard you say?"

"That's right, Banning," Rex replied, recognizing the tall, solidly built man as someone who'd played on the regional high school football team around the same time he did. "I've had some experience handling fireworks."

"Well, that's very impressive, Lovell. Maybe I'll rush right over there and tell the chief, maybe even the mayor. Tell them we've got ourselves a genuine fireworks expert here and see if they think this here situation calls for a little Gypsy voodoo.''

Chuck Banning grinned broadly, obviously tickled with his own humor and the chuckles he was drawing from those nearby.

''Tell me,'' he continued, as Rex looked past him toward the activity in the field beyond, ''just how is it you Gypsies handle a thing like this? Put a curse on it? Stew a few herbs and tree roots? Or maybe you just get a hose and whatever else you need the old-fashioned way—you steal it. Is that it, Lovell?''

There were more titters around him, but from long practice Rex tuned them out almost completely. He was so good at drawing into himself at such moments, that he nearly forgot that Jenny was by his side until she clutched his arm tightly.

''Rex, let's just get away from here,'' she said.

He looked down with a curt shake of his head. ''No. Not yet.''

''Please,'' she said, ''it's clear they don't want any help—''

''You mean it's clear they don't want my help,'' he corrected harshly.

''What difference does it make?''

''It doesn't. That's why I'm not leaving until I'm ready to.''

''Rex, please,'' she said again, her pleading tone drawing his full attention. For the first time he noticed that there was a look of fear burning in her eyes and felt the panic in her grip on his arm. ''I can't stand it here,'' she said. ''I keep thinking of how—''

He nodded before she finished, knowing what she was going to say. The fire and explosion reminded her of Jack, of course, and he should have known that without her having to plead for his attention. Immediately he circled her shoulders with his arm and tried to steer her back through the crowd that had already grown larger and was more actively pressing forward than when he and Jenny arrived just a few minutes ago.

"Excuse me," he said, slowly threading a path through the throng of onlookers.

"Where you running off, Lovell?" someone suddenly called out. It wasn't Banning's voice, and Rex looked around to see Ray Thompson a few feet to his left, looking as miserable as ever in a sweat-stained T-shirt and pants that rode below a gut that had been a whopper even back in high school. "I thought you was going to show us how a Gypsy fights a fire?"

"Looks to me like there's not much fire left to fight," Rex said in as neutral a tone as he could manage. All he wanted was to get Jenny away from there with a minimum of fuss and without an ugly confrontation. He'd say anything, bite any bullet, to do that. Even if it meant being civil to a hulk like Thompson.

The hulk seemed to have other plans. "Well, I should think you'd at least want to stick around for the rest of the show," he said, swinging his bulk sideways so that he was blocking their path. "On the other hand, maybe you don't want to be around when they start asking questions, huh?"

Rex stopped trying to find an opening. Dropping his hand from Jenny's back, he faced Thompson. "What do you mean by that?"

"Nothing much. Just that I seem to recall another fire here in town that you were involved in. What's that they say about history repeating itself?"

Distantly, Rex heard murmurs of agreement from others in the crowd and several even more blatant comments from Thompson's buddies standing by his side.

"I was never involved in any other fire here or anywhere else," Rex said, weighing the anger that was quickly reaching volcanic proportions in his belly against his concern for Jenny. "I was accused of setting that other fire. *Unjustly* accused."

"Says you."

"The police said so, too. They found the man who did set it, and they admitted there was never any real proof linking me with it in the first place. Just ugly, unfounded suspicion."

"You don't say?" countered Ray Thompson, throwing his chest out. "Well, I got a few ugly suspicions of my own right now. As to why there's always this kind of trouble when you're in town and as to why you were so Johnny-on-the-spot down here this morning."

"Half the town is here," Rex reminded him.

"Maybe so. But half the town ain't Gypsy, are they, Lovell?"

Rex felt Jenny stiffen beside him, and concern for her played havoc with his reflexes.

"Now maybe they didn't have any proof against you last time around, but I'm wondering if you got any proof you didn't start things this time?"

"Are you accusing me of setting this off, you pinhead?" demanded Rex angrily.

"Hey, who you calling a pinhead?"

"You," he retorted. "Since you're the only one I see around."

"Seems to me you're pretty anxious to start name-calling and change the subject here. Why is that, Lovell? Why don't you just answer my question?"

"Because your question is more stupid than you are, if that's possible. I've spent most of my life handling explosives, and I've got too much respect for their power and seen too much of the damage they can do, to ever intentionally misfire them."

"That sounds good, but it still ain't proof, is it?" Thompson asked the men gathered in a circle of support around him. They shook their heads, echoing his doubts and accusations. Dozens of others stood behind them, watching and listening with perverse curiosity. Rex felt a slow burn of humiliation and could only imagine what Jenny must be feeling.

"Proof, Lovell," Thompson said again, his double chin quivering with enjoyment. "You ain't got any, do you?"

"As a matter of fact, he does," Jenny said suddenly, stepping forward so that she stood between Rex and Thompson.

"Stay out of this, Jenny," Rex snapped at her, jerking her back to his side, but unable to shove her any farther behind him. Had he called her soft? he thought disgruntedly. Right now she seemed made of steel, inside and out.

"He has me for proof," she said.

"I told you to stay out—"

"No," she said, daring him a quick glance. Her eyes flashed angrily. "This jerk wants proof and he's going to get it. I think my word is still good for something in this town," she said, turning back to the suddenly wary group of men.

"No one's questioning *your* word—" Thompson began, but Jenny broke in.

"Good. Because I'm telling you that there's no way Rex could possibly have had anything to do with this explosion. I know that because I was with him last night—*and* this morning." Lifting her chin, she met Thompson's startled gaze and added emphatically, "All night."

"Damn it, Jenny," Rex growled after he'd half dragged her all the way back to the truck. "Why the hell did you have to go and say a thing like that?"

"Because it's the truth," she said, seeming utterly unaffected by the hostile confrontation they'd just endured or his anger.

He pounded the steering wheel and got no reaction other than a wry quirking of one eyebrow. "It also made it plain that we spent the night in the same bed, and that's the last thing you wanted the whole town to know."

"Actually, I don't mind at all if the whole town knows how I feel about you."

"That's good, because now they're all going to know. Probably before the day is out."

"Oh, much sooner than that. I'd say word will spread in a couple of hours, tops. This is Pleasure, remember."

Rex shook his head, an unavoidable feeling of satisfaction infiltrating his anger. "Jenny, I can't deny that it pleases me that you're so willing to let everyone know about us. And it makes me proud. But it worries me, too. There's bound to be talk, rumors." He watched her eyes, wondering if she had any idea what she might have unleashed on herself. "Not very pretty rumors."

"I know that. But I also know that if we handle ourselves with dignity, in time the rumors will stop. And if they don't, then maybe this isn't where I want to be after all."

"I thought that was the whole point of coming back here. You wanted a place the boys could call home."

"I want a lot more than that for them. I want them to have a real home, and my idea of what that means has changed. I've changed, Rex. Twelve years ago I didn't have the courage or confidence to stand up in front of all those people and tell the truth even though I wanted to...even though I was dying inside because I couldn't help you. And I've lived with that regret all these years."

"You shouldn't have," he said, reaching across the seat to touch her. "I understood why you couldn't say anything."

"I understood, too—it was because I was a coward. But today," she continued, "it was all different. I was different. I don't know whether it's because I love you or simply because I've grown up, but today I couldn't have stood by and not spoken up. And I don't regret a single word. The only thing I regret is that I didn't whack that slob Thompson in the head while I was at it."

"The violent type, hmm?"

"When the situation requires it, yes."

"Come over here and show me."

He pulled her across the seat, angling her between his body and the steering wheel for a long kiss that would give any citizens of Pleasure who happened by added spice for their story. As she clung to him, surrendering as much as he demanded, Rex felt his love for her exploding inside, becoming something so wild and unwieldy he didn't know how he would ever contain it.

Maybe, it occurred to him suddenly, he didn't have to. Maybe love wasn't something that you could use up, something that you had to hoard, like squirrels hoarding enough nuts to make it through the winter. Maybe love didn't have dimensions or time limits. Maybe it just kept flowing, replenishing itself.

His mother used to tell him that flowers were like that—the more you cut, the more that would bloom. Maybe his love for Jenny would grow like that, thicker and deeper, wiping out the pain of the past, making things he'd thought impossible, possible. After all, he thought as he brushed his lips back and forth across hers, just yesterday he'd believed this was impossible too.

"There might be just one other itsy-bitsy regret that I do have," Jennifer said softly, her arms wound around his neck.

Rex swallowed, bracing himself, not buying that *itsy-bitsy* smoke screen for a second. "What's that?"

"I sort of wish I'd had a chance to break the news about us to my folks before my mother hears it over lunch at the club or while she's trapped under the dryer at the Beauty Nest tomorrow."

Rex regarded her with a grim smile. "You're sure you want to be around when your mother finds out?"

"Very sure. You see, there's a certain protocol you have to follow with my mother. If you let her feel she's in on things, life can be a lot more pleasant."

"You might still have time for protocol," he suggested. "I could drive you out there right now if you like."

"I can think of a hundred places I'd rather have you drive me right now," she told him, withdrawing to her own side of the seat, "and a hundred ways I'd rather spend the rest of the morning. But under the circumstances, I guess I better go talk to them first."

Rex nodded and reached to start the truck. When they reached the Cahills' stately white Colonial, he shifted into to Park, but didn't turn off the engine. He didn't want to put any more pressure on Jenny.

"Would you like me to go in with you?" he asked.

"Very much. But I have a feeling it will be easier on everyone if I speak to them alone this first time."

"I could wait if you like, or come back and pick you up."

"Thanks, but this could take a while, and then I have to stop by and get the kids."

"Sure, I'll see you later then."

Leaning across the seat, she kissed his cheek before climbing out.

Rex watched her hurry up the wide brick walk, remembering the last time he'd dropped her off here. The place still looked the same—just as intimidating and off-limits. Worse, he was beginning to feel the same way he had that night, a desperate sort of hopefulness mixed with a gnawing sense of dread.

Maybe, he thought as he slammed the truck into reverse, things hadn't changed as much as Jenny wanted to believe.

Chapter Fifteen

Her mother had some inner radar system that warned whenever a car approached the property, and she was already swinging the front door open when Jennifer got there.

"Jennifer, what a lovely surprise. Have you heard about the terrible explosion at the field? I do hope that wasn't who I think it was who just dropped you off."

"Hello, Mom. Are you going to let me come in or just grill me here on the front steps?"

"Don't be silly, of course you're coming in."

She stepped aside, giving the waistband of her pale lilac warm-up suit a tug as she surreptitiously glanced from side to side. No doubt checking to see if any of the neighbors had witnessed her daughter's mode of arrival, thought Jennifer bleakly. She definitely had her work cut out for her.

"Where are the boys?" her mother asked as she closed the door behind Jennifer. "Nothing's happened to them, I hope?"

"They're fine," Jennifer assured her. "They spent the night camping out at the McVeighs'. And yes, I have heard about the explosion this morning. As a matter of fact I just came from there and..."

She hesitated as her mother sniffed the air around her.

"I knew I smelled smoke," she said. "I hope you didn't get too close with your allergies."

Her father joined them in the front hall, his reading glasses slipping on his nose, the morning paper tucked under one arm. "Hello, Jennifer. What's this about smoke?"

"Jennifer just came from the field where that fire is, and I told her she shouldn't have gone near all that horrible smoke with her allergies."

"Definitely not," her father concurred, his expression deadpan. "The next time you go fire watching, make sure you leave your allergies at home."

"Oh, Jim, honestly," said her mother, as Jennifer met her father's gaze and winked. "Is that why you came? To tell us about the fire?"

"In a way, yes. You see something happened while I was there and I wanted to tell you about it myself before you heard about it from someone else. I wanted a chance to explain things to you."

"Oh, Jennifer, I hope it doesn't have anything to do with that Lovell character. I just knew trouble was brewing when I saw you getting out of his truck. I've told you and told you that the man is an absolute—"

"Vicky," her husband cut in sharply. When she turned her startled gaze his way, he softened his tone and took her gently by the elbow. "Why don't we all go into the den and discuss whatever this is. It seems to me we've been telling Jennifer one thing or another all her life. Maybe it's time we listened to what she has to say."

The meeting went about as well as she could have reasonably expected, Jennifer concluded later. Especially since reason was not her mother's strong suit at such times. She had received the news that Jennifer and Rex were "involved"—a safe word, which Jennifer opted to let them interpret any way they pleased—with shock and dismay.

Jennifer did her best to block out her mother's more colorful and inflammatory remarks, but she definitely recalled something about being "the scourge of the neighborhood" and that it was a "phase she was going through." For a moment, she'd felt about thirteen again, listening to her mother compare falling in love with Rex to skipping school or cracking her knuckles.

Fortunately her father was more understanding. Cautious, true, and clearly skeptical of her glowing description of Rex, but understanding just the same. When she left, her mother still teary-eyed and upset, he drove her to pick up the boys and then dropped them off at home. He declined her invitation to come in for lemonade, saying he'd better get home and check on her mother.

Jennifer leaned in the open window to kiss him goodbye. "You know, Dad," she said, "I've been thinking a lot about what you said the other day, about the red balloon, I mean."

"You have, huh?"

"Yes, and the more I think about it, the more I realize that it wasn't just a wild impulsive choice on my part, that deep down I wanted the red balloon instead of the pink one all along. I just didn't want to disappoint anyone by saying so."

He nodded, both of them understanding that the "anyone" she referred to was her mother.

"I want you to know that I never regretted getting the red balloon. And I'm not going to regret this, either. Some things you just know in your heart are right."

"And Rex Lovell is one of those things?"

"Yes, he is. I love him, Dad."

"Then he's a very lucky man, sweetheart. I just hope your heart is right about him."

The boys were understandably disappointed about the cancellation of the town's Fourth of July celebration. Jennifer had learned that the explosion was still under investigation, and the soggy condition of the field had ruled out the concert and town picnic.

Their reunion with Mikki and Foxy wet a long way toward cheering up Jeff and Ryan. When Jennifer had finished cleaning up the mess that two small puppies can make when left alone for such a long period of time, she suggested they have their own celebration.

"We have plenty of picnic supplies," she told them, "and those sparklers we never got around to using." Over the boys' cries of excitement, she added, "We could even invite Rex to come over and join us."

That prompted more cheers, and while she gathered ingredients to make the dip, they ran across the brook to tell him what was happening. They returned a couple of minutes later looking glum.

"Rex isn't home," Jeff told her.

Jennifer hated the clutch of apprehension his announcement brought her. There were a hundred places he could have gone. Maybe he needed supplies for some work he was doing at the house and had made a run to the hardware store in town. On a holiday? She clamped down hard on the doubts and questions that were trying to take root. She refused to get caught up in that again.

"I'm sure he'll be home soon," she told the kids. "We'll just schedule our picnic for a little later."

The afternoon dragged by. The kids took the puppies for several walks, tiring them out so thoroughly that they wagged their tails and licked her hands when she commandeered them and plopped them into their box for a nap. While they slept, the boys worked on the fort they were building and collected bugs in a jar and crossed the brook a hundred times to see if Rex was home yet.

I'll see you later, then he'd said.

What exactly did *later* mean? Jennifer found herself wondering. Later today? Later in the week? Later this century? Again she shrugged off the gnawing doubt that kept trying to drag her under. Rex would be here. Or he would call. She was sure of it. This was not at all like the last time. They had settled all that last night, and she wasn't going to lose faith, no matter how long she had to wait.

After a trek to the beach and the ice-cream shop, she finally ran out of plausible reasons to postpone their little party any longer. Luckily, the boys weren't hard to fool and she didn't have to try too hard to keep them from suspecting how little she really felt like celebrating tonight. That all changed when her parents pulled into the driveway sometime around dusk.

"Hooray," shouted Jeff. "Grandma and Grandpa are here. Now they can come to our picnic."

"Picnic?" her mother echoed, her forehead wrinkling. "At this time of night?"

"We were waiting for Rex," explained the helpful young son Jennifer could have cheerfully throttled at that moment. "But now you're here instead."

"Indeed," her mother said, glancing at Jennifer. "Where is . . . Rex?"

"I don't know," Jennifer said, opting for the truth no matter how uncomfortable it was. "He may even have been called out of town. This is a big day in his business."

"He didn't call? Or leave a note? I'd have thought with you two being so . . . close, and all . . ." Her voice trailed off and she shrugged.

"We are close, Mom, and no, he didn't call or leave a note. Rex doesn't always do things the way other people do, but that's okay with me."

"Well, if you say so. Your father and I didn't mean to intrude on your dinner, but . . ."

"You know it's no intrusion. Stay, please. The boys would love it and so would I."

Her mother smiled at her. "We'd love to stay. It seems we never cook on the grill anymore. With just the two of us, it doesn't seem worth the bother. Actually, that's sort of the reason we came. I bought this big cake for the Fourth," she said, reaching into the back seat for a large white bakery box, "and now the picnic's canceled and we'll never be able to finish it by ourselves."

"Terrific," Jennifer said. "All I had for dessert were cookies."

"It wasn't just to bring the cake that we came," her mother said tentatively as she handed Jennifer the box. "We thought . . . I thought that I'd like to say I'm sorry if I overreacted this morning. But really, Jennifer, how you could just sashay in and spring such a thing on a person is beyond me."

Jennifer glanced over her shoulder at her father, who shrugged. Laughing, she put her free arm around her mother's shoulders and gave her a squeeze. Half-baked as it was, the apology had been a major concession, as her coming here had been.

"We thought it would be nice if we all celebrated the Fourth together," her father said, as if reading her mind.

By "we all" of course, he had meant all of them and Rex, and for a few seconds, Rex's absence hung heavily in the air between them.

Then Jennifer reached down inside herself and drew from an inner well of certainty that everything was going to work out all right, and said, "Then let's start celebrating, shall we? Dad, you can light the grill, if you like. Mom, you want to come taste this dip? I followed your recipe exactly, but something is definitely missing."

"Is it the dill? It must be. I warned you that you had to buy dill powder, not the seeds. Now if you're making cheese spread, that's a whole different story..."

The dip was tasted and rescued, the hamburgers eaten, the cake cut, and through it all there came no sound of truck tires on the gravel drive next door, no light broke the darkness on the other side of the brook. A hundred times the same question formed behind Jennifer's stubborn smile: *Where are you, Rex?*

Finally all that remained of the evening was the moment the boys had been waiting for—the sparklers. Gathering on the deck, she issued a few rules concerning their use and how far away they were to stay from the puppies, and then flicked a lighter to light the first one.

"Ryan first this time," she said, touching the flame to the top of the silver stick and holding it until it sizzled and sparked.

At the same instant there was a rolling crash like the ones that had occurred that morning.

"Oh, no," Jennifer cried. "Not again."

"It couldn't be," her father said. "There wasn't anything left out there to explode."

They were all standing when the second blast sounded and Jeff pointed into the sky. "Look, look, everybody... fireworks!"

He was right. Barely visible above the towering trees all around them, was a plume of red and gold. As they all craned their necks to see, there came another loud bang and another plume appeared overhead, this one blue and purple with silver threads darting this way and that at the center.

"It's beautiful," Ryan cried, clapping his hands excitedly.

"Well, I'll be," her father muttered. "The mayor's outdone himself this time."

"I can't see good, Mommy," Ryan complained after the fourth burst of color. "Can you move the trees?"

"No," she replied, thinking he was right. With the trees encircling them, they were able to see only a small fraction of the sky. "But I can move us," she said. "Come on, kids, grab Mikki and Foxy and we'll get closer to watch the rest of them. Do you want to come along?" she asked her mother and father.

"Sure, we'll come."

"We'll take my car," added her father. "It's blocking yours anyway."

"But the dogs..."

"The kids can hold them on their laps. Just hurry or it'll be over before we get there."

There was little worry of that. The explosions were still growing louder, the displays overhead more elaborate, by the time they got to the area of the field. Lots of other folks had the same idea. People streamed from all directions, some carrying hastily grabbed lawn chairs and blankets. Everywhere you heard exclamations of surprise and delight, and versions of the same questions.

"How the heck . . . ?"

"Where did they come . . . ?"

"Who in the world . . . ?"

They were Jennifer's questions, as well, but she had her answer sooner than all the others. When they reached the edge of the field, it was possible to see where the fireworks were originating from. On the far side of the field, a safe distance from the crowd, was a flatbed trailer. She overheard two men who seemed to know what they were talking about say that the technician must be igniting them from a computer control board because there were no old-fashioned torches in sight. She didn't need anybody to tell her that it was Rex's truck that had pulled the flatbed out there, or that he was the technician flipping the switches that had saved this very important day for everyone here, and kept a little bit of the town from dying.

Love for him filled her so completely and overwhelmingly that it took all her self-control not to run across the field to him. She knew it wasn't only her impatience that made this display seem longer and more elaborate than any other year's . . . as if someone had pulled out all the stops. There was more noise and more color and in addition to the usual plumes and pinwheels, there were actual pictures exploding in the sky...sparkling white eggs that burst open to release bright yellow chicks; sports cars and rainbows and what looked like emblems that no one seemed to recognize, but that were breathtakingly beautiful just the same.

At last the ear-splitting magnificence of the grand finale had faded from the sky and Jennifer started toward the truck in the distance. The boys, each hanging on to a leashed puppy for dear life, came with her. She knew many others were also headed this way, driven by curiosity about the mystery man who'd saved the day, but she was running all out and she made it there before any of them.

"You idiot," she said as Rex jumped down from the truck and she threw herself into his arms. "You wonderful idiot. I love you...and I could kill you for not telling me what you were up to."

Laughing and kissing her, Rex lifted her from the ground and swung her in his arms before putting her down. He was every bit as excited as the kids and puppies clamoring round them.

"I didn't think of it until after I left you at your folks, and then I didn't want to tell you where I was going in case I couldn't pull it off."

"How did you do it? On such short notice and with no help....?"

He shrugged. "All the shells were surplus. Some mistakes, some leftovers from other jobs. I own all the equipment I needed and I had access to the truck. It's no big deal, really."

His grin told her he was as aware as anyone what a very big deal it actually was.

"I think it was the most wonderful fireworks display I've ever seen, ever."

"Good," he said, his eyes like fire in the darkness, "because I did it for you. And for the boys. I knew how much they'd been looking forward to today."

"You can't fool me, Rex. You did it for more reasons than that."

"Maybe," he allowed, as the approaching voices drew closer. "Maybe I did it because I figured that if I was going to try to make a new life for myself here, it was time to build some new bridges. This seemed as good a way as any to start."

Bridges needed an anchor on both sides, though, thought Jennifer, tensing as the crowd reached them. Would they be as thrilled by the evening's surprise when they realized who had orchestrated it? she wondered. Would they be willing to let Rex's bridges stand?

Carl Haggard stepped forward first, wearing his police uniform. Right behind him, Jennifer recognized other faces, her parents among them.

"Rex Lovell," Carl said, his lean face fiercely unsmiling, "you responsible for all this to-do?"

"Yes, sir," replied Rex, "I guess I am."

He glanced at the truck. "You got a permit to be setting off explosives inside the town limits?"

Rex shook his head, his jaw rigid. "No, sir, I guess I don't."

Carl's grin exploded as unexpectedly as the first fireworks had. "Well, see that you get one first thing in the morning, you hear? The clerk'll backdate it for you— Just so everything's all legal and proper." He moved closer and whacked Rex on the back. "Hell of a show, Lovell."

"Good enough for an encore?" Jennifer asked Carl. Ignoring Rex's warning look, she added, "Say next year around the same time?"

Carl nodded. "Sure thing if I have any say-so, and I think I do. Now if you'll excuse me, I'm going to see to the traffic out there before we have a bottleneck situation that lasts till Christmas."

A few others stepped forward to offer thanks and praise before her parents reached their side.

"Great show, Rex," said her father. "My wife and I have seen a lot of fireworks, but this outdid them all."

"Thanks, Mr. Cahill," Rex replied, with a slight tensing of his muscles that only the woman he loved would notice.

"Wasn't this the best we've ever seen, Vicky?" Jim said, pulling his wife forward a little.

She licked her lips, "Yes, it was...Rex. Very impressive." She smoothed her hair back, the habitual gesture seeming to relax her a little. "Although I did notice you used a great deal of blue. I think the pastels are much showier...." She stopped and gave a little shrug. "Just a thought."

Rex smiled at her. "I'll bear that in mind next year, Mrs. Cahill. Pastels."

"Well," her father said, "that's all I wanted to say, except maybe one more thing, something I'd say is long overdue." He held out his hand. "Welcome home, Rex."

It took a long time for Rex to speak to all the people who wanted a word with him and to answer all their questions. He did it with patience and good humor, although Jennifer had no doubt he was as eager as she was to be alone together. Finally everyone had gone and he had transferred his equipment to the truck, planning to come back for the flatbed in the morning.

"Let's go," he called to Jeff and Ryan, who were playing tag across the field. He whistled, a short, familiar whistle. "You too, Mikki...Foxy."

Turning to Jennifer with a look of self-deprecation, he said, "Tell me I didn't just do that."

"Sorry, pal, I guess you're just a dust mop lover at heart."

He made a sound of disgust, but she noticed he was very careful about how he scooped up the puppies and deposited them in the back of the truck.

"It was a pretty good show, wasn't it?" he asked as they leaned against the truck and waited for the kids to make their way back on weary little legs.

"It was stupendous. Although I did wonder about those chickens."

"Leftover from a farmers' convention," he explained, shooting her a look when she laughed. "Does the expression 'never look a gift horse in the mouth' mean anything to you?"

"Sure, it's sort of like 'never count your chickens before they explode,' right?"

"Forget it." After a minute, he said, "There was one other thing I wish I'd had time to do though."

"What's that?"

"Make up a shell just for you."

Jennifer glanced at him, touched by the idea, but he kept his gaze trained on the stars overhead, their crystal twinkling a gentler sort of nighttime drama.

"What would it have been?" she asked.

"I don't know. A big pizza maybe, or you sitting at your desk, or maybe something real crazy like the words 'Marry me, Jenny' written in red against the black sky."

"Rex," she said, her heart suddenly pounding, "is that a proposal?"

"Yeah, it is." He turned to face her. "My kind of proposal anyway. I never really could have written it in the sky for everyone else to see."

"It doesn't matter," she said, moving into his arms. "My answer is still the same . . . yes. I love you, Rex . . . I'll always love you."

He framed her face with his hands and kissed her with a love that stretched from the past far into their future.

"I never planned too far ahead," he told her, his mouth still close to hers, "but all of a sudden I'm full of plans, plans for us, and the kids. I thought if you want we could live in my house for starters. It's bigger than yours and everything in it is brand-new and... You don't like the idea?"

"No, I love the idea," she assured him quickly. "I think it's a wonderful house."

"Then why did you give me that look?"

"It's a wonderful house and you've done a great job with it...except for one little thing. Now I know you've done a lot of painting recently and..."

Rex grinned and pulled her mouth back to his, hesitating before he kissed her, just long enough to say, "Any color you want, Jenny."

* * * * *

Silhouette

SPECIAL EDITION

™

Starting in January
be on the lookout for

MAVERICKS

LISA JACKSON'S
MAVERICK MEN

They're wild...they're woolly...and
they're as rugged as the great outdoors.
They've never needed a woman before,
but they're about to meet their matches....

HE'S A BAD BOY (#787)—January
HE'S JUST A COWBOY (#799)—March
HE'S THE RICH BOY (#811)—May

All men who just won't be tamed!
From Silhouette Special Edition.

SEMAV-1

VOWS
A series celebrating marriage
by Sherryl Woods

To Love, Honor and Cherish—these were the words that three generations of Halloran men promised their women they'd live by. But these vows made in love are each challenged by the tests of time....

In October—Jason Halloran meets his match in *Love* #769;
In November—Kevin Halloran rediscovers love—with his wife—in *Honor* #775;
In December—Brandon Halloran rekindles an old flame in *Cherish* #781.

These three stirring tales are coming down the aisle toward you—only from Silhouette Special Edition!

AMERICAN HERO

Every month in Silhouette Intimate Moments, one fabulous, irresistible man is featured as an American Hero. You won't want to miss a single one. Look for them wherever you buy books, or follow the instructions below and have these fantastic men mailed straight to your door!

In September:
MACKENZIE'S MISSION by Linda Howard, IM #445

In October:
BLACK TREE MOON by Kathleen Eagle, IM #451

In November:
A WALK ON THE WILD SIDE by Kathleen Korbel, IM #457

In December:
CHEROKEE THUNDER by Rachel Lee, IM #463

AMERICAN HEROES—men you'll adore, from authors you won't want to miss. Only from Silhouette Intimate Moments.

To order your copies of the AMERICAN HERO titles above, please send your name, address, zip or postal code, along with a check or money order for $3.39 for each book ordered (please do not send cash), plus 75¢ postage and handling ($1.00 in Canada), payable to Silhouette Books, to:

In the U.S.	In Canada
Silhouette Books	Silhouette Books
3010 Walden Avenue	P.O. Box 609
P.O. Box 1396	Fort Erie, Ontario
Buffalo, NY 14269-1396	L2A 5X3

Please specify book title(s) with your order.
Canadian residents add applicable federal and provincial taxes.

IMHER02